ANOTHER DAMNED DARLING

MYKA BOUND

TRIPAWD
PUBLISHING

This is a work of fiction. Names, characters, places, and incidents either are the product of the author's imagination or are used fictitiously. Any resemblance to actual persons, living or dead, events, or locales is entirely coincidental.

Text copyright © 2022 by Myka Bound

Cover design copyright © 2023 by Gina Rinderle

All rights reserved. Published by Tripawd Publishing in Grand Junction, Colorado.

No part of this book may be reproduced in any form or by any electronic or mechanical means, including information storage and retrieval systems, without written permission from the author, except for the use of brief quotations in a book review.

Contact info:
www.mykabound.com
books@mykabound.com

ISBN: 978-1-955466-08-0 (ebook)

ISBN: 978-1-955466-02-8 (paperback)

For my husband
I am damned lucky to have a ride-or-die like you.

CHAPTER 1

I checked my outfit in the mirror for the fifth time, doing my best to ignore my little brother's defiant expression in the reflection. "I told you, it's a date not a hunt."

He motioned toward the dagger he couldn't possibly see tucked safely inside my boot. "Then why do you have that?"

At seventeen, Matty was an observant little shit who had somehow managed to grow four inches taller than me while looking like the spitting image of our mom. At least what I remembered of her. And when he looked at me with that confident smirk and all too familiar tilt to his head, it took some serious effort not to hold the likeness against him.

I shrugged. "I have no idea what you're talking about."

"Come on, Nev. Let me go with you. I'll do everything you say." He traced an 'X' over his chest with one finger. "Cross my heart." His boyish smile always gave my heart a painful little squeeze, but it also reinforced my standing rule not to take him on hunts with me.

He was strong enough to handle the daylight-dwelling demons, but he was still a little too immature to go up against the real baddies that stalked the night. And entirely too immature to keep his mouth shut about it afterward.

Most of the world didn't know about the demons. As far as I knew, it was just us lucky Darlings who could see them moving through our world. The last thing I wanted was for him to end up locked up in some mental health facility because some naïve idiot decided he was delusional.

That had happened to our great-grandmother, and it wasn't the kind of legacy I wanted to continue.

"I'm going to a party." I turned to face him, planting my hands on my hips in my best big sister power pose. "An adult party, with my boyfriend. No demons. No hunting. And you have a makeup test to study for."

His upper lip curled. "I could ace it with my eyes closed."

"You sure about that? You already failed it once." I held up a hand before he had a chance to argue. "And falling asleep at your desk is not a good excuse." It was his own damn fault for staying up late playing video games the night before his big chemistry test.

Instead of shrinking under my sisterly stare, he eyed my outfit. "Where's your costume?"

"I don't do costumes."

"Everyone does costumes on Halloween, especially when they're going to a party."

"Clint didn't say anything about dressing up." I turned to check my reflection again, tugging the cropped leather jacket around my waist and giving my ass a little shake. It was truly amazing what the perfect pair of jeans could do for a girl's confidence, especially when she wasn't feeling much like socializing.

Matty flopped back on the mattress with a dramatic groan. "Why are you still dating that asshole anyway?"

I pulled a scarf off the mirror's frame, balled it up, and threw it at his face. "Language."

"I'm not a kid anymore. I can say asshole," he muttered through the thin fabric.

"Not around me."

"Killjoy."

"Brat." I walked over and lifted the scarf off his head to find him grinning up at me like an idiot. His playfulness could be so damned contagious. It was the only thing that saved him from a lifetime of being grounded after I'd caught him sneaking out. "Not a chance, and you are not to step one foot out of this apartment tonight."

He might have been a few months shy of adulthood, but the way he rolled his eyes at me brought back memories of the terror he'd been growing up. I loved him to death. Enough to walk away from a full-ride scholarship and my last year of college to take care of him after his dad skipped out. But that didn't mean he didn't get under my skin.

"Up, Matty. Go study." I pointed at my bedroom door.

"What about the trick-or-treaters? They're going to be a huge distraction."

The universe chose that moment to take his side as a knock invaded the apartment.

I stalked out of the room, shaking my head at his little crow of triumph. When I reached for the knob, I paused just long enough to plaster on what I hoped was a convincing aren't-you-just-the-cutest-thing smile before pulling the door open. A trio of tiny children in store-bought disguises held out their plastic pumpkin pails and screamed "trick or treat" at me.

"Aw, how cute," I cooed, praying the cringe wasn't showing on my face.

In this batch, we had a princess, a fairy, and a pirate, and I had the sudden, inexplicable urge to educate the poor kid on the truth about pirates and how they'd been grossly romanticized by modern society. Real pirates were little more than drunks and wanderers who had pillaged and raped freely, spreading fear and disease from port to port. They were deplorable. Disgusting.

But the kid was all of six years old, so I kept those delightful details to myself. Instead of ruining his night, I grabbed a handful of candy from the bowl and tossed it in his pail.

"Happy Halloween," I said with a tight jaw, waving them on down the dingy hallway to their next victim.

"You suck with kids. You know that, right?" Matty's smirk was somehow annoying and endearing. "Like, *really* suck."

"Bite me." I wanted to say something a little more cutting, but it wasn't like he was wrong. "You and Lily don't hate me, and that's all that matters."

I must have made a face because his laugh filled the tiny apartment.

"What?"

"Your poker face sucks too."

I shoved my hair out of my eyes and yanked at my jacket again, already feeling the energy suck that was socializing at one of Clint's parties. If it wasn't for the fact that he'd be there, I wouldn't even bother.

"Don't forget to feed Lily." The big brown mutt lifted her head from her permanent spot on the couch and grumbled an agreement. "And at least try to study. If you can't focus, then put on one of your old costumes and hand out candy. But don't leave. Got it?"

He plopped his lanky body on the couch next to Lily and snagged the remote off the table. "Roger that." Then the little shit flipped me the snarkiest two-fingered salute.

"I'm pretty sure I could convince a jury of my peers to let me off," I muttered, slipping out into the hallway and pulling the door shut behind me, but not before his parting shot drifted through the crack.

"Say hi to Dickhead for me."

I eased the door back open an inch, whispered, "Fuck off," and yanked it shut.

Way to act like the grown up, Never.

I stood there with my hand on the knob, torn between going back inside and trekking through the dark to meet my boyfriend, until a chaotic chorus of youthful voices made my decision for me. Turning my back on the gaggle of baby-faced goblins, I made a beeline for the fire escape and the freedom of the park beyond.

If I took the safer route around the park, the one with concrete and streetlights, it would take me a solid thirty minutes to get to the warehouse where Clint and his buddies held their parties. And if Matty had been with me, I would have done just that.

But the clock on the crumbling stone pedestal at the entrance ticked diligently, reminding me that I was already over an hour late. That's what happened when a girl had to work two jobs to pay the bills and feed a growing teenager. Clint knew the story. Not all the cringy details but enough to understand my situation. I pulled my phone out and checked the screen.

No messages. He knew I'd get there when I could.

I rolled my ankle in my boot, making sure my trusty blade was still secure, and rubbed my free hand down my hip, anchoring myself in the softness of my favorite jeans. "Fake it 'til I make it," I whispered. Then I headed into the darkness.

I cut off the main trail onto the familiar dirt path. It was just wide enough for one person, and after a few yards, all remnants of grass and concrete gave way to the crisp aroma of pine needles and damp earth. I breathed it in greedily, savoring the richness of it. The rawness of it. There was something seductive about people and places that smelled… wild.

It was even better this time of year, when a desperate tingle of electricity infused the air, like every living thing in the place was scurrying and scrambling to make the best of what was left of the season.

Just like I was going to make the best of what was left of my night.

I checked my phone again and smiled. In five minutes, I would be at the party with Clint's arm curled around my shoulder and a cold beer in my hand.

A groan pierced the quiet of the moment, chasing away my happy thought and replacing it with a shot of adrenaline. Instinct took over. I shoved my phone in my pocket and crouched to slip my knife free from its hiding place. Moving quietly, I pushed through the thorny brush, tracing that eerie moaning as I went.

I wasn't in the mood for a fight. Not tonight. But I couldn't just walk away. If I let a demon go unchecked out here and it hurt someone, that would be on me.

A few more steps and two shallow breaths brought me to a clearing. Instead of facing off against a monster lurking in the darkness, I found two half-naked bodies moving to their own carnal rhythm. My view of the guy was blocked by the woman, who was wearing just the hat and the bottom half of a slutty cop uniform, with the fake gold badge clipped to her skirt bouncing in time with her hips.

A relieved laugh bubbled up from my chest. I slapped a hand over my mouth to smother it and turned away. What two consenting adults did in the park at night was none of my—

"Yeah, baby, just like that." The guy's slightly slurred voice pulled me up short.

All the air rushed out of me, and a hot wave of betrayal crashed back in. "Clint?"

You have to be fucking kidding me.

It was him all right. My boyfriend of six months. Dressed like a goddamned pirate with a slutty cop rocking on top of him like he was one of the spring rider things at the playground. His shirt was one of those flowy pieces, with the laces in the front hanging loose so I could see the fuzz of his chest hair. Even on the ground, I could make out the gaudy, fake gold hoop earring hanging from one ear. And was that eyeliner?

The heaviness slowly faded from his features, and he tried to focus on me. "Never?"

Nope. No way.

I turned on my heel and bolted.

"Shit! Get off me," he hissed. I heard a feminine 'harumph' and the rustle of clothing, but I'd be damned if I was sticking around for an explanation.

"Never, wait!"

Like hell. I was already shoving the thorny branches out of my way as I ran, ignoring the sting and warm trickle of blood as one of the spikes caught the sensitive skin of my neck.

I didn't know how much time passed or how far I ran before I finally slowed, but it was enough that I didn't recognize the part of the park I ended up in. On the plus side, I couldn't hear Clint's whiny, pleading voice following me anymore either.

I leaned my back against the nearest tree and sank to the ground, sucking in air and cursing under my breath when the bark scraped down my leather jacket.

"Fucking perfect," I bit out, landing on my butt on the damp earth. "I hate this city." The only reason I was still in Charleston was so Matty didn't have to switch schools in the middle of high school. The kid had a hard enough time making friends as it was.

I pulled my legs up and propped my elbows on my knees, turning my blade over in my fingers. My breath eventually slowed, and I made the effort to talk myself down from going back to find my newly minted *ex*-boyfriend and stabbing him in the dick.

"It's not worth it." I let my head fall back against the bark and drew in a deep breath, inhaling the scents of moss and decomposing leaves. "Probably."

Branches snapped and leaves crinkled to my left, and I rolled my eyes. "Go away, Clint."

I expected to hear some half-hearted begging. Maybe a drunken attempt at an excuse. Instead, I was treated to a low, rumbling growl. I lifted my head slowly, turning my gaze toward the sound and focusing into the darkness.

I should have been afraid. Most reasonable humans would wet themselves at the sight of a green-eyed demon stalking them through the moonlit woods. But killing some evil piece of shit sounded like just what the doctor ordered.

"You picked a bad night to mess with me, fugly," I said, taunting the scaly creature and pulling myself to my feet with all the nonchalance I could muster.

The creature lifted its chin and sniffed the air, curling and uncurling its creepy ass looking claws like it was planning something. The thing had a vaguely human form, but with arms that were entirely too long and snake-like skin that seemed to absorb most of the surrounding light. It was a strange combination, sure, but it was the thing's hesitation that gave me pause. The way its glimmering eyes locked on mine made my skin crawl.

I glanced down at my dagger and back at the demon. "You wanna dance?" I had to fight the insane urge to giggle at my own clichéd challenge. I'd clearly been watching too many eighties movies with Matty.

The thing cocked its head like it could read my thoughts.

Was that a thing? I mean, it was a demon. Who knew what all it could do? For all I knew, the damned thing could fly. A tendril of alarm skated over my skin until I scanned its dull body again.

No wings. Thank Pete for small favors.

The creature sniffed the night air again, and I remembered Clint. What if he was still out here looking for me? The idiot didn't know the first thing about dealing with demons. Hell, he probably didn't even know they existed. If he stumbled into this weird little standoff, he would definitely piss his pants.

This time I really couldn't help the giggle that bubbled out of me, because some sick, twisted part of me would have loved to see that.

The demon cocked its head again and I shrugged, shaking off the humor. "What are we doing here, oh scaly one?" I flipped the blade in my hand. "Are you going to come at me or are you going to make me chase you?"

At that point, from the way it shifted and glanced around, I was pretty sure the thing was going to make a run for it. I rocked onto my toes to give chase, except it didn't run.

Of course not.

The freakish thing swelled, growing at least a foot taller right in front of me. Its scales took on an uneasy shimmer just before it lunged at me with claws that were now as long as my forearm.

I barely managed to duck away from the first blow and pivoted the blade in my palm to drive it into the creature's belly in three quick jabs. Hot, steaming blood as black as the night sky spilled over my hand. Then the smell hit me.

Oh, sweet baby Jesus.

It took every ounce of focus not to gag at the stench poisoning the air. I stumbled back away from the creature, throwing my free hand over my face as I went. The demon should have been squealing in pain or moaning like the slut in the cop outfit. It should have been giving me some sign that I'd done some vital damage. Instead, it just glared silently at me and sniffed the air again.

Not good.

The demon took another step toward me and sneered, revealing a row of small, spiked teeth. It pointed one long, black claw at my neck, and I instinctively pressed my free hand to the spot, wincing at the slick of blood beneath my fingers. Then it growled something bordering on coherent, and when my brain finally processed the word, my whole body went rigid.

My trusty four-inch blade suddenly felt like a prop in my hand, nothing more than a child's toy.

"Darling," it growled again. Its green eyes flared in the darkness.

What in the actual fuck? How did that thing know who I was?

"Do I know you?" It was a struggle to keep my voice level.

The demon's lips curled up on one side like I'd only confirmed its suspicions, and my gut twisted. That smirk was entirely too human, entirely too calculating.

Shit, shit, shit.

That was all the time I had to formulate a thought before the thing lunged at me again. I scrambled back and almost got clear, so freaking close, but it managed to hook its claw around my ankle and spin me, sending me diving face first into the dirt and damp leaves. I tightened my fingers around the knife—silently thanking the god of fuck that I still had it—and rolled onto my back. There was no way I was letting that thing slice me open without looking it in the eyes.

The demon stalked slowly toward me, moving like it savored the idea of drawing out the moment as I tried to scoot backward, until another hair-raising growl rolled in from behind me. We both froze.

I probably could have taken one of those nasty smelling demons down by myself. With a little luck. But if there were two of them?

Yeah, I was officially fucked.

HOOK

CHAPTER 2

I needed to get up. I'd been lying awake in my bed for what felt like hours while sleep, that elusive mistress, remained just out of reach. My sense of time had been skewed for a while, years maybe, and the pitch black of my seabound accommodations offered no assistance in gauging the time of day. And yet, despite deliberately cutting myself off from the world outside my shadowed quarters, I knew someone was waiting on the other side of the door. I could hear his hesitance as he shifted his weight from one foot to the other, building up the nerve to wake me.

Any minute now.

The tick of the clock on my mantle was relentless, growing louder with each passing second. Tick, tick, tick. Every sense zeroed in on that sound until it resonated in my chest, as if my heart had no choice but to match its pace.

Thump-thump, thump-thump, thump-thump.

I wasn't the least bit startled when the booming knock echoed through the room, but knowing it was coming didn't stop me from cursing under my breath. It was an invasive reminder of just how much enchanted rum I'd drunk in my attempt to force a night of restful sleep.

My failed attempt.

I pressed my palms to my temples and closed my eyes. "Come in, William."

The heavy door swung open, and my first mate swept into the room, pulling back the heavy, velvet curtains along the viewing wall with an unusually gleeful air about him. "The demon has escaped, sir."

My head was a fireball of pain. Every muscle in my body ached as though I'd taken a tumble down a very long, very steep flight of stairs.

I rolled my head, groaning at the way my pulse seemed to thump through every inch of it. "Thank you for the wonderful news, William. It's fantastic."

He ignored the sarcasm dripping from every syllable of my response as he moved around the room. "I thought you would be pleased to know your charge is no longer wallowing."

It was entirely too late to be pleased about anything. Or was it too early? I cracked one eye open and glared at the only man on my ship who would dare to interrupt me in the middle of the night.

"Are you not aware that every single time the creature breaks free, it runs to the same place? I was certain that fact was common knowledge at this point."

And I'd be damned if I'd ever tried to follow it back to that insufferable realm, especially when I knew it would be forced to come back, one way or another. It wasn't the demon's physical form that was trapped here. It was its shadow.

The demon's body could travel where it pleased, it just couldn't survive more than a day on its own.

William offered me a curt nod but didn't speak. Nor did he turn to leave.

Lovely.

The man rarely hovered, so when he did, it usually meant trouble was brewing.

A little of my already thin patience slipped away. "What aren't you telling me?"

"There are rumors…" His normally strong voice took on a

simpering tone that always wore on my nerves. It was so much worse when my head was throbbing and my eyes felt as though someone had thrown sand in them. I gritted my teeth against the sound and motioned for him to go on.

"The demon has supposedly found a lead on a new Darling boy."

Oh.

The first tiny whisper of excitement chased through my veins, and I propped myself up on my elbows. "I suppose that changes things, doesn't it?"

Back when I'd started my little babysitting duties, the demon had been a formidable opponent who had constantly kept me on my toes. I couldn't kill the creature. It was far too powerful. Keeping it trapped, however, confined to the island and surrounding waters, had quickly become a game.

Nay, a rivalry of sorts.

It was… entertaining.

Sadly, after centuries—or possibly millennia, it was so hard to tell with the way time slipped and swirled between the many enchanted islands in this realm—the demon's appetite for escape and revenge seemed to dwindle. Until eventually, there was no fight left in the creature.

Which left me with precious little to do aside from patrolling the terminally uneventful waters and drinking copious amounts of the delicious black rum my men smuggled away from the neighboring shifter island.

But a new Darling meant a new fight was brewing. The demon would lure the boy here and attempt to use his soul to break free of this cursed place.

There had been attempts with other souls. At one time, the number of lost boys—those whose souls had been claimed by the demon—numbered in the hundreds. Now? Only a couple dozen remained.

The demon had killed many of them. As had I. For some, it was a kindness. For others, not so much.

The Darling kids were different. Something about their bloodline made their souls a source of immense power for an immortal demon looking to escape a timeless prison.

I sat up and swung my legs out of bed with a renewed sense of purpose. "William, prepare a team. We'll be venturing ashore."

"In the dark, sir?"

"Do you really need to ask?"

A sly smile transformed the other man's severe features into something bordering on boyish. It was an expression I hadn't seen in ages, and it called an answering grin to my own lips. I wasn't the only one looking forward to a little adventure.

"We'll be ready, Captain." Then he pivoted on his heel and marched out, barking orders at the men on deck before the door to my quarters had time to swing closed.

I pulled my trousers up over my hips and tugged at the waist ties as I took in the glittering twilight view through the array of windows lining the wall. It was like a veil had been lifted from my vision and, for the first time in eons, things were a little brighter in my little corner of the universe. Even in the dead of night.

William, or Mr. Smee, as the other men referred to him, was spot on with preparations for the trip to shore, as always. The skiff was fully stocked and the six men he'd chosen to accompany us were both loyal and capable. Of course, if they hadn't been, they would have been tossed overboard ages ago. There was no room for laziness, disloyalty, or ill manners aboard the Jolly Roger, not in our cursed realm.

Large ships were mostly safe at night, at least when there were no storms roiling the seas and stirring the creatures who dwelled there. But traversing even a short distance through those restless waters after sunset in something as meager as a skiff could be a treacherous undertaking.

"Sirens, sir." William's voice was low, but there wasn't the slightest waver in his words.

Good form, old boy.

"Which side?" I asked quietly.

"Starboard, sir."

It warmed my heart to hear the formality in my old friend's voice. Such things might not matter to some, but rules and routine were important. They kept us grounded. Kept us level. And most of all, they kept us civil.

The waters surrounding the island were crystal clear, and the moonlight was more than enough to illuminate the beings meandering below the surface. I unsheathed my cutlass and laid the blade across my lap. "Do not look overboard, men."

William acknowledged the warning with a nod, but the others stared at me as if I'd just sentenced them all to a slow, painful death. The thing was, sirens rarely surfaced without provocation, and a simple skiff in the water wasn't enough to draw their ire.

A body flailing in the water? Yes, that was a time to be worried. Crafts, on the other hand, were typically only at risk during a storm.

"These waters and the creatures they house are no threat to us, so long as we abide by the rules." I glanced at the moonlit faces before me—too wide eyes and quivering lips—and suppressed the resigned sigh building in my chest.

Why was good help always so difficult to find?

When we drew close to shore, the two men at the front dropped into the water and pulled the skiff ashore as if their lives depended on it. A quick glance behind me revealed their hurried motivation: three dark forms moving in lazy circles several yards out.

The sirens had spotted us.

"How long do you figure we have until the demon returns," William asked, reaching out a helpful hand.

I waved him off and swung myself over the edge of the small boat, smiling as I dropped into the shin-deep water. "It could be as little as a few hours or as much as two days." Though I was betting on the shorter of the two.

It rarely took more than a day for the demon's body to begin to wither and crumble. At the end of two days, the stardust that created it would find its way back to the Nassa Realm and reform around the demon's shadow.

"Do you think it's true about another Darling boy?" one of the other men asked, his voice whistling quietly through the gap in his front teeth.

Such a thing could always be true. We existed inside a magical realm in which time passed at an unpredictable pace and where all manner of fantastical creature could be found. It was a place where simply believing in a thing could make it a reality, but only if you were unfortunate enough to find yourself in the vicinity of fairy dust.

I ignored the question and motioned to the skiff. "You and the others make sure to pull that up beyond the high tide line and lash it to something sturdy. I won't be the one swimming for it over a bit of laziness."

I scanned the shoreline, cataloging the rippled sand bars lined with wavy rows of colorful sea glass. Animal prints dotted the damp sand, but I saw no sign of humans aside from my men.

Good. That meant the Darling child hadn't made an appearance yet, which gave us time to set a few traps for him.

"What is the plan, sir?" William asked, stepping up beside me.

For the first time in ages, I felt a smile tug at the corners of my lips. It might have been a vindictive smile, but it was a welcome change all the same. "When was the last time you set up a snare?"

CHAPTER 3

If I died, I was going to be absolutely pissed. I would be the bitchiest ghost ever to beat her ethereal fists against the veil.

Why?

Because I had things to do in my mortal life, like getting Matty through his last year of high school.

The demon huffed in the darkness and took another step toward me with its green eyes shifting quickly between me and the trees.

What the hell was it waiting for?

I expected another growl, or for its monster partner to come up from behind to rip my face off, because those were the happy thoughts I needed to be having when I was in the middle of a fight, but there was only silence in those dark woods.

Had I imagined that growl?

I edged back slowly, but the demon zeroed in on the movement. So much for sneakily getting back on my feet. I pressed against the damp earth and tucked my body into a ball as I threw myself backward, executing what was probably the most graceful reverse somersault I'd ever managed, all while holding a sharp blade. My old gym teacher would have been so proud.

In half a second, I was on my feet with my knife at the ready, but my quick thinking did nothing to impress my new demon buddy. Nope, that bastard launched at me with its nasty gnashing teeth and curved claws. Fire lanced my forearm as it sliced clean through my leather jacket.

"Sonofabitch!" I flipped the knife to my other hand and plunged it into the thing's shoulder. "This is my favorite jacket, dick."

That wasn't a lie. It was my favorite, but I didn't actually care that much about it. It was a thing. Things could be replaced. But thinking out loud helped to keep me centered. When I let the words bleed out, it left me so much more space in my brain for strategy. The fact that my chattiness tended to confuse my opponents was just a happy accident.

The demon's eyes flashed again, and the thing shifted its weight, telegraphing its next move as clear as day. I waited for the lunge and ducked, hooking to the right. It took all of one racing heartbeat to realize just how badly I'd miscalculated. The thing wasn't telegraphing, it was feigning, and I'd stepped right into its trap.

Fantastic.

The monster batted the blade out of my hand like I was a child and its gangly arm coiled around my midsection, drawing me to within inches of its face.

Clear liquid dripped from its pointed teeth before it closed its mouth and inhaled deeply. "Darling." The word sounded grossly orgasmic coming from the creature, like I was some long-lost lover.

There was no way in fuck I was letting that thing turn me into its demon bride. I twisted and thrashed, fighting for even an inch of freedom, but its arm only coiled tighter, crushing the air from my lungs. Black speckles darted across my vision.

"Fight it," I growled at myself.

I could not let unconscious overtake me. My heart was hammering in my chest and my intestines felt like they'd been caught in a vice, but I kicked and twisted and tried to scream. A vicious snarl ripped through the underbrush, and the next moment, I was airborne. The demon flung me away like a rag doll and I tumbled backward, bouncing across the ground, and losing all sense of direction as leaves and dirt swirled around me.

One thought pulsed through my mind: Run.

Another snarl seared the air, joined a second later by an ear-splitting scream. I scrambled to my feet and finally got a look at the fight raging in front of me.

Shit.

"Lily!" I screamed her name as a different kind of panic slammed into me.

My hellhound, the sweet girl who had been part of my family since long before I was born, had the demon by the leg and was thrashing wildly.

I scanned the area, spotting my blade half hidden by the monster's body, and quickly debated whether I should go for it.

Fuck yes.

I dived forward and snagged the handle in a single move, then drove it into the creature's side once, twice. As I drew back to strike again, it let out a scream so loud I instinctively cringed back and covered my ears, but since I refused to drop my knife, all I could do was press my fist to my right ear. It felt like my eardrum was bleeding.

The sound must have hurt Lily too, because she abandoned the demon's leg and shuffled backward, sinking to the ground with a low whine. I'd already wanted to kill the demon, but now I wanted it to suffer.

Screw it. What's a little hearing loss between friends anyway?

I settled into a crouch, blinking away the tears as the whine grew, and got ready to take another shot at the thing. But, instead of facing me like a big, grownup demon, it ran like a little bitch. I debated letting it go, and I was leaning heavily toward good-fucking-riddance, right up until Lily shook out her glossy, rust-colored fur and took off after it.

"I'm not in the mood to play hide and seek," I called breathlessly out ahead of me.

She wasn't listening. Which left me exactly one option. I chased

Lily's path through the woods because I would rather stab myself in the head with a dull steak knife than let her face that thing alone.

I rounded a corner at a dead run and barely avoided tripping over her as she sniffed, impatiently circling a small area of freshly turned dirt. It looked like someone had taken a giant leaf blower and just, poof, cleared that patch of ground.

"How did we lose that nasty smelling thing?" I asked, trying to keep my tone playful through ragged breaths. She pawed at the ground, obviously frustrated by its disappearance.

"Hey, it's okay, girl. We'll get it next time."

She gave the ground a few more sniffs, sending up little puffs of dirt as she went, then she sat down and, no shit, grumbled at me like all of this was my fault.

"Honest to goddess," I muttered back.

Matty and I didn't agree on whether she was actually a hellhound. Yes, she looked more like a wolf than a creature who was raised from the pits of hell, but wolves didn't usually hunt demons, and they didn't live for twenty plus years. Seeing as how Lily had been around since before I was born and still looked the same as she had when I was barely big enough to walk, I was sticking with my hellhound theory.

I called Lily to my side and scratched behind her ears. "You did well. Good dog." I said that last bit because I knew it'd get a rise out of her. And really, that was just one more point in my favor in the great wolf vs. hellhound debate.

Lily looked up at me with her big silver eyes and grumbled again, only that time it sounded like she was scolding me. Which I was pretty sure she was.

I chuckled and held up my hands. "I know, I know. We just need to figure out a way to get Matty on Team Hellhound."

Lily tilted her head at me like I was stupid, then leaned against my leg with her tail swishing low in the night air. I scratched the top of her head gently, the way I knew would make her fall asleep with her oversized head in my lap if we'd been curled up on the couch rather than out fighting demons in the middle of a city park.

"Let's go home, muttlet. I'm done with this crappy holiday."

When I got to the apartment, all I wanted to do was kick off my boots, strip off my dirty clothes, and climb into a hot shower. A quick look at the black sludge on my hands had me rethinking that plan.

"Matty, I'm home," I called out as I headed straight for the kitchen sink. It took longer than I expected to wash the demon's gag-inducing blood off my skin, but I eventually succeeded. I washed my knife too, because, ew.

I was just tucking the blade safely back in my boot when I heard Lily whimper behind me. The sound sent a fresh wave of panic through me. She didn't whimper, ever. Then it hit me: Matty hadn't said anything when I got home. On any other night, he would be buzzing around me with a million questions about how my night went, but he hadn't made a peep.

Maybe he'd gone to bed early. I held onto that thought for as long as it took me to make it to his bedroom. The door was wide open and the light at his desk was on. All perfectly normal. What brought me to the brink of panic was the smell.

"Matty, where are you?" I tried to smother the fear threading through me, but there was no response.

I checked the closet, my room, the bathroom, under the bed, everywhere. Even places his six-foot-tall frame could never fit because I clearly was not thinking straight. Then I stomped back into his room.

"Matthew Michael Hinkins, I am not fucking around. Get out here, right now!"

Silence.

I took a closer look at everything in the room, searching for anything out of place. That's when I spotted the smear of black on the windowsill. It was small, barely noticeable with the sheers pulled, but when I bent down to check it, the stench was unmistakable.

The demon had been there. In my apartment. In my little brother's bedroom.

Yeah, I was going to make that piece of shit suffer when I got my hands on it again.

The question was, how exactly did I go about finding it? And what the hell was it doing in my house in the first place?

I remembered the way it sniffed the air, and the way it damned near purred my last name.

Darling was my mother's last name, which she'd graciously passed on to me, the unwanted product of a drunken one-night stand. Matty was spared that humiliation by his dad, who was adamant that any child of his would bear his name. Hinkins was better, a little.

My hand crept up my neck and I winced at the tenderness as my fingertips brushed the still-seeping cut there. Just lovely. I pulled my hand away and examined the thick red blood smeared across my fingertips. My vision narrowed to the streak of crimson, and the world around me pulsed. I couldn't explain the sensation. I'd seen my own blood a thousand times, but something about it in that instance felt… different. Powerful.

A frantic scratching noise stole my attention, and my gaze darted around the room. It wasn't coming from any of Matty's stuff.

"Now what?" Stepping quietly, I traced the sound back to my bedroom to find Lily flat on her belly pawing at something beneath my bed. Hope blossomed for a split second before logic kicked in. There was no way my brother could be hiding under there.

I got down on my hands and knees beside her and craned my neck to see what she was after. "It's just a box of old junk, Lily." I flattened myself on the floor and batted at it, dislodging the lid with my impatience. I hooked a finger over the lip of the box and dragged it out.

"See?" I said, motioning to the contents.

Lily sniffed hesitantly, then slammed her big paw down on the edge, flipping the box on its side and scattering my mom's old worthless crap all over the floor.

"What the hell, furball?"

She pawed at a few little trinkets before gently nudging something toward me with her snout. When I didn't reach for it, she picked it up gently with her teeth and brought it to me.

"What does this have to do with Matty?" I asked, taking it from her. Not that I expected an answer. Hellhound or no, she was still a canine. It wasn't like she could spell it out for me.

Did that stop her from huffing at me in the most condescending way?

Nope.

"What?" I snapped, tossing the necklace back on the floor with the other junk. "I obviously don't understand how a shitty bauble is supposed to help me here."

She would not let it go. She flicked the pendant with her nose, sending it tumbling back toward me. In a fit of tired, panicked irritation, I snatched it off the ground and glared at her. "I want to find Matty, not—"

I didn't get a chance to finish my rant, because the cursed thing sent a jolt of electricity up my arm so strong, I jerked hard enough to fling it across the room.

Holy shit.

I stared at it where it landed, then turned back to Lily. "What was that?"

She blinked slowly, then fetched the necklace and dropped it in front of me again. Only that time, when I reached for it, she backed away from me until she was standing in the doorway.

"Come on, really?" She had the balls to walk it over to me but not to stand within fifteen feet of me when I grabbed it? "Wuss," I muttered under my breath.

I let my hand hover over it for a second before I pulled back. It probably wasn't the best idea to latch onto the thing while I was sitting on my ass. I rolled to my feet and crouched over it, trying to convince myself to pick it back up.

What if it tries to electrocute me again?

But how could it? The thing was a dumb little necklace for Pete's sake.

Maybe I'm going insane? The whole batshit crazy thing does kind of run in my family.

I huffed out a breath and grabbed the chain before I could talk myself out of it. And, drumroll please... nothing happened. Lily watched my every move without moving a muscle, and when I looked over at her, she flicked her chin up like she was telling me to get on with it.

"Okay, what was I doing with it when it zapped me?" I asked, talking to myself, but roping Lily in whether she liked it or not. I held it, letting the amber pendant swing in front of me. "You flicked it at me. Then I grabbed it. Oh, but I grabbed the pendant, not the chain."

I rolled my shoulders back and sucked in a breath. "Here goes nothing."

I dangled the pendant over my open hand for about ten seconds before I convinced myself to drop it into my palm. Balling it into my fist, I braced for another shock, but nothing happened. "Seriously? Not even a spark?"

When I shot a glance at Lily, I swear to all the gods, the dog was looking at me like I was an idiot. I mean, I felt like an idiot, so that was fair. But still.

I thought back over every move I'd made. I was irritated, and Lily was being pushy. I'd grabbed the thing off the ground in a huff and told Lily I just wanted to find Matty.

"Is it one of those wish fulfillment deals?"

Lily's lips peeled back, revealing just a hint of her very sharp teeth. Not gonna lie, it was a little creepy.

"So, maybe if I think about what I want, it'll bring it to me?" It sounded insane, but so did a zap-happy necklace.

I thought briefly about testing it on something simple, like asking it to bring me a beer. But why waste the time? And really, what did I have to lose? If it didn't work, it didn't work. Then I would just have to find some other way to track Matty down.

Of course, I was operating under the assumption that the damned thing wasn't a summoning device.

"This isn't going to summon the demon, is it?" I asked, looking at Lily expectantly.

She gave me nothing.

Because she's a hellhound, Never. A big, bad version of a dog. Not the master of the universe.

"You know what? Never mind." I pulled up a mental image of my brother, gripped the pendant tight, and repeated what I'd said before. "I want to find Matty."

The hum started in my palm and spread like liquid fire up my arm, across my shoulders, and into my core, until my whole body was thrumming with a foreign energy.

Lily let out another whimper and laid down.

I opened my mouth to tell her everything would be okay, but I couldn't breathe. The air around me thickened, and my bedroom faded to darkness. Then came the pressure. And the wet. It rolled in all around me, filling my ears and my nose. Turquoise lights flickered and darted across my vision until I closed my eyes against the sting.

Am I drowning? That would be just my luck. Behold the foolish girl who picked up a magic necklace that drowned its unsuspecting victims.

More cool liquid pressed in around me, slowly crushing me. My lungs burned in my chest, desperate for a fresh supply of oxygen, and the growing pressure of the water against my body ratcheted up my anxiety. It took all my focus not to thrash wildly into a full-blown panic.

I forced my eyes open, ignoring the bite of pain long enough to find what I was looking for. *Light!* My heart leapt. It wasn't daylight, at least it didn't look like it through the burn of salt stinging my poor eyes, but it was enough to give me direction.

My chest was locked up tight, but I managed to force a little breath out without totally losing control. When the bubbles started to rise toward the light, I let the panic take over and used it to drive my muscles, to pull myself up and up, until I finally broke through the surface with a desperate gasp.

I managed to suck in more liquid than air with that gasp and ended up hacking it out painfully while I tried to tread water. For the first time in my life, I cursed my choice of footwear. Chunky leather boots were great for a party and decent for demon hunting, but less-than-ideal for swimming. And my leather jacket wasn't much better.

The pendant was still clutched in my fist, and I shoved it deep in my pants pocket, fighting the slowly rolling water. I kept my arms and legs moving as I spun in a circle, searching for anything that might help me stay afloat. Or, you know, land. I would have been cool with that too.

And there it was, a tiny tropical island with a white sand beach glowing in the moonlight... way off in the distance.

HOOK

CHAPTER 4

"Is she alive?"

The men backed away from the woman's body without a word, and I got my first good look at her. She probably wasn't from any of the islands I frequented, not with those clothes. And her hair was strange. It was probably shoulder-length when it wasn't plastered to her skin, but the color was what drew my attention; dark brown, almost black at the roots, lightening to a brilliant red at the tips.

I'd never seen anything like it. Blues and greens were common among the magical creatures in the realm. Even a few pinks here and there, but nothing quite so bold as that red.

Maybe she was some kind of hybrid. I'd seen some interesting adaptations in recent years, and most of those stemmed from a union between a shifter and a mer.

Her chest hitched and a tiny groan escaped her lips. The dangers of drowning didn't end just because a person made it to dry ground, especially if she'd inhaled too much saltwater. From the look of her, that was a real possibility.

I crouched beside her and tried to gently roll her on her side to keep her from choking, but the minute I touched her, her eyes snapped open.

"Get the fuck off me!" Her fist connected with my jaw with surprising force, knocking me off balance.

No question it would leave a bruise, for a moment.

My men all took a step forward, and I held up a hand to stop them. Touching her without permission was my misstep, however well intentioned.

The woman looked at my men, narrowed her eyes, then turned that fierce gaze back at me. "Oh, come on." She groaned the words.

Before I could ask what she was talking about, her eyelids fluttered shut. She drew in a deep breath.

I considered warning her against doing it again, given the way her damp shirt clung to her curves, but she collapsed back against the sand with a dull thud. Her whole body went into convulsions. I finally managed to get her on her side—this time without catching a fist to the face.

She came round enough to spend the next several minutes coughing and gagging up an impressive amount of water. Truly. It was a miracle there had been any room in her lungs for air. When the shudders finally died down, I eased her onto her back.

I had questions, starting with what she was doing on my island, but when I ran a finger down her cheek, she didn't react in the slightest. I used my thumb to gently pull one of her eyelids open and let it fall shut again.

"She's out cold," I said, more to myself than anyone.

I scanned the beach for any belongings that might have washed ashore with her, but only weathered seashells and decaying strips of seaweed littered that particular stretch of sand.

Staring down at her and that wild hair of hers, I couldn't fathom leaving her out in the elements. "We'll take her back to the ship."

One of my men moved to grab her arms as though he intended to drag her to the skiff like a sack of flour, and it was all I could do not to pull out my cutlass and gut him right there. He must have sensed the violence pulsing from me because he backed away from her with his hands up.

"I will take her," I said, a tad alarmed by my reaction and the possessiveness in my voice.

That didn't stop me from standing and resting a hand on the pommel of my cutlass to make sure my meaning was clear. William gave me a strange look, but he didn't question me.

"Come on, men," he said, motioning down the beach. "We still have a few more traps to set now that the sun is up."

"Make sure to set a few where the streams reach the sand!" I yelled after them.

There was no guarantee where the Darling boy would end up on the island, but fresh water was something every human needed for survival. Which made laying traps along the streams a good bet.

It was only when the others were headed toward the wall of greenery lining the beach that William stepped closer to me, keeping his eyes on the men with his voice at little more than a whisper. "Is everything all right, sir?"

Well, I'd just had the urge to slit a man from crotch to chin for thinking about touching a woman I'd never met. That was a *little* unusual.

"Nothing to worry about."

He studied me for another second, then nodded once. "We'll meet you back at the skiff shortly, sir."

"Very well."

I waited until he joined the others beyond the border of the beach before turning back to the woman. She had a beautiful face when it wasn't contorted with rage. I knelt beside her, tracing the lines of ink decorating her wrist. I did this in part to see if it would wake her, but also because I wanted to. Needed to.

Pulling back the sleeve of her jacket revealed even more ink, and I imagined both her arms were covered shoulder to wrist in those delicate, swirling black tattoos, without a hint of color to be seen.

Interesting.

I'd seen plenty of women with tattoos, but they were always small, discreet, and without fail, colorful. This strange woman wore her dark artwork out in the open, save for the jacket that currently kept it hidden. Based on just what I could see of it, the designs would have taken an enormous amount of time to ink, not to mention the prolonged pain she would have endured.

I traced my index finger lightly along another fine black swirl. "What do these mean to you?"

I stayed with her like that for several minutes, but she didn't stir. So I gently hoisted her into my arms and headed back across the beach toward the skiff. We were just a hundred paces or so away when she shifted in my arms, blinking up at me with devastatingly blue eyes. I thought for a moment I could drown in those eyes, until they narrowed dangerously.

"Fucking pirate." She hurled the words at me like a weapon then bucked violently in my arms. I fought to keep my grip on her, but the woman was wily. I had no choice but to drop her, not if I didn't want to hurt her.

She didn't waste a second after she hit the sand, rolling deftly and leaping to her feet before taking off up the beach.

Every calm, rational bone in my body said I should let her go.

The woman clearly didn't desire my assistance. She also wasn't from the island. Of that I was sure. Which meant she had no idea of the twisted evils that awaited her in the shadows of that lush forest.

I probably had at least a few hours before the demon made it back from the human realm with its new prize. That time could be spent waiting impatiently, or it could be spent in a more interesting way. A smile crept across my lips as I jogged toward the tree line.

The woman might not have known where she was going, but I had a pretty good idea where she'd end up. Perhaps she'd be a bit less combative once she'd had a chance to burn off a little of that wild energy.

CHAPTER 5

Yep, I was lost. And not like 'I couldn't find my car in the parking lot' lost. Palm leaves and reaching ferns slapped against my skin with every step that drew me deeper into the strangely dense tropical landscape.

From my shitty little apartment in that crap city to... wherever the hell I'd ended up. That was fine by me, so long as my path took me away from the wannabe pirate. I had more important things to worry about, like finding my brother.

Was I in a forest? Or was it called a rainforest when it was so close to the ocean?

No, that didn't sound right. Not that it mattered much. Trying to figure out worthless crap like that was just how my brain worked in moments of stress.

Giant palms stretched up toward the sky, but a jumble of other trees and plants effectively blocked my view, blotting out the sun before it had a chance to shine down into the shadowed, humid world below. And holy hell was it humid.

I paused, taking in the sounds surrounding me. They seemed to grow louder the longer I stood still, as if the chirp of a million tiny birds worked to multiply the swelling buzz of insects. The place was teeming with life, activity, and movement. And it was playing hell on my senses.

Leaves rustled softly and tiny particles of something, maybe dust, glittered in the rare rays of sunlight that managed to pierce the shroud of darkness above. But how could there be dust when it was so damned humid? I stripped off my jacket and held it out in front of me, wincing at the state of the poor thing. Fighting demons was why I couldn't have nice clothes.

It was also the reason I didn't get attached to much; I could find a way to ruin anything eventually.

Now that was a chipper thought. Way to let that inner positivity flow, Nev.

I tied the sleeves around my waist and kept moving. There was no time for self-loathing when I was lost in the forest. Lost and thirsty. My stomach growled loudly, and I rolled my eyes. Of course, because hunger was the perfect companion to my already stellar situation.

There had to be a trail around somewhere, right? Something to show me I was on the right path.

"Who exactly do I think I'm kidding? I have no clue where I'm going." I glanced behind me only to find myself fully ensconced in that dense green undergrowth. I couldn't even tell where I'd come from.

Some people had an internal sense of direction. *Lucky bastards.* If I had a landmark to reference, I could find my way. But surrounded by a forest of trees, vines, and ferns that all started to blend together? That wasn't really the best situation for my directionally challenged ass.

The lush landscape around me shifted and shimmered as I picked my way through the foliage, pushing glistening palm fronds out of my way. Succulent, ropy vines sprawled across the ground and spiraled up the trunk of nearly every tree in sight. It was gorgeous. Suffocating, but gorgeous.

A brightly colored bird squawked and chirped as it flitted from one vantage point to the next.

"Maybe that's what I need, higher ground."

I kicked a cluster of vines out of my way and sidled up to a tree that looked promising. Tilting my head back, I followed its trunk up and up, until the gnarled, papery bark disappeared beyond the canopy.

"Yeah, this will do nicely. I just have to figure out how to climb it." I talked myself through it. "Maybe if I wedge my hand there and my boot here?"

I managed to pull myself up all of three feet before the creepy crawlies figured out there was fresh meat invading their domain. Tiny bites stung my hands and chest and I yelped, letting go of the tree and stumbling to the ground.

I rolled and flopped on the damp dirt, slapping at my chest and stomach, flinging my jacket off and to the side. Then I scrambled to my feet, shaking my head violently in case any of those mean little bastards decided to hitch a ride. I followed that up by brushing off every inch of my body. Well, every inch I could reach.

But that creepy, crawling sensation refused to fade.

The forest around me was oblivious to my tantrum, though that brilliant blue bird with the orange beak perched on a branch just out of reach honked noisily at me. If I didn't know better, I might have thought the damned thing was laughing at me. When it flapped its wings happily and honked again, I flipped it my own version of the bird.

Karmic retribution for my treatment of the animal was swift when I turned to find my jacket soaking in a puddle of thick, brown mud.

Perfect.

I plucked it from the slimy pool and shook it off as best I could, giving it a little test sniff before tying it back around my waist. At least it didn't smell foul. And I'd learned a valuable lesson: No climbing trees without checking for insectile nasties first. Noted.

A few minutes later, I was entirely too focused on the angry red welts forming on my hands as I pulled my shirt away from my sticky skin, that I almost stumbled into the most breathtaking lagoon I'd ever seen. Not that I'd come across many lagoons in my near total lack of travels. Unless the manmade versions at the city zoo didn't count.

A moss-colored toad with a bright yellow stripe down its back croaked lazily at me from the edge of the crystal water.

"Hey, buddy." I crouched a few feet from it to get a better look. The area was calmer than the rest of the forest, quieter, and a gentle ripple a few yards out into the pond drew my attention.

A homely, middle-aged woman emerged from the pond, gliding forward slowly until she was only waist-deep in the blue-green water. I didn't see her lips move, but a gentle, soothing hum filled my ears, and a tiny sigh escaped my parched lips.

She motioned for me to come into the water with a sweet smile, like a mother beckoning her small child, and even though little alarm bells were ringing in the back of my mind, I couldn't help myself. My feet moved before my brain had time to process what I was doing. Even if I'd wanted to stop, I didn't think I could. But the thing was, I didn't want to. Every atom in my body wanted to go to her.

I was just one short step from the water's edge when strong arms banded around me and hauled me backward.

"Close your eyes." The man's whispered voice was abrasive, cutting through that growing feeling of serenity like a chainsaw.

I bucked and bent to get away from him, to get closer to the woman in the lake, but I couldn't move.

"Don't let her in your head." His warm breath in my ear sent a shiver through me, triggering a flood of warmth in my core. "Close your mind to her." My eyelids fluttered, and I leaned back into his hard body, willing him to chase that whisper with his lips against my neck.

Wait. What am I doing?

The vibration humming through me changed, morphing from warm and welcoming to urgent. It called me to the water, demanding my obedience, but the arms around me were steel bars anchoring me in place.

I wrenched myself forward and twisted back, elbowing my captor in the face hard enough to send a jolt of pain up my arm. The man grunted and released me, but I felt his fingers reaching out and grasping my thin shirt as I stumbled forward. I landed on my knees at the edge of the pond, the blessedly cool liquid soaking through my jeans.

It felt divine compared to the pressing heat of the day. How incredible would it be to wade out into that cool spring?

Gods, how I wanted to.

But part of me wanted to listen to the man too. To obey.

Where the hell was that coming from?

His heated voice tried to coax me back, but the woman in the water never took her eyes off me. I could feel her want, her need, so thick I could taste it with each breath.

It was all too much.

I inched backward, slamming my eyes shut as I moved. "Leave me alone." My voice sounded like it was a million miles away. Soft mud squished between my knuckles, and I dug my fingers into the ground at my side, sucking in a deep breath. "Leave me the fuck alone!"

The hum raised in pitch until it felt like a banshee was trapped inside my head. A familiar, coppery taste filled my mouth and warmth dribbled from my nose. Could the woman in the lake kill me with her mind?

I shoved myself back as hard as I could and when I opened my eyes, the picturesque lagoon was gone, replaced by a stinking black pool of sludge and slime.

And the woman—*oh gods*—I fought back a gag.

She must have sensed that her spell had been broken, because she rushed the water's edge screeching like a madwoman. Her rotten green teeth showed through her sneer and the purple, bruised flesh of her face and neck sagged in the most sickening way.

What would happen if I wrapped my hand around that water-logged neck? Would the skin slide and peel off under my fingers?

I retched again, dragging myself to my feet and stumbling.

The woman cackled like a lunatic, a sound so unsettling it made my stomach roll, before melting back into the darkness. The moment she was out of sight, the air around me shimmered and the illusion of an enchanting, breathtaking lagoon returned.

"Definitely not in Kansas," I whispered.

"It's a glamour." The man's coarse voice still stirred something in me, but when I turned, I found myself face to face with the asshole from the beach.

"Oh, for fuck's sake. What the hell do you want with me?"

He tilted his head as he wiped blood from his split lip. "'Thank you' is the generally accepted response when one has been rescued from meeting a rather grotesque end."

I planted my hands on my hips and instantly regretted the move when I realized my palms were still coated in foul-smelling mud. Then I remembered the taste of blood in my mouth and spit on the ground in front of me.

"That was part of the glamour too." He was studying me now and doing nothing to hide it. "Most people who get that close end up as siren food."

I clenched my jaw so tight my teeth ached. "Thank you," I gritted out.

One side of his kissable lips quirked up in a smile, and he looked almost impressed.

Wait. Kissable? Did I hit my head?

"I only got you away from the water, miss. You're the one who broke the siren's connection."

"Well, goodie for me," I muttered. Then I glared up at him. "Were you following me?" I stalked forward, stopping just out of arm's reach. "You know what, no. Let's back up a little farther. Why were you carrying me across the beach?"

He folded his arms over his chest and lifted his chin, looking down at me with all the arrogance in the world.

"Answer me," I snarled at him, but his response was a maddeningly calm lift of his brow.

"I don't owe you an explanation." He dropped his arms and took a step toward me. "If anything, you owe me an apology for accosting me."

I glanced at his split lip, and a twinge of guilt snaked through me. But why? I mean, yeah, he probably saved my life, but he'd also manhandled me. The memory of his whisper in my ear sent a wicked chill through me, and I clenched my fists, digging my short fingernails into my palms.

"I was defending myself."

That fucking smirk made a comeback right before he tilted his head back and laughed. "You are an ungrateful little thing, aren't you?"

"You're the one who should know better than to sneak up on a woman."

"Even a foolish woman who runs herself right into a siren's lair?" He held his hands up and backed away a few steps. "Never fear, my lady. It is not a mistake I will make again." Then he turned and walked away.

Was he fucking kidding me?

"I am not foolish!" I stalked after him, telling myself it was because I wasn't done with the conversation yet. "Where were you taking me earlier?"

He didn't turn to look at me, but when he drew a short sword from the scabbard at his hip I paused. "Holy shit, are you a *real* pirate?"

That got his attention at least. "As opposed to imaginary?" When I didn't respond, he shook his head. "I assure you, I am quite real." He swung his blade down, clearing a path through the underbrush.

Whatever the hell he was, if he'd followed me out here without getting lost, then he probably knew more about the island. Which meant I might be able to use him to find Matty. It wasn't like I'd found any other leads.

"Wait, please?" I tried to inject some remorse into my voice, but I was pretty sure it just came out sounding needy. Great.

He didn't stop, just kept slicing his way through the reaching ferns and vines.

"Please. I'm lost out here." Now I was pleading with a pirate. That was what my life had come to.

He paused and turned his head, but not far enough to make eye contact. "You don't say."

That flicker of irritation growing inside me suddenly ignited. "You know what? Fuck off. I've had a shit day an--"

He moved so quickly that I barely had a chance to suck in a breath before his big body was looming over me. His light brown eyes, with just a hint of amber at the edges, burned through me, but my gaze drifted down, first to his lips, then his neck, before zeroing in on the way his artery pulsed beneath his skin.

What would he taste like if I licked him there? Saltwater and sunshine?

He cleared his throat, just loud enough to snap my focus, and I glared up at him.

"Your beauty does not excuse your language." Despite the whisper of a smirk on his face, his voice was low, dangerous. "Do not speak to me like that again."

Every rebellious instinct in me screamed for me to punch him in the throat or grab him by those broad shoulders and shove my knee into his crotch.

Instead, my body betrayed me in the worst way. Warmth flooded my cheeks, slinking down into my neck and chest as I shuddered under the command. I licked my lips to respond, trying to find words that simply would not manifest.

His gaze followed the movement and his pupils flared, dilating until his irises were little more than slivers rimming the dark depths before he turned away.

I stood there for a minute, with my chest strung as tight as a drum, trying to make sense of my body's reaction. Was there any sense to be made of it? How deeply damaged was I to actually get turned on by that command, or by him?

Really fucking damaged.

Even just thinking the curse word triggered a rush of saliva and a flush of heat between my thighs.

What would he do if I said it out loud?

I was still trying to remember how to form a coherent sentence when he spoke without looking at me. "Stay close." His shoulders and back were fixed in stone, but his voice had a deliciously raw edge to it. "I'll make sure you arrive back at the beach unharmed."

HOOK

CHAPTER 6

"What's your name?" she asked.

It was impossible to ignore her trailing behind me, stomping through the underbrush like a tiny, angry elephant. In the fifteen minutes she'd been following me, the woman hadn't made any attempt at stealth. Yet the sound of her voice still prickled my skin.

"Ladies first." I slashed through another web of vines crossing our path back to the ship. After a long stretch of silence, I almost turned to make sure she hadn't fallen prey to one of the many dangers lurking in the woods.

"Never."

I had to smile at the hint of defiance in her voice. "Then I see no reason to share mine."

"That's my name, genius. Never."

I stopped and turned to find her features set in a mask of irritation. I knew exactly how she felt. "What kind of parent would name a child Never?"

A slash of pink brightened her cheeks and her eyes narrowed. "You're an asshole."

Ah. Now we were getting somewhere. She either didn't want me to know who she really was, or she disliked her real name so much that she didn't use it. "Your real name, miss. What is your given name?"

She crossed her arms over her chest. "Quid pro quo."

I had to press my lips together to stop the grin trying to form there. The flippant use of Latin was a bit of a surprise coming from the lips of such a foul-mouthed creature. A contradiction that bordered dangerously on delightful.

She shook her head with another little. "It means something for something. I offered you something personal about me, and now it's your turn."

I laughed. I couldn't help it. It just burst out of me. "I am aware of the meaning."

Her jaw worked overtime, clenching and grinding, and I considered, for one very brief moment, giving her what she'd asked for.

But where was the challenge in that?

I turned on my heel and headed for the beach, which was only a few yards ahead of us. The ivory sand peeked through, a beacon guiding me from the darkness lurking beneath the canopy and drawing me back to my ship.

If I could get her to the beach, then at least she'd have a fighting chance. Besides, I had my own tasks to see to.

I glanced behind me before stepping into the dappled sunlight at the edge of the trees, but the infuriating woman hadn't moved an inch. She stood there in the shadows with her hands on her hips like she controlled the world. It was enticing in a way, that confidence, but it also made a part of me long to take her down a notch.

She was watching me with a look that said she could stand there until the sky crumbled around her. Luckily, the natural world, in its infinite wisdom, saw fit to lend me a hand.

"You're welcome to remain here, if you like," I offered in my best, most genial voice. "Though you may wish to reconsider choosing that particular spot." I motioned with my cutlass to the branch just above her.

She speared me with a vicious glare before reluctantly glancing up. The scream that ripped from her throat was indecent, and my cold, hard heart melted just a little at the thought of making her scream like that in my bed.

Never ducked to the side and checked her surroundings, presumably to make sure there were no more chameleon constrictors dangling from the trees near her, then she marched toward me. From the fury sparkling in her deep blue eyes, there was a good chance she was about to take a swing at me. I braced for it, ready to catch her hand and spin her into me if she tried.

I wanted her to try.

But she stopped just shy of arm's reach. "No one calls me by my real name. Ever."

I flinched back from the venom in her voice. "Is it truly that bad?"

She tilted her head back and let out a sigh that sounded eons older than she looked. The muscles and tendons in her neck flexed and pulled with the movement, and the mental image of wrapping my hand around her slender throat flipped a long dormant switch in me, bringing my cock to attention.

There was no way the woman was human. Not *just* human, anyway. She must have been part succubus or siren because nothing had piqued my sexual interest in years.

Decades.

"Will you only help me get out of here if I tell you?" She was studying me now, and I shifted my stance to disguise the bulge of my growing erection.

"Those are my terms, yes."

The stubborn woman looked down and rubbed her hands up and down her thighs like she was preparing for some monumental task. "It's Moira."

My stomach twisted. "Moira what?"

And for the love of all the worlds, please don't say Darling.

"Moira Darling, but if you ever call me that, I'll cut off your tiny little balls and feed them to my hellhound as a snack. Now, quid pro fucking quo."

I pressed my lips together, barely able to suppress the growl that burned my chest. Why had I expected anything different? Clearly her presence was a trick of some kind. The demon wouldn't bring a woman to the island for any other purpose.

And certainly not a Darling woman. Not after what Wendy had done.

Oh, but the demon was certainly clever using a woman as attractive as the creature before me. Quite clever. The woman had a pull that was undeniable.

Only now, I'd seen through the ruse. She was a distraction. A ploy meant to keep me from finding the Darling boy in time. And someone was going to pay dearly for playing with me.

I spun and headed for the beach without another word.

"We had a deal!" A thread of panic laced her words, but I didn't bother looking over my shoulder.

I kept moving, intent on putting some distance between me and the devil woman. She'd played her part well, that much was certain. When I brushed through the final barrier of lazy ferns and rustling palms, an errant thought snagged my attention.

What if she was telling the truth?

Her clothes, her language, they weren't native to the island. And those tattoos.

I took two more steps, my boots sinking into the fine white sand. That was where I waited until she followed me out of the shadows, blinking against the sudden brightness.

"Why are you here?" I asked.

"I don't see how that's any of your business, pirate." Moira, aka Never, mumbled a string of startlingly colorful expletives under her breath as she stalked past me.

"Wait." She didn't stop moving, but it only took two quick steps to catch up and grab her arm.

She wheeled on me like I'd assaulted her. "What?"

My men were watching the exchange from the shore with mixed expressions of surprise and amusement. Was it a trick, or wasn't it? I honestly couldn't tell.

"My name is Atlas."

She ran her tongue along the edge of her teeth. "Atlas what?"

"I have no surname." Because the offspring of a titan and goddess didn't need one.

And yet someone in this cursed realm had bestowed one upon me all the same. *Hook.* It was an unpleasant moniker, one meant to belittle and demean, and one I hadn't heard in more years than I could count. Likely because it tended to trigger a violent response from me.

"But most people call me Captain," I offered.

I didn't know what reaction I was expecting from the woman at my offering. Maybe a little softening, perhaps a touch of acquiescence.

Her bark of bitter laughter definitely wasn't on the list.

"Captain?" She cocked her head and gave me the most condescending look. "Seriously?"

She glared out at my ship, anchored a fair distance from shore, and rolled her eyes. "I'm trapped in a place that looks like Neverland, and I'm talking to the captain of a pirate ship. Why not jump right in and introduce yourself as Captain Hook? James Tiberius or some shit. I suppose next you're going to tell me that if I wanted to fly my ass off this crappy island, all I'd have to do is believe." Her lip curled up in a snarl and she yanked her arm free of my grip. "I don't have time for this shit, *Hook.*"

Fury rolled over me, thick and hot, bringing my anger to the surface in a rush. Nearly a century had passed since anyone in my enchanted waters had dared to utter that name aloud. And the last person to say it to my face...

Well now, it'd been the infamous Wendy Moira Angela Darling.

A murmur of unease filled the space behind me, reminding me that my men were back there, watching everything.

I gripped the pommel of my cutlass hard enough for the metal to morph under the strain. "Detain her."

The girl put up a vicious fight, drawing blood from four of my sailors before they finally managed to subdue her. Even then, calling her subdued wasn't entirely accurate. She'd kicked and squirmed the whole way back to the ship. There were a couple moments where I'd seriously considered dropping her into the water and letting the merfolk deal with her.

It had been a tempting notion.

But we'd made it to the ship without her flailing capsizing the skiff.

Which was why I now had a very angry, very colorful woman bound to the chair in my quarters. I'd been standing at the helm trying to get my bearings since our return, despite the fact the anchor was still down, and we weren't going anywhere anytime soon.

I just needed time to think.

I would much rather have been on the island with my men, checking the traps in case we managed to snag the Darling boy. Instead, I'd left a small team on shore, and I was here. And that damned woman wouldn't stop running that mouth of hers.

Not gagging her had clearly been a mistake.

Even my men were giving the closed door to my private room a wide berth as they went about their duties.

I sucked in a steadying breath and stepped away from the wheel. "Keep an eye on things, William."

He lifted one bushy eyebrow my way, then reached in his vest pocket and shook out a nearly pristine kerchief. "You're going to want this."

I took the offering, turning it over in my hand. "For?"

He chuckled, his cheeks glowing pink with humor. "I imagine it's the only way you'll get a word in with that one." He cocked his thumb toward the door.

We'd been back on the ship for two hours, but somehow, the mysterious woman who claimed to be a Darling was still yelling. The vibrant, creative insults she hurled about in that empty room were enough to make even a seasoned sailor blush, and a quick glance around the deck confirmed my assessment.

"She certainly has… endurance," I said with a shake of my head. William laughed again, a full belly laugh, and I let myself smile for a moment. "It's good to hear that sound again, old friend. It's been too long."

His amusement died down to a chuckle, and he nodded as he grabbed the helm.

We had been sailing the same pristine waters day after day, week after week, for decades on end, just waiting for something to happen. That wasn't living. It was existing, and I'd taken to medicating with an inordinate amount of enchanted rum to maintain that bleak existence.

For the first time in a very long time, I didn't want to feel numb.

Below deck, Cook was already hard at work preparing the evening meal, and I let him know to send up a tray of food and drink the moment it was ready. Then I headed for my quarters.

The cool metal of the ornate knob centered me when I stood in front of the door. The woman's yelling had finally, blissfully ceased, but I still needed to walk into that room and establish dominance. She needed to know who she was dealing with.

So why was I hesitating? It was my room she was in. My personal space. She was only locked in there to keep her from finding a way to throw herself overboard. That, and to give her a modicum of privacy, away from the lust-laden gazes of my men. Not that any of them were showing an ounce of interest in her after her profane tirade.

I turned the knob and shoved the door open, expecting to see Never glowering up at me from the center of the room. It took half a second to realize the room was empty before movement in my periphery caught my attention. I ducked a split second before something heavy crashed against the door frame above my head. Wooden splinters exploded every which way, raining down around me like the world's worst confetti.

Chains rattled in the confines of the room, and something hard smashed against my shoulders, driving me forward before I had time to pull myself fully to my feet. I stumbled over something, wheeled for balance, and swung around in time to find myself face to face with a woman possessed.

Violence contorted Never's delicate features, and she took another swing at me, using the arm of a chair as a bludgeon.

My reading chair?

I winced inwardly at the loss but managed to catch her arm before she connected. I wrenched the makeshift weapon from her grip and tossed it aside, pulling her in close.

Too close.

The thought flickered like a warning, but I shoved it aside. No one attacked me in my own home. Not even a creature as enticing as her.

Her breath came in ragged gasps. The rise and fall of her chest against mine felt unexpectedly erotic, sending a wave of fire rolling through me. A flame I'd thought was long forgotten to the endless span of time.

Her pink lips were angry and chapped, but that did nothing to quell my sudden need to taste them. To taste her.

I leaned in slowly, locking my gaze with hers before our lips met.

The flash of rage in those gorgeous eyes registered a heartbeat too late.

She whipped forward, driving the hard curve of her forehead into my face. Half a second sooner and she would have connected with the bridge of my nose. Instead, she connected with my mouth, and pain flared as my upper lip split open again. I clenched my hands tighter around her small arms.

No one had made the mistake of causing me pain in a very long time. Let alone twice in the same day. The rush of desire that had been building in me morphed into something else, dark and dangerous.

A jagged thrum of unchecked emotion coiled inside and had me grinding my teeth while I fought for control. I hadn't let my temper get the better of me in ages.

A man in my position couldn't afford to lose control.

But the woman seemed intent on taking every ounce of discipline I possessed and tearing it to shreds. I scowled down at her, relishing the feel of the hot blood trickling over my bottom lip.

"Are you quite finished?" The words came out in a snarl, and she shrank away from me.

Oh no, she was not getting off that easy.

I shook her, hard. "Answer me."

The hate dripping from her glare only fueled the new storm growing inside me. I tossed her like a rag doll to the floor. She hit hard but scrambled to her knees with so much defiance pulsing from her I could taste it in the air.

I hauled her back up, pulling her close enough that I could see the threads of black slicing through her deep blue irises. Another command danced on my tongue. My fingers twitched, and she whimpered. It was a tiny sound, but it sent a shot of ice through my overheated veins.

And there was real fear in her eyes. She was burying it under a mountain of anger and hatred, but it was there.

Shit.

I needed to back off. Now.

Pushing her away, I shook my head. "It was not my intention to hurt you."

What the hell was happening to me?

Fear and anger warred for dominance in her features, and that blistering hatred rolled off her in waves.

My calves hit the settee and I dropped onto the upholstered cushion, fisting my hands in my hair as I leaned back. I sucked in a sharp breath and closed my eyes. She had every right to attack me. Every reason to feel like she needed to defend herself.

I was a monster, after all.

The waiting was the worst part. Waiting for her to launch her next offensive. Waiting to feel the burn of a blade slicing through my chest or the burst of agony from a heavy object striking the side of my head. Would she try to wrap one of those cold chains around my neck and choke the life out of me?

I wouldn't try to stop her. After the way I'd just handled her, I deserved it. All of it.

CHAPTER 7

The clink of the shackles at my wrists and ankles reverberated in the loaded silence of the room. It wasn't completely quiet though, not like a padded room or recording studio. There was a clock somewhere, ticking away, and the hollow thump of boots outside.

That asshole had left me in here for *hours*. At least it'd felt like hours. I'd yelled, begged, screamed at the top of my lungs for help, but no one on his godforsaken ship had even bothered to check on me.

And every minute I was trapped in here was another minute my brother was at the mercy of a demon that I had no idea how to find. I still didn't even know where the hell I was, let alone why that cursed pendant had brought me here.

If it was supposed to zap me to my brother, it'd missed its mark. By a long shot.

I swallowed painfully, trying to clear the gravel from my throat as I moved closer to the small couch. Hook stiffened but didn't move, not even to protect himself.

Why? And why had he looked apologetic when I winced?

Hook—that was what I was calling him because I was pissed, and I could tell it got under his skin—he'd just said he hadn't intended to hurt me. But he was a pirate, right? Why should I believe him?

"Kidnapping 101, genius." The rasp in my voice was unavoidable, but when he flinched at the sound, that tiny reaction eased my nerves a little. "The very least you can do is offer your captive water."

He sat forward, resting his hands on his knees and cast me a wary look. "You didn't try to attack me just now. Why not?"

Before I could answer, a knock filled the room. The fiery, confusing pirate beside me didn't take his eyes off me.

When I didn't answer, he let out a small huff and stood, brushing a few splinters of wood from his clothing. "Come in, Cook."

The door swung open on silent hinges, and a short, stocky man with a round belly entered the room carrying a massive tray loaded with silver-domed dishes. I didn't recognize him from the beach. Which meant he hadn't had a hand in tying me up. I made a mental note to let him live if I managed to get out of this ridiculous floating jail.

He stepped carefully around the remnants of the shattered chair, paying no further attention to the destruction while he set the tray on the table and began laying out dishes. When he was finished, he straightened, then turned and offered me a bow.

"Never, this is Cook," Hook said with a casual air, like he was introducing two friends at a dinner party.

"At your service, miss."

"At my service?" I lifted my hands, showing him the shackles and chains. "So far, the service on this ship is shit. Zero stars, do not recommend."

Confusion pinched his plump features and he turned to Hook. "Did you understand that?"

"It would appear she thinks our hospitality is lacking, though the star reference is peculiar."

"Oh!" Cook hustled back to the table, filling one of the fine metal goblets and bringing it to me with an apologetic smile. "Here you go, miss."

I hesitated, glancing between the men.

Yeah, not really in a trusting mood right now, guys.

Hook chuffed out an irritated breath and poured a little of the clear liquid into his own glass. "It's not poison." He took a drink. "See?"

It was all I could do not to rip the cup from the man's hand. My throat was raw from yelling, screaming, fighting, and nearly drowning, and I gulped the contents down greedily. What I didn't account for was the cold. The shock of it was too much for my tender throat, and I doubled over in a violent coughing fit before collapsing gracelessly to my knees.

I didn't hear him move, but when I looked up through the tears of exertion stinging my eyes, Hook was crouched beside me holding the goblet.

"Easy, love." His voice was warm and the concern threading through it almost sounded sincere. "Small sips."

A ragged laugh rattled out of me, at least until my throat convulsed again and a new bout of coughing savaged my already pained windpipe. Black spots dotted my vision, and I squeezed my eyes shut.

Don't gasp. Easy, shallow breaths, dummy.

The sound of boots on hardwood and a door closing quietly seeped through the haze. I wrapped the chains around my hands and squeezed, forcing myself to take careful, controlled breaths, focusing my mind on the sensation of the cool metal biting into my skin.

When I could finally breathe without fire licking its way up and down my trachea, I pried my eyes open. The goblet was on the floor beside me, but Hook wasn't. Sitting back, I grabbed the goblet and brought it gingerly to my lips. I scanned the room as I took that first careful first sip, only to find him staring back at me. He was back on the loveseat thing, leaning forward with his elbows on his knees, watching my every move.

"Feeling better?" he asked quietly.

I eyed him over the rim of the cup, then took another tentative swallow. My throat was in no condition for conversation, so I gave him a small nod.

"Good." He stood and walked to the table, lifting one shiny silver dome at a time and examining the contents. "Are you up for a meal? Cook really is quite the chef. It looks like our choices are fish, poultry of some kind—probably gull—and a selection of fresh fruits and grilled vegetables from the island."

He glanced over his shoulder, one eyebrow raised, but I wasn't moving from my spot on the floor. If I did, I was afraid the effort would trigger another fit of coughing and hacking. I wasn't sure my throat could take much more.

I shook my head and tried another sip of the cool water. The taste was crisp and clean, like a rush of rain over my tongue, and it soothed the worst of the angry burn when I wasn't trying to gulp it.

Hook scowled at the table, replacing the covers on the food before returning to me and holding out an expectant hand. When I hugged the goblet to my chest instinctively and tried to scoot away, he let out an impatient grumble.

"You do want more water, don't you?"

My heart sank a little when I looked down and saw the goblet was mostly empty. I was so freaking confused. And tired. And more than a little pissed off about being manhandled. Yes, I wanted more water, but I certainly didn't want to give him the satisfaction of doing me any favors.

I tipped the last of the cool liquid into my mouth and clutched the metal cup tightly, lumbering to my feet. Once I was upright, I shot him a triumphant glare. "I can get it myself, thank you." My voice was hoarse, barely more than a whisper, but I smiled inwardly when I got the words out without hacking up half a lung.

He moved away from the table, giving me ample room to pour my own water without him hovering. It would have been a thoughtful gesture, in theory, except I didn't understand the man or his motivations.

I took another drink of that gloriously cool water then set the goblet on the table. "Will you unshackle me?" I asked, holding my hands out toward him. "Please?"

His eyes narrowed just a hint. "Why would I do that?"

"Because I've done nothing wrong."

"You accosted me with a piece of furniture and ruined my favorite reading chair." He motioned to the pile of broken wood and torn upholstery.

"You chained me to it!"

Ouch, that was a bit too much. I pressed my hand to my throat and grabbed the goblet, taking a small sip. Then I tried again, a little quieter. "Your men chained me to the fucking thing on your orders. If you didn't want it smashed up, maybe you shouldn't go around kidnapping innocent bystanders."

His nostrils flared as he folded his muscled arms over his chest. "You hardly strike me as innocent, love."

"I'm not your *love*, asshole." The desperate urge to stab him was riding me hard.

I bent, pretending to reach for my knife.

He thought he knew exactly what I was doing, the arrogant asshole. One eyebrow winged up and another slip of a smile lifted his lips. Despite the fact that I already had multiple reasons to hate him, *legitimate* reasons, that look made my stomach flutter.

I rolled my shoulders back and gave him a little sneer. "Tell me where it is, and I promise not to slit your throat with it when I get it back."

He laughed, actual big bellows of laughter. "I'm not a fool, love. Your dagger is safe, but you're not getting it back until you can behave in a more civil manner."

It was his confidence that was getting to me. He wore that cockiness like a second skin. What he didn't know was that I'd found a dagger in the nightstand. His men took my blade when they chained me up, so I'd taken his. And I would let him go on thinking I was unarmed, for now.

At least until someone unchained me.

Hook studied me for a long moment, long enough that I had to fight the urge to break eye contact. Was it a challenge of some sort? A test? He finally looked away and I felt like I'd won something, some tiny but significant victory.

"Very well. I will remove the shackles." He reached in his pocket and pulled out a small, black key. "But the dagger stays with me until after we eat."

I thrust my wrists out in front of me. "Deal." Sucker.

He moved slowly, dancing the key across the back of his fingers as he stepped toward me. I wanted to look up, but my gaze was locked on that shiny black piece of metal. The way it flipped and floated over and between those strong fingers was mesmerizing.

I slammed my eyes shut. *How could I be so stupid?*

"Were you seriously just trying to hypnotize me?"

His dark chuckle rolled over me like a caress. I lifted my chin and opened my eyes, keeping them firmly locked on his. "Not cool."

Another low chuckle filled the diminishing space between us. "It was purely for my own safety."

"Ha!" *Again, ouch.* I swallowed delicately. "I'm the hostage here, remember?"

"Who has already proven to be a flight risk, and a violent one at that." He pressed a knuckle to his lip.

His perfectly shaped, perfectly unwounded lip. The one I was sure had split when I'd smashed my forehead into his annoying face. I also couldn't think of any great comeback since he wasn't wrong. So, I just held my wrists up a little higher, silently insisting he unlock the stupid shackles.

He pointed to the loveseat. "Sit."

A sharp retort curled on the tip of my tongue, but the fire rolling through me had me keeping my mouth shut and shuffling over, dropping onto the elegant fabric like a good little captive.

"Lean back."

A little tingle chased up my spine. "Why?"

His gaze raked over me from head to toe and back up. "Must you question everything?" He shook his head, not allowing me time to respond. "Give me your hands."

I leaned back and held them up with suspicion crawling across my skin. His grip was strong, but not painful, as his fingers wrapped around my forearm. The first shackle clinked and fell free. The relief was instantaneous, and I rolled my wrist gently in his grip.

His brow knitted. He ran his thumb in a light circle over the angry red skin there, but I tugged my arm back before he could put words to what he was thinking.

"I can do the other one," I said, turning my palm up.

He paused, then nodded once before dropping the key in my hand and wrapping both of his hands around mine. "Don't try anything, lo —Never."

I gave him a smile that was all teeth. "Wouldn't dream of it."

He narrowed his eyes, keeping his hands on mine for a moment, then he let go and took a step back.

I didn't waste any time unlocking my other wrist, though it was a bit more challenging than I'd anticipated. Bending down to release the shackles at my ankles wasn't much better. Every bone in my body groaned with the move.

Hook reached out a hand. He probably meant for me to return the key, but that fucker wasn't getting off that easy. I grabbed his outstretched hand and wrenched myself up, swinging as I rose.

He was fast, much faster than me, and managed to duck out of the way with my knuckles barely grazing him. To make matters worse, his grip on my hand didn't falter. He used my own momentum to spin me, curling me into him and clamping his arms around mine. Ropes of hard muscle enveloped me and a massive, wholly inappropriate thrill shot straight to my core.

His breath on my neck sent a shiver through me. "We had an agreement," he said, keeping his voice low.

"I said I wouldn't stab you," I ground out, bucking against him. "And I didn't." I tried to twist free, but those delicious bands of muscled steel were unyielding.

"I warned you not to try anything," he asked.

I could hear the smile in his voice, and it just pissed me off more. "Let me go!"

"No." He paused, holding me against his solid body while my heart rate notched higher and higher with every quiet tick of the unseen clock. "Here's the thing: I don't particularly enjoy being hit, and I would like to have a civil conversation with you, if you are, in fact, capable of civility." He paused again, letting his words sink in. "So, how shall we proceed?"

"You can start by letting go of me." I wriggled in his grip but froze when he sucked in a sharp breath. Something hard and long pressed into my backside.

"Unless you're eager to find yourself chained up again, I suggest you behave." His voice sounded different—strained—and the desire in the threat sent a chill racing through me.

But the moment his arms fell away, the rage inside me bubbled back to the surface. I balled my hands into fists and spun. I should have hit him with a quick hook to the jaw and a jab to the ribs. My body knew all the moves, but something in his expression stopped me.

Which just irritated me even more.

He lifted a brow. "Can we be civil now?"

Despite my better judgment, I took a step back.

"Then sit," he said, turning his back on me.

Hook moved to the table and pulled the covers off a few of the dishes. When the smell reached me, my stomach growled audibly. I tried to ignore the flash of heat across my cheeks when he gave me a little smirk. His mood changes were truly jarring. Then again, so were mine.

"Do you have a preference, Miss Darling?"

Now he was going to be all overly formal?

Fine. Whatever. At this point, I was too hungry to care.

I examined the available food, but it all looked equally delicious. Except for the fish. *Ugh. Why did people leave the head on fish when they cooked it?* I didn't want to look into the concave, soupy eye sockets of the thing I was about to eat.

"Anything but the fish."

He put the silver cover over the offending dish. "Poultry it is."

I sat stiffly, not allowing myself to show just how awkward I felt. He cut a large chunk of meat, then grabbed my plate and loaded it with a little of everything. When I reached for it, he shook his head and I let my hands fall into my lap.

The whole situation was weird.

He laid the plate in front of me, then set to work filling his own dish. I picked up the fork and checked around the table. "Do I not get a knife?"

"You won't need one." He dipped his chin with a little smile. "Nice try, though."

"I wouldn't stab you." He gave me a knowing look. "I probably wouldn't stab you. Right now. Is that better?"

"You've broken your word once, Miss Darling. I'm afraid that means trust is not something we share."

Well, that stung. Where did a filthy pirate get off accusing me of being untrustworthy? I gripped the fork tightly and considered driving the dull tines into his thigh the next chance I got. It might not do the same damage as a knife, but it would get the point across.

"My name is Never."

He took a seat at the opposite end of the table, safely out of reach of my murderous fork. After he flipped a napkin into his lap, he finally looked up at me. "Yes, I recall."

"Then why do you keep calling me Miss Darling?"

His eyebrows winged up and he cocked his head, studying me. The silence stretched until the air between us was heavy with tension.

"All right, can we be straight with each other?" I put my fork down and folded my hands in my lap. He followed my lead, only his movements were smooth, languid, and I found my mouth watering for a whole different reason.

Get it together, Nev. You're pissed at him, remember?

"I don't know what I did to upset you back at the beach, but I'm not here to cause you any trouble." I shook my head. "Because I don't even know where *here* is."

CHAPTER 8

Her gaze darted around the room, landing on the stretch of curtains along the back wall. They were drawn tight. All the light in the room came from a few colorful oil lamps and flickering candles.

If I was being honest with myself, she did seem lost. Lost but determined.

"What brought you here?" I asked, keeping my tone casual. The girl was inordinately suspicious, but her reactions to some things were still unpredictable.

She pressed her lips together and stared back at me.

Right.

"Okay, let's start with something a little easier. Where are you from?"

"Charleston."

That was it. That was all she deemed fit to offer, the name of a place that meant nothing to me. "Is that a village or perhaps another island?"

It wasn't one of the islands in my waters, I knew them all by every name they'd ever been given. Not to mention the Darling factor. If she really was who she said she was, then I had at least an idea, but I wanted to hear it from her lips.

"It's in South Carolina." She quirked her head at me, then closed her eyes and let out a little huff. "I've been trying to convince myself none of this shit is real. If I was dreaming, then the bushel of crazy in this place would make total sense. But I'm not dreaming, am I?" She looked up at me with an expression I couldn't quite place.

"I'm afraid not."

Never pulled in another breath, a little shakier than the last. She shook her head like she couldn't believe what she was about to ask. "Where am I? What is this place?"

And there it was, confirmation. I threaded a hand through my hair. "Still on Earth, if that's what you mean."

Her eyes narrowed and she leaned her elbows on the table. "That's not an answer."

"Technically, we're on a different plane than the one you came from." That was the easiest way to explain it, even if it wasn't entirely accurate. The realm we were in was more like a pocket carved out between dimensions, but she didn't need to know that. She just needed to know she wasn't in her world anymore, not really.

"Fuck." The word came out on a harsh whisper. She slumped in her chair and scanned the room again.

"What are you looking for?"

"A way out."

"Ah." I picked up my fork and speared a small piece of meat before motioning to her plate. "Eat something."

Her eyes drifted back to the curtains, and she pulled her bottom lip between her teeth. The effect it had on me was immediate and unnerving. Heat raced through my abdomen like a flaming blade, and the bulge of my growing erection pressed uncomfortably against the seam of my pants.

I tore my eyes away from her lips, locking my focus on my food. "It's already past dusk, and we're leagues from shore. I'm afraid you're stuck here until sunrise." When I dared a glance up, she was glaring at me again, thankfully without that plump little lip of hers pinched between her white teeth.

"I know how to swim." Her tone was defiant, challenging me to question her and further cementing how little she knew of my realm.

"How did you get here?" It was a fair question. Anyone from the enchanted islands would have known the open water wasn't safe at night, at least not to swim in.

Her expression closed off tight and she crossed her arms over her chest. That topic was off limits, apparently.

"Would you at least be willing to tell me if you have a reason for being here?"

Never looked longingly toward the curtains again, then back at me. "I'm looking for my brother."

The food turned to stone in my stomach. I'd suspected her arrival might be a repeat of the original Wendy situation the moment she'd told me her real name. I might not have been fond of the family, and gods knew Wendy had hated me in the end, but I certainly didn't want to curse Never to the same fate.

"And that search brought you here. How?"

"I don't know exactly. One minute I was at home and the next I was here." She motioned toward the curtains and the windows beyond. "Well, out there."

"In the water?"

She nodded once.

So, not the way Wendy came. At least we had one difference.

Wendy had arrived in my realm in a literal fire storm, dragging more than a dozen vicious demons through the rift in her wake. And they had not been happy about the relocation. It had taken me and my men years to find and subdue them all.

"Like I said, I can swim. Just let me go and you'll never have to see me again."

"There are creatures that prowl these waters at night. Violent, malevolent creatures who would love to get their claws in you. Letting you go now would be sending you to your death."

She snorted. "I did it last night and I was fine."

That got my attention. Surviving the waters of this realm at night was no small feat. In fact, unless she'd had help from some of the day creatures who were, for some reason, willing to risk their own lives to intervene, the sirens and nymphs would have torn her to ribbons long before her feet ever touched sand.

"Setting aside the fact that you were unconscious when we found you this morning—which suggests your survival was tenuous at best—I'm afraid the odds of repeating such a feat on an empty stomach are unfavorable." I motioned to her plate.

The woman was stubborn and even though I'd heard her stomach rumble more than once, she still refused to work with me.

I closed my eyes and leaned back, drawing in a steadying breath. Were all women from that horrid world so difficult? "Perhaps we can strike a deal."

"No deals." Her chair slid back across the wooden floor, and I opened my eyes to find her gripping the table as though she planned to flip it.

I held up a finger in warning. "Don't. I will not tolerate you wasting Cook's hard work by tossing it on the floor. If you don't want to eat, then don't, but do not disrespect his effort."

Her combativeness was getting under my skin, goading me, tearing holes in the net reining in my temper.

Her palms bit into the edge of the table. "Why should I do anything you say? I woke up to you trying to haul me off to your little boat, then you chased me through the trees. Yeah, you saved me from the gross looking lake lady, thanks for that, but then you were a condescending prick all the way back to the beach. And then…" Her voice rose in volume as her rant gained momentum. Color filled her cheeks and the bright red tips of her hair danced around her face. "Then you dragged me back here, chained me to a fucking chair, and left me in here for hours. Why in the name of fuck would I make a deal with *you*?"

She speared me with an angry glare that would have made a lesser man wither. To be fair, it did have an effect on me, just probably not the one she was hoping for.

I gathered my napkin from my lap and set it on the table as I stood. "Because you are not leaving here tonight."

The way she narrowed her eyes at me made my cock throb. That should have bothered me. An attraction to such a brash woman was illogical, but it obviously wasn't just anger she stirred in me.

"I will take you to the shore in the morning. You have my word on that. But if you try to sneak away or leave this ship before the sun is fully risen, I will chain you below deck and leave you there to rot."

Defiance flickered in her expression, but she took her time, clearly weighing her options. "Give me back my dagger."

"Not a chance, love."

She sneered viciously at me, then crouched beside the table, keeping her eyes locked on mine. There was a quick rustle of fabric and when she stood, she drove a small, gleaming blade into the tabletop with surprising force. I recognized it immediately as mine, from my very own nightstand.

"I could have killed you half a dozen times already."

She certainly wasn't short on surprises. "Remind me to have a chat with my crew about doing a better job of keeping weapons away from our captives. It appears they have become lax in their duties."

"Give me my dagger. Then I'll sit here and eat a meal with you like a good girl. But don't get any ideas." Her gaze cut to my bed.

My stomach tightened and adrenaline raced through my veins, but I shut the feeling down before it could spread. "Even the suggestion of such behavior is an insult, Miss Darling."

A muscle in her jaw twitched and she drove her fist down on the table. "Quit calling me that! My name is Never."

"Very well, I will call you whatever you wish, so long as you agree to do me the favor of not insulting my integrity by suggesting, or implying, or even thinking, that I would attempt anything of a sexual nature with you. I may be a pirate, but even I have standards."

Never flinched away from the last, and I wanted to claw the words back the instant they were out of my mouth.

"No problem. Thank you for the clarification." She yanked the blade free of the wood. "And I'm keeping this. Try to take it from me and you have *my* word that I'll drive it into your heart before the night is over." She slammed it down on the table, then dragged her chair back, sat down, and started shoveling food in her mouth in the least ladylike way imaginable.

CHAPTER 9

I just stood there, staring like a fool. I'd gotten under her skin with my comment, but I truly hadn't meant it the way she'd heard it. Was it worth trying to explain that to her? To explain that I'd meant I would never touch an *unwilling* woman in that way? And she was obviously unwilling.

When I didn't move, she pointed the tines of her fork at me and swallowed. "What?"

No, definitely not the right time to try to explain our misunderstanding. "I'll be right back," I said quietly. "Please continue."

She didn't, of course. Instead, she tracked my every movement as I crossed the room, opened my bureau, and retrieved the dagger she so desperately wanted.

I set it on the table beside her. "Consider this a show of faith and an offering of peace." Then I took my seat across from her and dug into my own dinner.

A solid minute ticked by before she continued her meal, but she didn't take her prize from the table. She left it in plain view.

Perhaps that's her way of acknowledging my gesture?

"You still owe me a name," she said just before taking an enormous bite of food. Her eyes fluttered closed for just a second.

"I told you Cook was good."

She studied me as she chewed slowly and swallowed. She reached for her glass and sipped at the water. "Cook is good, I'll agree with you on that, but it won't distract me from the name issue. Remember, quid pro quo."

"I already told you; I have no true surname." I cast her a wary glance. "Though I find it odd that you're circling back to this when you already used that insulting slur I was cursed with forever ago."

She cocked one manicured eyebrow and waved her fork in a small circle. "I get that this is some *other* place, different from my world. I'm willing to get on board with that after seeing that creature in the lake. But that doesn't make me psychic."

I leaned back in my chair, resting my forearms on the curved wooden arms. It was almost amusing how stubborn the woman was being, refusing to put the pieces together.

"Hook, Miss Darling. My name, in this realm, is Atlas Jameson Hook."

Her blue eyes narrowed, silently assessing me, until a bitter laugh huffed past her lips. She pointed her fork at me again. "You're trying to be clever? Okay, ha ha. Now I want the truth."

"I am not trying to be clever."

"That's a relief, because if you are, you kind of suck at it." Her fork scraped across the plate as she cut what remained of her food into smaller pieces, but instead of bringing any of it to her lips, she just stared at it. "Look, you don't grow up with a name like mine, with a family like mine, without being subject to more than your fair share of ridicule. I can't make you tell me, but don't mock me for something I have no control over."

"Miss, I assure you, I am not mocking you."

Her body stiffened and her grip on the fork tightened. I'd hit a nerve, clearly, but I wasn't sure how to show her the truth. Then her whole rant at the beach came back to me.

Never set the utensil down slowly and finally looked up. "Do you honestly expect me to believe that bullshit? Every kid knows that story. Peter Pan, Neverland, Wendy Darling, and Captain Hook." Anger laced with venom spilled from her lips as her voice ticked lower with each word. "Why not tell me your name is Kris Kringle or The Easter Bunny or fucking Thor?" Her gaze raked up and down my chest. "I think it's because you're an insecure asshole who likes to poke fun at people who don't cower when you have a little tantrum."

Speaking of tantrums...

She knew she wasn't in her world anymore, she'd said as much, but she also didn't believe in mine. At all, apparently.

I could have let her continue to eviscerate me with that double-edged tongue of hers while she burned herself out, but when the truth actually settled, I doubted she would feel good about her words.

No, what I needed to do was find a way to make her believe. "Can I show you something?"

She leaned back in her chair, kicking one of her booted feet up on the carved base of the table. I supposed that wasn't a no, technically, so I stood and moved across the room to the curtains, pulling them back one by one until my quarters were awash in cool moonlight.

"Come here, please." I motioned to the windows.

She stayed in her seat for several heart beats, but then it scraped back against the wooden floor and she stomped over to me. "What?"

I drew in a deep breath and tried to find the right words. "You accept that this isn't your world, correct?"

She gave me a sharp nod.

"Which means you accept that other worlds or realms exist?"

"Obviously." She ground the word out through clenched teeth.

"Then what is it about this place, about who I am, that would lead you to believe I'm being dishonest?"

"Because what you're talking about is a made-up story. A hallucination told by a mad woman that was twisted into a fairy tale for entertainment. It's pure fiction."

And there we had it, the root of the problem.

"Who was the mad woman?" I thought I knew the answer, but a little confirmation might help her convince herself of the truth.

"Seriously?" She slanted her eyes toward me, then sighed as though she carried the weight of the universe on her shoulders. "She was my great-grandmother, the first Wendy Darling. According to the police reports, she and her brothers ran away from home, but only Wendy was ever found. She'd always insisted the boys were taken to a magical island in the middle of nowhere by a demon. In her version, she'd found a way to that island, tried and failed to save her brothers, then found her way back to London.

"No one believed her. And when she refused to tell the truth about what had really happened to her brothers, she was put in an asylum. Eventually, a writer got hold of her story and flipped it into the fairy tale everyone knows and loves." Sarcasm dripped from the last few words.

"Is that why you hate your name, because of her?"

"It was more because of the story, originally. Then it became about the truth behind the tale, that it was based on the nightmares and delusions of a raving lunatic. Darling is synonymous with crazy in my world."

I ran a hand over the back of my neck. Hearing what had happened to Wendy all those years earlier was almost tragic. Almost. "She was telling the truth, at least partly."

Never turned abruptly and stalked back to the table. "And now I'm done playing."

"Give me five minutes." I didn't know if that was enough time to explain what had really happened, or to convince her to believe it, but the woman couldn't go on refusing to see what was right in front of her.

She didn't answer right away, but when she sat down and picked up her fork, it felt like I'd won some small measure of trust.

"You have until there is no food left on my plate. After that, this conversation is over."

I nodded once. "Agreed." I didn't give her time to interrupt me or to set any more restrictions. I tilted my head toward the windows, careful not to take my eyes off her. "That island is called Nusthena.

Well, some people call it that. It has been known by several names through the span of time. It means, roughly, *nowhere*. The girl you speak of, your great-grandmum, did find her way to the island to try to save her brothers and she did fail."

Never shook her head a little at that, but she didn't interrupt. She also wasn't shoveling food in her mouth to cut my time short, which I took as a glimmer of hope.

"Those were things she was telling the truth about, more or less." I moved to the row of cabinets on the far wall and knelt to open one of the lower doors. The book I wanted was buried behind a wall of others.

Its worn leather cover was cold against my fingers as I headed back to the table and placed it next to Never's plate. She eyed it suspiciously but didn't reach for it.

I took my seat across from her again, leaning back. "I am Captain Atlas Hook, though the Hook moniker had become something of a cruel joke long before I met Wendy. You should know, no one who finds value in keeping their intestines on the inside of their body typically dares to use it. Now I go by Captain or, to my dearest friends, Atlas."

She finally glanced up at me, her expression unreadable.

"Wendy's brothers were taken by the demon, lured to the island with lies and magic. It's something that has occurred many times, sadly, but Wendy's intervention was a first. For your great-grandmum to get here, she had to siphon the power of a very powerful demon from your world. I found her wandering the island, listened to her story, and agreed to help her try to save her brothers."

Never set down her fork, her meal still unfinished, and pushed her plate away. "I'm still miles away from believing you, but at least you spin an interesting tale."

"I'll take what small victories I can at the moment. When Wendy arrived, she was scared, but still full of humanity and hope. She was young, maybe seventeen, if I recall. We worked together for three days. That is how long it typically takes to break down a boy's defenses and separate him from his shadow."

She pressed her lips together like she was biting back a giggle, and I paused. "What is it?"

Never leaned her elbows on the table and folded one forearm over the other. "The shadow thing? Really?"

"That was in the story, I take it."

"Yeah, but it was Peter Pan who was separated from his shadow."

"Of course." She had said Wendy's story was twisted into a fairy tale. "That part isn't entirely wrong. The demon's shadow is a separate entity, but they are linked. Though, perhaps the terminology is an issue. In this usage, one's shadow is one's essence, the thing that makes a person who they are."

Now she was smiling at me. It was a wonderfully delicious expression, with a hint of mischief in her curved lips. "So, Pan is the demon that lures boys to Neverland to steal their souls?"

I gave her a confirming nod.

"I mean, it's a very demony type thing to do, sure, but it seems like an awful lot of work to cross dimensions for teenage boy souls. Especially when there seems to be an abundance of pirates who could stand in." She paused and I waited to see where her thoughts were leading. "Unless you're all a bunch of soulless bastards."

I bit the inside of my lip and closed my eyes. She was not taking me seriously. When I opened them, I leaned forward and slid the book in front of her. "Look at the title page."

She gave me a triumphant little smirk, but did as I said, showing absolutely no regard for the age of the book.

"Careful, please."

She held her hands up and cocked a smartass eyebrow at me. "What? Is it dangerous?"

I let out an irritated sigh and got to my feet, moving around the table. "Not to touch, but it is old." I leaned in and carefully lifted the front cover, tapping the name written on the bookplate in fading ink. "This belonged to her."

She examined the page with a suspicious glare, tracing a finger over the aged signature. I would have paid my weight in gold to know what she was thinking right then. Something about the book or the signature was important to her because her breathing picked up and the crease in her brow disappeared, replaced by wide, questioning eyes.

Never let the book fall closed in front of her and she looked at me again, only with a new air of fear surrounding her.

I inched away, putting my hands up. "I am not a threat to you, Never. I wasn't a threat to her either. I tried to help her."

She pushed up out of her chair slowly, her hand sliding toward her dagger. "No? Because I read her journals. She sounded like a nut job, Grade A fucking bonkers, but if she wasn't lying—" She snatched the blade, stepped back, and pointed it at me.

"There's more to the story."

"There always is," she spit back.

"That power she siphoned from the demon to get here, she didn't know how to control it once it was in her. Like I said, she was vibrant, sweet, hopeful. In the beginning. The more she used that power to find her brothers, the more it corrupted her mind and her soul. By the end of those three days, she was damaged. Irreparably."

Never's jaw ticked, but her blade was steady in her hand. "So, you didn't kill her brothers?"

I froze where I stood. Lying at that moment would have been a mistake, I knew that, but the truth wasn't much better.

She took a step forward. "It's a simple question with two possible answers; yes or no. Which is it?"

"Wendy killed them. With her own hands."

CHAPTER 10

"Why?" My skin crawled with frustration, prickling in an almost painful way. "Why would Wendy do everything she did to try to save them, only to turn around and kill them?"

Hook—Atlas—whoever the fuck he was, shook his head and gave me a pitiful look that made me want to punch him in the throat. "We didn't get to them in time."

I waited for what felt like an eternity, but apparently that was all he was going to give me. "What does that even mean? If she killed them, that means she got to them while they were still alive, right?"

"It's not that simple," he said, backing toward the bed. He sat on the edge, spread his legs in that cocky, masculine way some men had, and leaned forward, elbows on his knees. "The demon had already succeeded in separating the boys from their shadows. Killing them was the only humane option."

A hot rush of panic flooded my system, making my head pound in time with my increasing pulse. *I only had two days left.* My lungs couldn't hold enough air. I let my hand fall to my side but kept a painful grip on the dagger's handle. "I'm going to need you to show your work here, because you aren't making sense. If this is Neverland,

and there is all this magic, is there really no way to save someone like that?"

Understanding softened Hook's face, but it didn't soothe the need for violence raging in my heart. And I decided in that moment, I would be calling him Hook for eternity. He could go fuck himself if he didn't like it.

His eyes took on an eerie glow, reflecting the moonlight back at me. "It consumes souls as a source of power. Once they are gone, all that's left is a husk. Still living, but a slave to the demon's whims. There are dozens of such creatures on that island, children who were forever trapped, forever under the demon's control." His voice fell to almost a whisper. "Killing them is a merciful act."

"Fuck." I felt breathless. I looked down, glaring at the knife in my hand and my short fingernails digging into my palm around it. "Fuckity fuck." I paced in front of the table. "You're telling me this douchebag demon turns kids into lesser demons?"

He watched me, saying nothing for long enough that I was tempted to repeat the question, only louder and with more colorful phrasing.

"They're not demons," he finally said. "Demons *do* have souls. It's how the ancients were able to trap it here. The demon's shadow, soul, whatever you wish to call it, is bound to the island. The demon's physical form, however, is not. It can leave this place, but only for short periods of time. If the two remain separated for too long…" He waited until I looked back at him to pin me with a serious look. "The magic that keeps the shadow tied to this place will drag the demon back."

"Why does he want the souls? You said he consumes them, but for what? Are they like some gross delicacy?"

"Consume might not have been the right word. Souls are powerful, the most powerful magic in the universe. Incredibly strong magical barriers were erected to keep the demon's shadow tied to this place, but each time the demon succeeds in luring a boy here and collecting his soul, it absorbs that power."

I continued my pacing, trying to work through the implications of what he was telling me.

"If you keep that up, you're going to make me dizzy," Hook said with a slight quirk to his lips.

I paused. "You're a pirate. Don't you kind of need to be immune to motion sickness for that job?"

He leaned back on his hands, crossing one ankle over the other. "Doesn't matter. I got you to stop moving for a moment."

"Yay for you. Can we get back to the demon?"

"That depends."

"On?"

His head tilted to one side and the edge of a scar peeked out from the open collar of his shirt. "Do you believe me?"

I kept my eyes locked on that scar as I straightened and adjusted my grip on the blade. My intention wasn't to stab him, at least not right that moment, but having something in my hand helped me think. Kind of like my mom with her cigarettes when I was a kid. She always had one burning between her fingers, but sometimes she would just hold it and stare at the ember on the tip, letting it burn away to nothing as it filled our tiny kitchen with pungent smoke.

Did I believe Hook? I felt like a crazy person, but yeah, I guess I did. "So far."

"Fair enough. The demon and those soulless boys have the run of the island. The sirens and other creatures that are a danger to you have no interest in tangling with them. They don't have enough power to manipulate a creature with no soul."

"Does anything have that kind of power?" I asked.

"To manipulate? I can think of one or two things. To kill? No. The demon is immortal, and the soulless are nearly immortal."

"So, that means the lost boys can be killed?" That's what I was hearing.

He watched me for a long moment. "They can, but it takes a great deal of... dedication to get the job done."

So, if my brother was with them, he was being held hostage by an immortal, soul-sucking demon, and his soulless, almost immortal minions. Awesome.

Something from the story came back to me. The made up one.

I held up a hand. "Are pixies real?"

He nodded. "They are, but to my knowledge, there's only one left in this realm."

"Don't tell me. Tinkerbell?"

"Is that from the journal?" He cocked his head, looking entirely too comfortable resting on his bed, and I had to force myself to look away. *Oh look, windows.* I headed toward them on legs that felt like jelly.

The view from his room was stunning. I hadn't taken the time to appreciate it earlier, but now that I wasn't seething and intent on his immediate destruction, things looked, you know, a little brighter. Scents of warm leather and citrus swirled around me, and I breathed them in deep, letting the delicious combination caress my senses.

"Do you like the view?"

I jumped at the question because his voice was close. Too close. When I glanced back, he was standing just behind me, taking in the view over my head, and the heat radiating from his body tugged at me in a dangerous way. "It's not smart to sneak up on an armed woman."

"I didn't realize I was sneaking." Then the bastard winked at me.

I ignored it and tried to block out that intoxicating scent, looking back out at the softly rolling waves. "You're lucky I didn't just stab you." Tiny, luminescent specs of turquoise glittered in the sky. "And yes, Tinkerbell is from the story. Wendy never mentioned her in the journals I read, but I didn't have access to all of them. In the story, though, Tinkerbell was this mischievous little pixie who was always hanging around Pan and the lost boys."

"Was she portrayed as a conniving, petty creature who was deadly with her dust?"

So, she *was* real. And so, apparently, was her fairy dust. I might be able to make that work in my favor.

Hook's voice was a hot, gravelly distraction. "She and I have crossed paths. She's a piece of work."

"Not a fan, I take it?"

A low growl rumbled from his throat and the sound sent a tiny thrill zinging through me.

Seriously, what was my problem?

"If we ever run into each other again, I will gladly slice off her treacherous little head." He paused. "You mentioned lost boys. Is that what they called the boys who were trapped on the island?"

"Yeah, but in the story, they weren't trapped. They were orphans who didn't have a home to go back to, so they stayed in Neverland, never aging, never growing up." I expected some kind of response to that, but Hook was silent behind me. "What happens next?" I asked, turning to face him.

His strong jaw was lined with dark stubble, a few shades darker than his thick, messy hair. His tongue darted out, wetting his full bottom lip. Christ, that gaze was intimidating. The man was a study in ruggedly handsome, attractive in a wild way, and he carried himself with a confidence that made it clear he didn't give a damn about it.

"Are you finished with your dinner?"

I nodded, trying to focus on anything other than his mouth.

"Then let me show you something." He stepped aside and motioned to the door.

I let him guide me out across the deck, trying to ignore the curious glances from the other pirates. They didn't look quite like one would expect. Their clothes were clean, they weren't all scruffy, and there was no stench of BO wafting my way as they passed by.

I really wanted to ask if that was typical or if he just ran an exceptionally clean ship. If his own appearance was any indication, he was at least part of the reason they didn't all look like disease-riddled ruffians.

Since this was my first time on a ship like this, on any ship, actually, I craned my neck to look up at the towering masts. He chuckled low behind me, and I did my best to block him out. He already knew I was a tourist in his world. There was no use in hiding it.

Hook murmured something to one of the men on deck, who took off in the opposite direction. Then he escorted me to the railing, his hand hovering over my low back but not quite touching.

"I mentioned these waters were dangerous at night, but there is a difference between being told a thing and seeing it with your own eyes."

He pointed down to the water and I leaned over, casting him a sidelong glance as I did. "This isn't all some ploy to get me out here so you can toss me overboard or make me walk the plank, is it?"

He pressed a hand to his chest, just over his heart. "You wound me, love."

I narrowed my eyes at his use of the nickname, but that just made his smile bloom. The man had a smile that could make a girl's panties combust. "What am I supposed to be looking for?" I asked, dragging my focus back to the water.

"Do you see those shapes moving just below the surface?" He leaned over the rail beside me, close enough that our arms brushed.

I squinted into the darkness, trying to get a clearer view, but the movement of the ship and the breeze sent tiny ripples across the water, distorting everything. "Sort of. They look like giant fish. Or dolphins maybe?"

The pirate he'd whispered to earlier hustled up beside him with a bucket of something foul smelling. The stench brought tears to my eyes, and I threw my arm over my face, burying my nose in the crook of my elbow.

"What is that?" My voice was muffled, but Hook had no problem understanding me.

"Chum." He hoisted the bucket onto the railing.

"It smells horrible."

"No argument there, but it will bring the creatures up from the depths." He dumped the contents over the edge, then handed the bucket back to the man at his side. "Thank you, Linus. That will be all."

The man nodded quickly. "Yes, Captain." And he scampered off into the darkness.

"Keep your eyes on the water, love. By now, they've smelled the blood."

CHAPTER 11

"The frenzy will only last a moment," Hook said, his voice pitched low.

Sure enough, the shapes ceased their aimless, lazy circling and converged on the growing splotch of black in the water beside the ship. When a human face broke through the surface, my instinct to get down there and pull the woman from the water kicked into high gear.

Hook's hand clamped around my upper arm, anchoring me in place. "Just watch."

Next, a man surfaced but only to his shoulders. The woman's face contorted, and she lunged for him, gnashing her teeth so violently I swear I could hear them clash together. Those teeth would give me nightmares, all sharp and pointed, like a saw blade in her mouth. My eyes flew wide as she lifted partially out of the water. From the waist up, she could have passed for human, assuming she never, ever opened her mouth. From the waist down, though, she resembled a fish, complete with scales and a tail fin. Three more creatures joined the fray, all appearing to be some variation of human-fish hybrid, and they all thrashed wildly in the water, fighting over the larger scraps of guts and gore sinking around them.

The whole thing lasted maybe thirty seconds before the five

creatures dived back into the depths and darted off in different directions, but my heart rate was a long way from recovering.

"Were those mermaids, mer-people?" I asked, silently cursing the wobble in my voice.

"You're thinking of merfolk, and no. Merfolk only patrol these waters during the day, and they're a friendly bunch, for the most part. If a man goes overboard when the sun is up, they'll go out of their way to see him to safety." He leaned against the railing and stared down. "What you saw down there were sirens."

"Like the creature in the lake?"

"Yes, but hers is a unique case. Sirens typically live in open water because they like to roam, and I imagine it's easier to hunt. Efinia was cursed eons ago, bound to that tiny pond the way the demon is bound to the island and the surrounding waters. No one knows what she did to find herself landlocked, but swimming in that same tiny pool of acrid water for centuries has taken a toll."

"Those sirens seemed just as crazy as her." I pressed a little closer to the railing to get a better view of the water beside the ship.

"They were hungry. Blood in the water always creates a frenzy, but they're devious too. They all have the ability to sing beautifully, to lure men and women in with their voices, but only a few have the power to create glamours like Efinia."

"That's why you won't let me leave." My stomach rolled uncomfortably when I thought about the night before, about how far I'd had to swim to make it to the beach. An unfamiliar memory flashed through my mind, just a blink, but I definitely remembered fins and scales and bright blue hair.

Hook turned and hiked his hip up on the railing. "You look a little green, love."

I inhaled deeply and released the breath slowly, carefully. "Do they ever…" I didn't know how to ask the question. "Do sirens save people?"

He tipped his head from one side to the other. "On occasion.

Though, usually just long enough to watch them suffer. Why do you ask?"

"I was in the water last night." I had to turn away from the edge, from the dark stain of blood dissipating in the sea below. A girl's face filled my mind.

He glanced toward the island. "Sirens mostly stay clear of shallow water and they only venture close to shore if they think they can lure someone out into the depths. I doubt you were in any real danger."

Was he being a condescending ass or just a dismissive one?

"I wasn't near shore," I said, hoping I didn't sound as whiny as I felt. "I was farther out than this, actually. The moon was pretty bright, and I could see the island. It looked so far away. I started swimming and..." And what? I didn't remember dragging myself up the beach or sprawling out in the sand.

"How did you get all the way out here?" Hook's question pulled me from my thoughts.

Should I lie or tell the truth? Maybe a half truth?

"It's where I landed, I guess, when I got here." I chewed on my bottom lip.

Glancing up, I shoved my hands into my pockets. The necklace was still there, pressing against my hip. Stars twinkled happily in the night sky, which by itself wasn't the least bit usual, but no matter how long I stared, I couldn't seem to recognize a single constellation.

"How *did* you get here? If you're from Wendy's world, you must've gotten your hands on some powerful magic to make the trip. Unless you managed to hitch a ride with demons?"

I rolled my eyes. "If I'd traveled piggyback with the demon who kidnapped my brother, you can bet your ass he'd be in pieces right now."

"Undoubtedly." He paused, his amber-tinted eyes tracing over my features and down my neck. The fire in his gaze was like a caress all its own and a shiver raced through me. "Cold?"

His voice triggered a shiver that coalesced into a pool of heat in my core. "More like a hot mess," I muttered.

"Come with me." The smirk on his face spoke of trouble, deliciously sexy trouble, and I stayed firmly planted where I was.

"Let's say I accept the theory that I'll need to stay on your boat tonight—"

"Ship." He patted the railing lovingly.

"Whatever. I get that I'm staying on your *ship*. Where will I be sleeping?"

"If you come with me, I'll show you." Now his voice was playful, like he was goading me to take on some challenge. I looked down at his outstretched hand and shook my head, crossing my arms over my chest.

"Nope. Not a chance, asshole. I've given you points for being decent to me for the last, oh, hour or so. But that doesn't negate the fact that I'm stuck here because of you, when I could be on that island finding my brother. Don't hold your hand out to me and flirt like we're going to run off and be fuck buddies in the night."

His taunting smirk faltered, and he straightened. "Never fear, miss. Even on my most desperate day, I wouldn't dream of bedding such a foul-mouthed creature."

Okay, that kind of hurt. A simple, *go fuck yourself* would have been sufficient.

His gaze raked up and down my body. "Your blade is still in my quarters, correct?"

Was I dumb enough to leave it lying on the table?

Yes, yes, I absolutely was that much of a mouth-breathing moron. The way I pressed my lips together must have answered his question, because when he moved, he didn't hesitate.

And he was quick.

Hook ducked and tossed me over his shoulder, anchoring his arm around my thighs.

Oh, hell no.

I screamed and kicked out, but my bucking had zero effect. When I elbowed him in the back of the head he stumbled and let out a little *oof*.

Ha, take that.

"Let me go this instant!" I threw as much authority into my voice as I could, but he didn't respond. No chuckle. No yelling. No taunting words. He just stalked silently across the deck.

When we got to his room, the door was wide open, and I had just enough time to reach out and grab the door jamb on each side. The sudden resistance threw him off balance and by some miracle we didn't both end up flat on the floor. I kept my grip on the wooden frame, enjoying the small victory, when he shifted and I felt a sharp sting across my ass.

"Did you just spank me?!" An unexpected heat filled my core and my nipples hardened to sensitive nubs.

Not cool, body. Not fucking cool.

I twisted, trying to ignore the damp heat blossoming between my thighs, but I didn't let go. "I'm not sleeping with you, pirate," I said between gritted teeth.

A dark, promising chuckle reached my ears a heartbeat before another sharp slap resonated across my ass. Fuck. He was not playing nice. That smack had some bite to it, and for some super twisted reason, my body responded like it was the best foreplay of my life.

What the hell was wrong with me?

When I felt him shift like he was going to do it again, I let go of the frame and pulled my arms around behind me, protecting my backside from another blistering spank.

"Good girl," Hook whispered as he stepped into his room and kicked the door shut behind us.

No, no, no. I was not okay with what was happening. I flailed, but the moment I pulled my hands from my backside, I felt the threat of another smack and kept them firmly in place.

Then I was falling backward. I hit something lusciously soft with the perfect amount of bounce, and that mingled scent of warm leather and citrus surrounded me again, making my mouth water and my skin prickle. I was on his bed.

I scrambled back toward the headboard. "I don't know what you think is happening tonight, but if you try anything—"

Hook held up his index finger and ticked it back and forth. His eyes were slightly hooded, like the thought of bedding me was arousing to him, but the scowl on his face was a bit confusing.

"Do not insult my honor again. I have never and would never take an unwilling woman sexually." He was standing at the edge of the bed, glaring down at me. "Don't get me wrong…" His gaze slid over me, every inch of me, and that heat pooling in my middle turned positively molten. "The thought of stripping you naked and making you come so hard that your body melts in the afterglow. . ." He licked his lips. "It is enticing."

A jolt of need—purely sexual, animalistic need—almost had me clambering to my hands and knees and crawling toward him. When he licked his lips again, the wet heat of my pussy soaked into my panties. Goddess save me. How could a pirate be that freaking hot?

He inhaled deeply, his eyelids fluttering for a moment, before exhaling in a rush and shaking his head. "Or it would be enticing, if it weren't for that mouth." Then he turned on his heel and headed back toward the open door. With his hand on the knob, he said, "The key to this door is next to your dagger. Lock it the moment I leave and do not open it again, for any reason, until sunrise."

HOOK

CHAPTER 12

I stood on the other side of the door and closed my eyes as I listened. She didn't move off the bed right away.

Had I managed to scare her so badly that she wouldn't dare to move from the place I'd left her? Surely a woman with her fire couldn't be that fragile.

But what if she was? What if that grit was all for show?

I ran a hand through my hair, tugging at the ends. My behavior was completely unacceptable. Never in all my many years had I spoken to a woman that way; at least, not one I hadn't already bedded. And I swatted her bottom, twice!

The memory of how that sting felt against my palm sent a dangerous tingle across my scalp, but when I heard the lock engage, a little of my frustration bled off. Then something slid against the door and plopped softly on the floor. A peek through the gap beneath, showed me the hem of her leather jacket and just a hint of her lower back. The ink swirling across her soft skin there did nothing for my self-control.

Was she saying something?

I pressed my ear to the cool wood, but I could only make out a couple of her words. It clearly wasn't a conversation she'd intended anyone else to hear. A gentleman would have stood quietly and edged away from that door. He would have given the woman the privacy she deserved.

When it came to Never, I was anything but a gentleman. I moved slowly, quietly sitting on the ground outside my own room, and leaned back against the door, just the way she was.

At least an hour went by with us sitting like that. Her mumbling had stopped about twenty minutes in. I'd expected to hear her get up after that, but there was a gentle thunk against the wood, probably from the back of her head, and she'd stayed where she was.

One of my men approached me with a curious look on his face, but I pressed my index finger to my lips and motioned for him to keep moving. He hesitated, but the don't-question-me look I gave him was enough to convince him to move on. Never was finally calming down; I could feel the shift in her energy in the air, and I didn't want to move from that spot until she'd settled.

A few minutes later, a feminine yawn drifted to me, and she scooted away from the door. Good. With any luck, she'd lay down and try to get some sleep. The trek to find her brother in the morning wouldn't be an easy one.

I finally pulled myself away and made my way up to the helm, nodding to William as he stepped aside. "Anything to report?" There was a sharpness to my voice that even I didn't recognize.

William, ever the professional, ignored it. "No, sir. I suspected your little show and tell with the girl might bring the urchins out in force, but something else must have their attention this evening."

I glanced over my shoulder at the heavy clouds slowly rolling in from the south. "What do you make of that?"

"Might be a problem." We both looked toward the flag fluttering on the bow. "It appears to be headed this way, though not too quickly," he said with practiced indifference. The weather around and between the islands was unpredictable. Winds could shift on a penny, and storms, even the largest and most devastating of them, could dissipate in seconds.

I grabbed the handles on the wheel and adjusted my stance. "Tell the men to stay below deck and get some rest. I'll take watch tonight. If the swell looks like trouble, I'll sound the alarm."

William folded his hands behind his back and offered me a perfunctory nod. "Yes, sir. What about the girl?"

Part of me wanted to send William in to check on her, to make sure she'd found her way to bed, but a new face likely wouldn't help anything. "Leave her be. I've given her the interior key. With any luck, she'll stay holed up in there until sunrise. Speaking of…" I held my hand out. "I'll need your key for the night, just in case."

He pulled the worn cast iron key from his pocket and dropped it in my palm with a sly smile. "Just in case."

"Don't go getting ideas, William. There's a world of unknowns surrounding that woman."

"Of course. I would never presume. Is she…" His words trailed off as he glanced toward the door.

I nodded grimly. "Yes, if she is to be believed, she truly is one of Wendy's descendants."

"And the madness?"

Something in my chest twinged painfully and I adjusted my grip on the rudder wheel. "No sign, yet. She has, so far, been unwilling to share what brought her here, but I don't think she used Wendy's method."

"How can you be sure?"

"If she was speaking the truth, she arrived at the compass late last night."

His eyes widened and his gaze bounced from me to the door and back. "The compass? And she made it to shore?" His voice was threaded with just a hint of awe. "That girl is lucky to be alive."

I rubbed my hand across the back of my neck. "There's no way she got there without help, not in the middle of the night."

"You don't think the shifters had something to do with it?" he asked, keeping his voice low.

Our long-time alliance with the shifter colony on a neighboring island had grown fragile in the aftermath of Wendy Darling's chaotic visit. The daughter of the alpha, one of my dearest friends for many centuries, had gone missing the same day that wretched girl escaped the confines of the island. I'd helped search for her for years. Even now I kept a careful watch each time we visited the islands, but there was only so much I could do.

We all suspected Wendy had a hand in her disappearance, but with no proof and no way to track her down, the blame had eventually fallen on me, at least in the eyes of some. I was the one who'd helped Wendy in the beginning. The shifters had helped her too. I wasn't the only one she'd tricked into believing she was nothing more than an innocent seventeen-year-old girl.

I stared out across the water. "It would be unwise to rule them out."

Lightning flickered across the horizon, drawing slowly closer to our position. The distant thunder was barely audible over the crash of the waves against the ship's hull, but I took it as a warning all the same. "You and the men should turn in. I have a feeling I'll be waking the lot of you before the night is out."

"I would be happy to keep lookout, Captain," William said.

I waved him off. "No need at present. Besides, I could use some time to myself." My mind was churning trying to figure out the significance of Never's presence. At best, she was a distraction. At worst, well, she was a Darling.

William nodded and pivoted on his heel, leaving me to my thoughts as the sounds of the night sea rushed in around me.

Two hours later, I shook William awake gently. Not because I wanted to, but because the distant storm was no longer so distant, and the black clouds were threatening to break open directly over the ship.

He looked up at me groggily, blinking against the light from my lantern. "Is everything all right, sir?"

"The storm found us. I need you and the men to stay down here and lock everything up tight."

He sat up, rubbing his hands down his face. "What about the girl?"

"Still locked in my quarters. Remember the signal, and do not open the hatch until you hear it."

I shook my head when he tried to argue with me. "I'll be fine. Not to worry. We both know I can't actually die."

"Maybe not, but that doesn't mean being torn apart by sirens won't have you wishing for death."

My joints creaked as I straightened, a sure sign the downpour was imminent. "Remember the signal, William. No arguments." I headed up the stairs and closed the hatch before he could respond. Icy wind yanked at my hair and stung my face as I rapped on the hatch twice with my fist. I barely heard the heavy beams slide into place above the squall.

Waves crashed against the hull, picking up force by the second, pitching the ship to and fro at ever steeper angles. The first fine drops of rain struck my face and dusted the deck. I latched onto anything in my path that would allow me to keep my balance.

The cursed song of the sirens filled my ears a split second before I reached my destination. *Almost time.*

Pressing my back against my bedroom door and turning my face to the sky, I sent a silent prayer to the powers that be.

If anyone is still out there, please, help me keep her locked in that room.

Millennia had come and gone since the last time I'd asked for their help. I didn't expect any response. I was, after all, persona non grata in the proper immortal world, but it couldn't hurt to try. I unsheathed my cutlass and locked my eyes on the railing. If the clouds opened up and cursed my ship with a downpour, that railing was my first line of defense.

A crack of electricity tore across the night sky an instant before a deafening clap of thunder rattled my teeth, and that gentle sprinkle of rain transformed into a torrent.

CHAPTER 13

"Don't you know how to drive a boat?!" I yelled, dragging myself up off the floor. Well, that's what I was trying to do anyway. The floor beneath me rocked the opposite direction I was moving, and I stumbled in the darkness, banging my shin against the hard corner of the bed frame and careening onto the mattress.

I knew there was a storm outside. I could hear the wind and thunder, but I was still blaming Hook for being thrown out of bed. Warmth trickled down my leg as I moved to the center of the bed, and I pressed my hand to the throb.

Yep, I was bleeding. Awesome.

"This is going on the list of reasons why I hate you!" I shouted.

When I finally got my bearings enough to make an attempt for the door, I scooted to the edge and used the post to brace myself as the boat rocked and tilted. In my head, I ran through where the objects were in the room before the whole thing had turned into a tilt-a-whirl. What were the odds the table was anchored to the floor? I knew the chairs weren't.

Why hadn't I been smart enough to leave at least one candle or lantern lit? I closed my eyes, because even though it was pitch black, it signaled to my brain to stop wasting energy trying to use that particular sense. Every sound in the room multiplied, bouncing off the walls despite the heavy curtains dampening the sound coming from the windows.

Now, there was an idea. Instead of trying to make it to the door in the dark, what if I tried for the windows? It wouldn't offer much light, but a little would be enough to keep me from falling and breaking a wrist or something. I shoved my hand in my pocket and wrapped my fingers around the heavy key. Good. I left it there. My blade was tucked neatly in my boot, which I'd been too damn tired to bother taking off before I'd finally dragged myself to the bed earlier.

"Light first," I said, pushing away from the bedpost and stumbling forward waving my arms in front of me. The thought of the ship shifting violently and pitching me into, and then through, the fine glass windows made my knees wobble. The second my fingertips brushed the jacquard fabric of the drapes, I grabbed handfuls of it and pulled myself flush with the glass.

I worked my way across the fabric panels, yanking them aside one by one as I found the seams, but there wasn't much to see. In fact, it was nearly pitch black out there too. I grabbed another handful of fabric and yanked just as a bolt of lightning creased the clouds.

And I screamed like a little bitch.

A man was hanging in front of the window looking in at me, eyeing me like I was edible. His gnarly, moss laden teeth made me cringe and his black tongue flicked out rapidly.

"Ew."

Fortunately, the light disappeared just as quickly and I was left with just an outline of a man, butt-ass naked, with his junk pressed against the glass. *Was* he naked though? I squinted at the silhouette and could just make out scales tracing down his hips and legs—another jolt of lightning hit—and yep, even his dick. The dude had a scaly dick.

The urge to gag doubled me over and I flipped the curtain closed.

"Was that a siren? Or whatever you called a male siren?"

The crazy chick at the lagoon had legs, at least for a little bit. Did that mean they could shapeshift?

I stayed where I was for a second, waiting to see if the leering, scaly bastard on the other side tried to bust his way in, but when I pulled the curtain back and peeked out again, he was gone. I should have been thrilled, or at least relieved, but instead I got a sick, sinking feeling in the pit of my stomach.

What if he wasn't the only one?

I knelt and pulled the blade from my boot, then I waited. When the next flash of lightning illuminated the room, I sprinted for the door, leaping over an overturned chair that slid into my path as the boat tipped again. The movement shifted my landing off balance, and I stumbled forward, finding the door much earlier than expected, with my face.

"Christ-all-fucking-mighty-on-a-goddamn-slut-cracker!" Hot blood poured from my forehead, and I pressed the heel of my palm to the gash. "Head wounds always bleed more, Never. It's nothing to worry about."

I'd almost convinced myself of that too, right up until I heard the screeching from beyond the door. There were more of those nasty creatures out there on the ship. I might not have liked Hook or his men, but there was no way I was cowering in his room until those gross bastards found their way in and cornered me.

I wiped my blood on my shirt and searched along the door for the keyhole. When I found it, I clenched the handle of my knife between my teeth, pulled the key from my pocket, and slipped it in the lock. The ship pitched hard, rocking me with it. I managed to keep my grip on the knob, barely, but the damned key clattered to the floor.

"Fuck!" The word came out muffled since I was yelling around the handle of my knife still between my teeth. I dropped to all fours and slid my hands across the polished wood boards. Seconds ticked by, even with the racket I could hear the clock, and the room seemed to sink deeper and deeper into darkness.

My heart was doing an unwelcome gallop in my chest. I was

getting myself worked up, which wasn't good. I stopped searching for a second and focused on my breathing, drawing in a slow breath, willing my heart rate to slow with it.

The boat pitched again, and something small and metal bumped my fingers. I snatched at it, dragging my nails across the polished surface as I did. The sensation made my teeth ache, but I shoved it to the back of my mind and focused on crawling my happy ass back to the door.

The wailing and screaming outside grew louder, but the violence of the storm was still winning. I found the door, pulled myself back up, and braced my legs wide as I slipped the key in the lock and twisted.

Ha ha! Victory!

I yanked the door open and realized a second too late that I'd made a huge mistake. Massive.

In the dim light of the few remaining lanterns on deck, I saw a figure not too far in front of me surrounded by sirens. He was slashing and stabbing, but the moment they realized there was more fresh meat on board, half of them turned my way. Red seeped into my vision from the cut on my brow and suddenly, sickeningly, a vivid image of the sirens in the water fighting over scraps of meat hit me.

Fuck my life.

I grabbed the knife from between my teeth and pulled the door shut behind me so those slimy bastards couldn't shove me back in. Then I did what I did best.

"Come on, bitches. Show me what you're working with."

A siren to my right didn't appreciate my taunting, because when she opened her mouth, the sound that came out nearly made my ears bleed. It was a horrible, eye-watering, screeching wail, and it took everything in me not to slap my hands over my ears and slide down into a fetal position until it stopped.

What was the best course of action here?

I sucked in a deep breath and screamed back at her like a lunatic.

She stopped wailing immediately. In fact, she stopped entirely, because every other creature on deck turned my way.

Oops.

Maybe that wasn't the best plan.

The figure with the sword froze too. "Get back inside!" It was Hook. He was out there fighting, guarding the door, by himself from the looks of it.

"Not a chance!" I wasn't sure he could hear me over the roar of the storm.

Four sirens moved in at once, and I managed to slice up the face of the one who'd screamed at me. She flailed backward, but a male monster was quick to take her place. His scaly penis was fully erect, and the moment my eyes landed on it, I decided that was my next target. I knew guys got hard from fighting because of the flood of adrenaline and all that, but looking at that fish skin appendage pointing at me would probably scar me for life. Removing it was the only reasonable option.

He lunged and I ducked low, hitting him with two quick jabs to the side before taking a sweeping slice down the front of him. His gross looking dick flopped onto the deck and the sound coming out of him changed from a wail to more of a squeal, like a stuck pig.

I shoved him away and turned back toward the brunt of the fight, but I was nearly knocked off my feet when Hook slammed into me. His shirt was shredded, plastered to his skin, and he had four deep wounds across his chest. I spotted another three gashes down the side of his neck. He was losing a lot of blood. Too much blood, too fast. His sword dipped and he nearly dropped it before I snagged it from his loosening grip. I shoved him behind me, and he slipped to his knees. I took a step back, pinning him between me and the door.

"Stay down!" I yelled over my shoulder, though I wasn't even sure he was conscious at that point.

The sirens darted in at me and pulled away like they were playing a game, except each time one of those wretched fish people got close enough, I made them bleed for it. One dived for my legs, and I cut his head clean off with a single blow of Hook's sword.

"Okay, that was cool." I kicked the head like a soccer ball, and it rolled awkwardly toward the surging mass of sirens. "Who's next?"

Another female made like she was going to charge, but it was a distraction. I managed to sever the hand of the male siren trying to creep in on my left, but he'd gotten a little too close for comfort.

It was time to stop playing defense.

I took a step forward and slashed with Hook's blade, slicing across the female's stomach. Her screams fell silent, though her mouth hung open. She pressed her hands to the wound. Try as she might, some of her intestines still slipped out between her fingers. The smell, even in the rain, was beyond nauseating.

That shit was nightmare material. I'd fought all manner of demon before, but they'd always looked like monsters. The bastards on the deck all looked like people from the waist up, well, mostly. Except for the teeth. Either way, it was a little disconcerting.

I shifted my grip on the blade and scanned the faces, trying to read their body language. Either my eyes were playing tricks on me, or the gap between us was slowly growing.

Were they backing away from me?

Holy shit, was I winning?

"Really? That's all you've got?" I shouldn't be taunting them. I knew that, but seriously, the minute I started acting instead of reacting they all turned cowardly on me? That wasn't normal.

In unison, three of them turned their faces to the sky, and that was when I realized the rain was slowing. A few stars were starting to peek through the tiny breaks in the clouds. And then, as if they'd all received some secret signal, they scattered, darting to the railing and diving back into the sea.

I stayed where I was. I'd seen enough scary movies to know there was always one more.

Hook groaned at my feet, and I glanced down. "Hang tough for one more minute." I tried not to let any concern slip into my voice, but with his blood pooling around my feet, it wasn't the easiest thing in the world. Panic tried to seep in. If Matty was here, in this world, was he facing this kind of attack right now too?

My blood turned to ice in my veins. If something bad happened to him, I would destroy every evil creature in this realm.

I counted to ten in my head before turning back to Hook and squatting beside him. "Where is everyone else?"

He didn't respond. My heart skittered for a second before I saw his chest was still rising and falling. It was shallow and weak, but I would take it.

"Where is your worthless crew?" I pressed my lips together and stood, trying to remember where the pirates had all been going when they were moving around the deck. I spotted a slanted hatch off to one side and stalked over to it. Using the sole of my boot, I stomped hard on the panel three times. It was solid, but I could hear the booming racket I was making down below.

"Hey!" I stomped again. "Wake up, you fucking pussies, and get your asses out here! Your captain is dying!" I felt a sharp pain in my chest at the thought but shoved it away. It was just adrenaline, just the excitement from the fight. Because I wasn't developing feelings for the guy. That was a big nope to me hooking up with a pirate. No pun intended.

Normally something like that would at least bring a smile to my lips, but I wasn't even in the mood for my own stupid jokes. I was worried about my brother. And now, apparently, I was worried about my captor.

I heard a noise below and stepped back. When the hatch swung open, a slender man with a sharply angled face that still somehow managed to be handsome stared up at me. He spotted the sword in my hand, did a double take, then climbed up the stairs with his wide eyes locked on me.

"Where?"

I used the sword to point to where Hook was curled on his side, and the guy took off across the deck without another word.

CHAPTER 14

Two hours later, Hook was locked in his room and William, the guy from the hatch, was filling me in on all things siren. Like, apparently, they could only shapeshift in water. Which meant the rainstorm was the only reason they were able to climb up onto the ship.

"Does this happen often then?" I asked, motioning to the blood-stained deck. The crew had already finished off the injured sirens who weren't able to drag themselves off the ship and unceremoniously pitched their remains overboard.

He shook his head. "We usually sail through the storms rather than remaining anchored close to the island. It makes it harder for the sirens to latch on."

"Why stay anchored tonight then?"

"The captain said he would take you to shore in the morning. He wanted to remain close to the island so he could keep his word." He gave me a look like I was just the most adorably foolish girl he'd ever met. I should have been offended, I wanted to be, but I could tell he wasn't doing it to be a jerk. The man really thought that was something I should have known.

"So, instead of being a little tardy delivering me back to the island, now he's on his death bed. That'll make it a little tough for him to live up to his commitments, won't it?" I held up my hand. "You know what, forget it. I don't care." I glared over at Hook's door. "Shouldn't someone be in there with him, making sure he's not choking on his own blood or something?"

"He'll be fine. Miss..." He motioned to me. "The captain has indicated you are not fond of your family name. What would you prefer I call you?"

"Call me Never."

"Very well. He'll be fine, Miss Never. He's not—"

"Just Never. No miss, no ma'am, none of that."

William's right eye twitched like his brain couldn't process what I was saying. "It's not proper to call a lady—"

"See, that's where you're getting your wires crossed. I'm no lady."

He offered me a curt nod. "Never it is. Just, bear with me, please." He paused, straightening his blood-stained vest. "I am not accustomed to speaking so casually with a woman."

"It's my name, William. See, I'm using yours. It's not that hard. Try it again." I lifted my brows and flipped my hand in a circle.

"What I was saying, Never, is that the captain will be fine. He is not like us." He motioned between us. "He is—"

"Not fond of his first mate sharing details that aren't his to share," Hook said, buttoning up his shirt as he walked toward us.

William jerked to a stand, a stuttered apology spilling from his mouth.

I ignored his groveling and studied Hook's chest. "How are you upright?" I got to my feet and started to take a step toward him, but he held up a hand.

"They were minor wounds, and I heal quickly."

"Minor, my ass. I saw those gashes." I charged forward and yanked his hands away from his shirt. There were four angry red lines on his chest and three on his neck, but they looked more like deep scratches than the ragged gouges that had been pouring blood a few hours earlier. "What the fuck?" My voice was a whisper as my finger traced the length of one of those scratches before I fully realized what I was doing. A barely noticeable wave of goose flesh broke across his skin and his breath hitched.

He grabbed me by the wrist, holding me in place but not pulling my hand away. "Like I said, I heal quickly. Another hour or so and I'll be right as rain."

The phrase hit me all wrong and I glared up at him. "Are you trying to be funny?" I yanked my hand free and shoved him. Hard. "I thought you were dying."

He held up his hands. "Settle down, love."

I balled my hands into fists and clenched my jaw tight. Every colorful word I knew flashed through my head, but I was riled up enough that I couldn't even pick one to hurl at him. Which didn't make the least bit of sense. Why would I be upset that he was okay?

"When can I get off this fucking boat?"

"I'll take you to shore at sunrise." His voice was annoyingly patient for a guy I'd thought was on his death bed.

"When is that?" I flung my hand at the sky. "Because all I see are a bunch of stars I don't recognize. I have no reference for time here!"

"Three hours, give or take."

"Great. Wonderful. Thank you, so much."

"Never?" My name was honey on his lips, and my anger began to melt even as I tried desperately to cling to it.

"What?" I snapped back.

"If I might be so bold…" He held out his hand like I was supposed to take it.

"Yeah, not happening." I crossed my arms over my chest, casting that outstretched hand a wary look.

"You need sleep. The hike to the demon's camp takes the better part of a day in the best of conditions. If your brother is here, and not caught in one of our traps, that's where he'll be."

A sick feeling snaked through my middle as visions of Matty caught in human-sized versions of animal traps flooded my mind. "What do you mean by 'your traps?'"

"We have several traps set at various points on the island, and part of my crew is out there monitoring them. The intention isn't to kill, it's to capture. We intend to get him off the island before the demon gets to him."

Hope tried to bloom for one brief moment before he opened his mouth again.

"You managed, what, an hour's worth of rest before the storm? Maybe two?"

I narrowed my eyes. "Were you spying on me?"

Hook pinned me with a glare. "I was devising a plan for the morning." He scrubbed a hand over the dark stubble shading the line of his jaw. "Now that I have one, I would also like to get some sleep. However, in order for that to happen, I need to know you have yourself safely locked in your room."

"It's your room," I corrected.

His stern expression turned even harder. "For tonight, it is yours. No one will bother you until sunrise."

A wave of exhaustion rolled through me, and I swayed a little on my feet. "Give me your word. Promise me no one will enter that room without my permission, and I'll march my smug little ass in there right now." I couldn't believe I was asking a pirate, of all people, for his word on anything, but some deep part of me desperately wanted to trust him.

He dipped his head, never taking his eyes off mine. "You have my word."

I hesitated for a moment, then shoved my hand in my pocket and pulled out the key. "Then I won't need this," I said, tossing it to him before turning and heading back to his room.

There was a pause, but his quiet words filtered through my thoughts as I stepped inside. "Thank you for your help earlier."

I turned with my hand on the door. It was still dark, with only the flickering of a few scattered lanterns lighting the way. The gentle rocking of the ship kept that dim light moving, casting shifting shadows at sharp angles across the deck. Hook's face was partially hidden in the gloom, but a dark shiver trickled through me when I saw him watching me. His eyes glowed orange for a moment, like they were picking up the light from the lanterns and reflecting it back. Then he turned away and retreated into the night.

I let the door close, releasing the breath that had locked up in my chest. My chances of getting even a little sleep had just gone from slim to none. Unless...

I eyed the freshly made bed and closed my eyes. How wrong would it be to give myself a little... sedative?

HOOK

CHAPTER 15

How did I end up here?

Simple, I'd heard a noise. A feminine moan, low and muffled, like someone was trying to smother the sound. It was something a mortal would never have picked up on, and the fact that it'd come from my room had sent a jolt of adrenaline through my system. I'd raced for the door and grabbed the handle, ready to burst in and take out whatever new threat was trying to get at Never.

The woman was apparently a magnet for supernatural villains.

Except bursting in wouldn't necessarily have given me the upper hand. So, I'd slid my cutlass from its sheath and turned the handle slowly, quietly. I'd opened the door just a crack, just enough to get the lay of the land.

I was ready for anything. A siren, a vindictive shifter, a misplaced demon. I would have taken on an army of them to keep her safe, even if she was beyond infuriating. But what I saw stole the breath from my lungs.

Never was sprawled on my bed, naked from the waist down with one hand between her legs and the other fisting my pillow.

I'd stared dumbfounded, frozen, suddenly on fire on the inside. She was a creature of beauty lost in a moment of self-pleasure, and I was ashamed to admit I'd watched for longer than any gentleman would. Tempting thoughts shot through my mind. How would she taste if it was my face between those luscious legs? My tongue making her writhe? Would she tangle her hands in my hair and pull me closer, urging me on as she shook with pleasure?

On the heels of those erection-inspiring visions, another question surfaced: What if she opened her eyes and caught me watching?

A sliver of ice had slipped through the flames chasing the blood in my veins. Would she scowl, or maybe scream? Would she invite me in?

That was when I'd closed the door, quietly. Well, as quietly as I could with the tremble in my hand.

I'd told her no one would go in that room. I'd made her that promise in good faith. Despite her unveiled disdain for pirates, for me in particular it seemed, I would not fail in that promise.

Which was how I ended up standing outside my own door in the pitch black with one hand splayed on the smooth wood and my other hand fisting my swollen cock.

Technically, I was keeping my word.

I should have walked away and tried to forget what I'd seen. That would have been the right thing to do, the honorable thing. But I could just make out her little moans of pleasure through the barrier and I couldn't bring myself to move my feet.

I gripped my cock a little tighter and slid my hand up the length of it, rubbing my thumb over the tip and dragging the bead of precum down. It didn't offer much in the way of lubrication, but I didn't need much. I was already close to the edge before I'd ever touched myself. Seeing her like that, hearing her, stirred something in me I hadn't felt in eons.

I stroked a little faster as I listened. My blood pulsed through me, and with each slide of my fist, it got a little harder to control my breathing. When her cries grew louder, I closed my eyes and pumped harder. She didn't know I was out there, imagining I was the one wringing those sounds from her, but that didn't stop me from wanting to meet her beat for beat.

One more sharp cry rang through the night air just before it was smothered. The sound of her climax broke me. The muscles in my lower body pulled taut, and I shifted my grip to the door frame, anchoring myself to it as I gave my cock three more rough pumps. My jaw clenched painfully, and I bit back my own groan, erupting with a violent shudder.

My knees went soft, and I had to lean my weight against the frame to keep my balance. I hadn't made myself come in ages, but I didn't recall it ever feeling quite that good. That delicious feeling lasted for one short beat before the doorframe creaked under my weight.

"Is someone out there?" Never's voice carried a mixture of fear and irritation, and I silently cursed myself for interrupting her peace. If she caught me out here...

I didn't waste time entertaining the thought. Moving quickly, I wiped my hand on my shirt, tucked my still rock hard and surprisingly sensitive cock in my pants, and retreated like a thief in the night. And was I not a thief? Had I not just stolen a moment of her pleasure and made it mine? I'd taken without permission, without her knowledge.

What the hell was that woman doing to me?

She must have possessed magic of some kind. That was the only reasonable explanation for my reaction to her, and for my less than admirable behavior. Never had to be an enchantress, and if my depraved behavior was any indication, she knew her craft well.

I rounded the corner and ducked back into the safety of the shadows. Yellow light spilled from my room when she cracked the door and peeked out. I expected to see anger or frustration in her gaze, but unless I was mistaken, she looked disappointed.

Of course. I could have smacked myself for my foolishness. An enchantress would have been disappointed to realize her magic had failed.

I couldn't let her get to me like that again.

CHAPTER 16

Morning took an eternity to arrive, and I hadn't slept a wink in the interim. When the pink and orange shocks of color painted the sky, I maneuvered the ship closer to shore and had my men ready the skiff.

"Morning, sir," William chirped.

"Aye," I grumbled back.

He eyed me. "I take it you didn't sleep much after the siren attack." It wasn't a question, so I didn't respond. He'd been my closest friend for centuries and he knew better than anyone how my mind worked. "Would you like me to see to Miss Never now or wait until we're a bit closer?"

The urge to growl at him bubbled in my chest and I froze. Why would I react like that to my oldest friend offering to simply wake the woman? I shook my head. "I'll do it. Take over here and bring the ship round to the west beach. You know the spot."

"Yes, sir," he said, not even trying to hide the twinkle in his eye.

What the man didn't realize was that I was going in there to wake her up so he didn't have to deal with her volatility. It was entirely possible, given her previous behavior, that she was inclined to come awake swinging. Technically, William healed more quickly than I did these days, but I still wouldn't put it on him to risk taking that blow.

That was what I told myself when I got to the door. I knocked gently and listened, but the only sounds my heightened senses picked up were the slap of waves against the hull, the cry of a gull flying toward the island, and a faint, feminine snoring.

It was an unexpectedly adorable sound. A reluctant smile curved my lips, but then the vision from a few hours earlier filled my mind.

My indiscretion.

It had been wrong in so many ways, and very likely a setup by an incredibly talented enchantress. None of that stopped my cock from coming alive at the memory or prevented my mind from stitching together her moans of pleasure with the sight of her fingers dancing in small circles between her thighs.

I should have knocked again. Louder. But I turned the handle, pressing the door open quietly. I opened it just enough to duck through without giving any of my men a peek inside, in case Never had fallen asleep as I'd last seen her.

The thought made my scalp tingle, and I tried not to imagine her sprawled half-naked in my bed.

Fortunately, the woman was fully dressed, save for her boots and jacket. She was curled on her side on top of the covers with her arms wrapped protectively around something.

That was odd.

I edged closer to get a better look and recognized the book right away. A fresh twinge of irritation snaked through me. Had she gone through my things?

She mumbled something in her sleep and shook her head, burying it deeper into my pillow. Her grip on the book loosened and it slipped from her grip, sliding flat onto the silky duvet. Before I realized it, my feet carried me to the edge of the bed, and I plucked the book from its resting place. It was the one I'd been reading before this whole debacle with the demon and Never had started.

So, maybe she hadn't gone snooping through my belongings. I vaguely recalled leaving the title in the top drawer of the nightstand. I flipped through the pages, but there were no creases in the dogeared pages. No sign of ill treatment.

"That's one of my favorites." Her voice was laced with sleep, but her eyes were piercing even in the near darkness.

I covered my startle by opening the nightstand and putting the book back in its place. "Aye, mine too."

"I gathered that from the condition of it. How many times have you read it?" She asked the last bit with a groan as she stretched her limbs taut, arching her back just a little.

My body's reaction was instantaneous, and I turned abruptly from her. She could not be allowed to witness the effect she had on me.

"What are you, Never?" The question came out unintentionally brusque, rough, and I hated myself for not having better control over my own voice. Silence filled the space between us, save for the ticking of the clock, marking the seconds she spent conjuring an answer.

I wheeled around and pinned her with my gaze. "I asked you a question."

"I heard you, but I don't know how to answer. Human? Is that what you're looking for?"

Fine, if she wanted to play games, I could play too. Enchantress or no, I knew for a fact I had an effect on her. That attraction I felt, however warped, was not one-sided.

I hoped it wasn't one-sided.

She propped herself on her elbows as she watched me. Her eyes followed me to the bottom of the bed. When I grabbed her ankle and pulled her toward me, she didn't scream or cry out. No, she let me slide her closer without any fight at all.

Enchantress or temptress? One was magical, the other was just… insatiable.

My cock pulsed uncomfortably as I imagined stripping her out of her pants and running my hands up her legs. I shoved the thought from my mind. What I was doing was not for me. It was a test. A challenge to see how she would react.

How far could I push my little charade?

If she was an enchantress, she would let me take it all the way to the end, riding out the pleasure, consuming it all as she pulled it from me. Enchantress, succubus. They were effectively the same.

I let her foot fall and grabbed the other, pulling it flush with the first and pressing them together. Her eyes bore into me as I climbed onto the bed straddling her body, just barely letting the strings of my shirt graze her clothes while I worked my way up. It wasn't real contact. I doubted she could feel a thing, but a visible shiver raked through her, and her breath caught.

Those were not the reactions of a creature bent on stealing the pleasure of others. Doubt bled slowly into my mind. Was I wrong about her?

I pulled myself up so I loomed over her. Even on the heels of somewhat restless sleep, with dark circles beneath her eyes and her hair tousled around her face, she was alluring. I lowered a little of my weight onto her and she stiffened but didn't protest.

"I'll ask you only once more. What are you?" I kept my voice barely above a whisper.

She shifted beneath me, pressing herself into my throbbing erection with a sly smile.

Definitely a succubus. The realization stung. Why had I been hoping she was anything else?

Then that sting manifested as a sharp pain that lanced up my side. She bucked violently beneath me, her wicked smile morphing into a sneer. I pitched sideways and Never rolled off the bed, landing lightly on her bare feet. She squared her body to mine with the bloody tip of her dagger pointing at me accusingly. The tip vibrated ever so slightly.

What the hell just happened?

An enchantress would *not* have bucked me off. I pressed my hand to my aching side and pulled away a palm slick with blood.

A succubus wouldn't stab its intended target, at least, not before it got what it wanted.

Which meant she was neither, and I'd made a huge mistake.

"You're an asshole."

"Never." I held my hands up defensively. "I believe I owe you an apology."

"No shit." An emotion flickered across her features, betraying the rage seething at the surface. Hurt. I'd hurt her. She pointed the blade at me. "The sun's up, right?"

I nodded slowly, keeping my hands in plain sight. I'd mucked things up royally with her and my mind was racing to find a way to fix it. She wasn't a succubus, nor an enchantress. She might be a temptress, but I was starting to understand it might not have been intentional. Was the woman even aware of the effect she had on me?

"Are you going to take me to shore or will I need to swim for it?" Her gaze darted around the room.

She didn't want to swim. Good. I could work with that. There was little risk to her now that the sun had crested the horizon, but I kept that to myself. When I pushed off the bed and stood, she took two quick steps backward, maintaining the distance between us.

"My behavior was unacceptable. Please know that it was a misunderstanding." How could I explain the situation without giving too much away? Or should I even bother? She might not have been a supernatural being bent on possessing me in some way, but I seriously doubted she'd missed the signals my body was broadcasting. A vision of her in my bed from the night before seeped through my guilt, sending a jolt of pure lust through me that set my heart racing. I slammed my eyes closed before my arousal shined through. "I am sorry. I will take you to shore, as promised."

Silence stretched between us. I couldn't shut the thoughts of her out. The black and gray tattoos swirling up from the top of her left foot, snaking around her taut calf and chasing a path up her thigh. The way her slender fingers circled, almost lazily, like she loved the sensation of exploring her own body almost as much as she enjoyed bringing herself to climax.

It was beyond sexy.

And keeping my eyes closed definitely wasn't working.

I turned my back to her and forced them open, focusing on the bed. Another wave of heat rolled through me at the sight of the rumpled duvet and dented pillow. Not good. I was like a randy teenage boy trapped in the body of an immortal.

Goddess, help me.

I tried to find something innocuous to anchor my lecherous mind to, but everything in my room was potential kindling for the fire growing inside me.

"Are you feeling so guilty you can't even bear to look at me now?" Her bitter accusation finally sliced through the flames.

"Go wait on the deck with William." My voice sounded foreign to me, rough and thick through the roar of blood rushing past my ears. "I will join you shortly."

Again, the silence between us grew until it felt like a mile-wide chasm. I wanted to explain, to reassure her that she was safe with me, but if we were being honest, I wasn't entirely sure that was true. I'd never felt this kind of attraction to anyone. It was all-consuming and more than a little terrifying.

Her clothes rustled gently as she slipped on her boots, but I didn't dare a glance over my shoulder. I could still feel the power coursing through me, barely in check. The door opened and the cool ocean breeze swirled with her scent. I breathed it in deep.

"For what it's worth, I'm sorry if I upset you with the book. I know I had no right to touch it. It just—"

I waited, breathless with her invigorating scent trapped in my lungs. Did she really think any of my reaction had to do with the book? Was she really so oblivious to her own appeal?

"It reminded me of home," she said quietly.

The door clicked shut and I let out my breath in a rush, the tension retreating from my body with the exhale. Then I turned and sat heavily on the edge of my bed, scrubbing my hands over my face. "What is wrong with me?"

CHAPTER 17

The trip to the beach in the skiff wasn't as bad as I'd expected, though the silence was awkward. Hook refused to meet my gaze, keeping his attention focused on rowing the little boat through the slow, iridescent waves.

I'd checked the water at least a dozen times for any sign of lurking sirens, despite Hook's assurance that they were traditionally nocturnal creatures. When a brilliant head of bright pink hair popped up in the water a few yards away, I yelped and grabbed for my blade.

Hook's head snapped around, following my gaze, then his low chuckle threaded through my growing panic. "It's fine, Never. That's a mermaid, not a siren." He set one oar in his lap and waved the creature over. "Come say hi! You're scaring the poor girl."

The girl reference stung a bit, but I shoved my irritation away. I shouldn't give a crap what Hook thought of me. I was using him to get me back to shore, then we were going our separate ways.

The pink-haired creature disappeared beneath the water, then popped back up right beside the skiff a half a breath later. I scooted back away from the edge.

"Hi!" The mermaid waved excitedly, sending little droplets of water into the boat. "I'm Hemisa." She batted her long lashes, the same neon pink as her hair, and dipped her head. Then she pulled herself up so she was resting on her forearms with her bare breasts pressing against the edge of the craft.

"You're naked." I instantly felt like an idiot.

Smooth, Never. Super smooth.

Hook and Hemisa both laughed. "She lives in the water. Do sea creatures in your world wear clothes?"

I shrugged, trying to look her in the eyes, but my gaze kept wanting to dip down to her pert little breasts. Her skin shimmered in the sunlight, like it was made of a million tiny, ethereal scales. Which it probably was.

"I, uh…" Seriously? I'd seen naked women before. An errant thought hit me, and I couldn't smother the snort that followed.

She watched me curiously, then looked to Hook. "Do you know what she finds humorous?"

I shook my head, pressing my lips into a flat line to get myself under control. When I could finally speak, I still couldn't seem to control the amusement in my voice. "I just realized how men must feel sometimes." I motioned to her bare chest to make my point, but she only tipped her head in confusion.

Hook's bark of laughter let me know at least he understood where I was coming from.

She eyed us both with one eyebrow raised, and I held up my hand. "We don't have real mermaids in my world, but in the movies, the females always wear clothes, at least on their top half." I held my hands in front of my chest to show her what I meant.

Her irritation quickly turned to curiosity. "Why? We live in the water. Clothing would drag in the current."

She made a solid argument and I nodded. "I think it's a modesty issue. It isn't typically acceptable for women in my world to walk around topless."

Hemisa tugged herself up a little higher and flipped her tail out of the water. She gave it a little wiggle, winking playfully when the move splashed more droplets over me. "Good thing I'm not a human woman then, huh?"

Her tail was a thing of beauty, making the gentle shimmer of her upper body pale in comparison to the rich pink and blue hues of her scales.

"You are stunning." The words were out of my mouth before I realized it, and heat filled my cheeks.

She smiled coyly and batted those lashes again. "Thank you." Hemisa reached a hand out and ran a finger down my cheek, sending a shiver through me. "You are an exceptional beauty yourself."

A low rumble pierced the spell she'd cast on me, and I turned to see Hook scowling at her. "She is off limits."

Her lips quirked playfully. "Is that so?"

If I hadn't been staring at him in horror, I would have missed the flash of orange in his eyes. Her lips dropped into a pout, then she released her grip on the skiff and flipped backward into the water, sending a wave of the cool liquid cascading over a very grumpy looking Hook. When she resurfaced, the mischievous grin on her face was infectious.

"Hemisa!" Hook yelled at her. "What has gotten into you?"

She winked playfully at me then turned her attention to him. "I thought you needed to cool down a bit, lover boy."

He froze at the accusation, like a deer in headlights.

"You might want to get a handle on that before you-know-who figures it out." She swam lazily closer to the edge and motioned me over with a crook of her long finger. I leaned out and she whispered, "You're a very lucky girl."

"What?" My brow pinched in confusion.

She tilted her head to one side, kind of like a dog, then her pink lips spread wide in a breathtaking smile as she glanced between us. "Oh." Her giggle sounded like raindrops on a wine glass. "You two are just too cute. This is going to be so much fun." She pushed away from the skiff.

"Wait!" Hook yelled, leaning out over the edge.

She swam up next to him and he leaned in close, whispering something in her ear. Her eyes fluttered closed at the sound of his voice and a twinge of displeasure lanced through me. Then her eyes flew wide and settled on me. When he finished being a secretive prick, she nodded once. "Of course."

"I need your word, Hemisa. This is not a game."

"You have it."

After the shimmering creature with her annoyingly perky attitude finally left, I leveled him with a glare. "What was that about?"

He picked up the oars and continued rowing without so much as a glance in my direction, which wasn't the easiest thing in the world, since I was basically sitting right in the broody bastard's eyeline.

"Well?"

"That was insurance." He still wouldn't look at me, but at least we were talking again.

"For what?" I fought the urge to cross my arms over my chest because doing that on this little bench on a tiny boat would have me listing from side to side with every gentle wave that rocked the craft. Instead, I wrapped my fingers around the edge of the bench at my sides and dug my nails into the sealed wood.

What did I get in return? Silence.

Hook's jacket was draped neatly beside him, which meant the outline of his muscled frame was clear and cut beneath his flowing white shirt. Every time I'd seen a man in a shirt like that before, he'd always resembled a boy dressed up in women's clothing, but Hook wore that damned shirt like he'd invented the look. He owned that shit.

Watching the muscles of his shoulders and arms flex and pull with each sweep of the oars didn't hurt either. The guy was ripped. Not giant, bulky, walks like a wooden toy kind of ripped. I liked a man who had enough range of motion to wipe his own ass, thank you very much. And Hook was the kind of muscular that was all long and lean with just enough mass to make my mouth water.

And that was the reason for my attraction to him. The only reason.

Ignoring, for the moment, my track record of dating guys who'd turned out to be giant assholes, if I looked past the grumpy, broody, bossiness of the man, his sex appeal was undeniable. That didn't mean I liked the man himself. It just meant he was sexy enough to daydream about and to think about when I'd made myself come in his bed.

Heat flushed my cheeks even before I realized he was watching me damn near drool over him.

A crease formed between his drawn brow. "Are you feeling ill?"

Great. Apparently my aroused look bore some passing resemblance to sea-sickness. "I'm fine." I tried not to choke on the words, swallowing hard to clear the frog from my throat. "What kind of insurance were you and fish girl talking about?"

"Merfolk are not fish."

"What are—" I cut myself off with a wave of my hand. "You know what, I don't care. What were you two whispering about? And why did she give me that weird look?"

"It was just a precaution. Nothing for you to worry about."

I covered my mouth with a fist and fake coughed my response. "Asshole."

A muscle in his jaw ticked. "I haven't been on my best behavior of late, which is something I am trying to rectify. You would do well to work on yours as well. Name calling isn't remotely lady-like."

"I never said I was a fucking lady," I fired back.

His Adam's apple bobbed as his throat worked silently.

"Does my language still bother you?"

He swallowed again, then glanced over his shoulder. "We're nearly there."

"Yeah, I can see that. Thanks." I grabbed the edge of the skiff. "What do I need to do?"

"Nothing. Stay right there."

"I'm a big girl. I can help." I looked over the edge. The sandy bottom was clear through the water. "What is that, like two feet deep? Maybe three?" I hoisted myself up.

"I wouldn't."

It was too late. I swung over the edge and sank into the water. Then I kept sinking. When my boots finally hit the soft bottom, I was chin deep and sputtering.

"Hold onto the edge," he said, irritation and humor battling for dominance as he rowed the skiff closer to the beach.

By the time we touched down and dragged the skiff up past the high tide line, my embarrassment was well on its way to being replaced with frustration. I stripped off my poor jacket and shook it out, then plopped down in the sand. I unlaced my left boot and dumped the saltwater out of it, feeling a bit like a drowned rat. My hair was plastered to my cheek, and when I tried to shake it loose, it didn't budge.

Of course.

I shoved my foot in my boot and yanked the laces tight, then repeated the process with the other side. Hook, on the other hand, just stood there watching me.

"What?" I asked, making no attempt to mask my irritation.

"Do you have a habit of diving headfirst into situations even after people advise you otherwise?" He had one hand on the hilt of his sword-thing and a look of absolute confidence on his face, like he was so fucking sure he had me pegged.

"Only when I don't trust the person doing the advising." I lifted one eyebrow in a silent challenge. I wanted him to take the bait, because gods, I was in the mood for a fight.

But he wouldn't even give me that satisfaction. He lifted his chin and looked up to the sky, drawing in a deep breath. "Very well."

That's what I got? Very well?

Very fucking well to you too, buddy.

"You can go now. I've got it from here," I said, motioning to the foliage crowding the sand in a thick green wall of leaves and vines.

Hook ignored my dismissal, scanning that same terrestrial line. "I'll help you find your brother."

What if I didn't want his help? I almost asked the question out loud, but the reality of my situation wasn't difficult to see. It wasn't like there was a trail head with a weatherproof sign that would point me to Pan's camp. I pulled myself to my feet, checking for the pendant tucked in the coin pocket of my jeans as I brushed the sand off my clothes.

"Why would you help me?" It was a question I actually wanted an answer to. As far as I could tell, the man had no real reason for wanting to help me. But then, I didn't know all that much about him.

He pulled in another deep breath. "The demon and I have a lengthy history."

I waited for him to say more, because that wasn't anywhere close to a useful answer, but apparently that was all he was going to give me.

"Could you, maybe, elaborate on that a little?" I tried to keep my voice light, but damn, it was tough. I'd never been good at shielding my emotions. I was more of a you-get-what-you-see kind of girl, and at that moment I was all over the place. I desperately wanted to find Matty and get him home, but I also wanted to know what Hook's damage was.

He shook his head, but his gaze never stopped scanning the trees behind me. "Not here. Are you ready?"

I rubbed my hands together to knock the last of the sand off and picked up my jacket. "Tally ho, sailor."

"Captain," he corrected.

Tying my jacket around my waist, I eyed him warily. Even first thing in the morning, the island was considerably warmer than the deck of his ship, and a tiny, superficial part of me longed for deodorant. At least I'd have a few hours before the BO stink really kicked in, thanks to my chin-deep seawater bath. I refrained from lifting my arm and performing a quick sniff test, barely, and chose instead to poke the bear. "I'm not calling you Captain."

He zeroed in on me, and my body wanted to squirm under the heat in that glare. The man was a fucking master of silent intimidation.

"Glare all you want," I said, shoving past him. "Hook."

CHAPTER 18

I made it exactly three steps into the trees before his hand landed on my shoulder and I flinched involuntarily. How had he gotten so close so fast? His touch was gone in an instant and he stuttered an apology.

"No need to grovel." My attempt at easing his guilt clearly failed, because when I glanced at his face, he looked almost sad. "I grew up with a demon-fighting mom who taught me just enough about the bad shit in the world to give me a lifetime's worth of nightmares before she skipped town. It made me a little jumpy."

Hook reached a hand out and gently touched my arm. Even just that light contact sent tiny waves and tingles across my skin. It was the kind of touch I *should* have pulled away from. Yet, somehow, he made the soft press of his fingertips against my forearm feel intimate, and every cell in my body wanted to lean into it. Every cell save for the few neurons in my brain that were still functioning properly.

I took a half step back, hoping he couldn't see me mentally shaking off the sensation. "You do know where we're going, right?"

The landscape looked beautiful from the outside, from the safety of the beach where I could hold my arms out at my sides and spin in a big, girlish circle without touching anything. But the previous day's adventure had opened my eyes to one of the realities of strolling through a rainforest. Well, two actually.

First, there was no strolling, not unless we managed to find a handy dandy trail. Between the trees, vines, shrubs, puddles, erupting roots, and animals, getting through the dense vegetation would be nothing short of a slog. Second, and the thing that had my skin crawling, was that everything was much, much too close for comfort.

I desperately wanted to find Matty and get him home but standing there with the toe of one boot edging into the shade already had my chest constricting. I just hadn't noticed as much the day before because I was running from Hook.

"I do know where we need to go, and it isn't through here." He took a step back and motioned to the long stretch of untouched sand with a little bow of his head.

The vise tightening around my lungs eased back a notch, and I nodded gratefully.

"The island isn't all bad. There is a lot of beauty here, but like all beautiful things. . ." He paused and glanced over at me. "It comes with its share of danger."

"Like that cursed siren from yesterday? Or the snake that tried to pounce on me from that branch while you just watched?"

His lips curled up in a hint of a smile before he headed down the beach. "Snakes do not pounce, and that one was not dangerous. It was merely trying to say hello. And the siren is avoidable. It's just a matter of keeping a safe distance from her putrescent little pond."

I had to move quickly to keep up with Hook's annoyingly long legs, though he didn't appear to be in a hurry. "How do you know where Pan is keeping my brother?"

His hand drifted up and his fingers pressed to his chest absent-mindedly. "The demon has a routine." He glanced down at his hand, yanking it away with a little huff of disgust. "Your brother must have used a summoning spell. It is the only way the demon would have been able to leave this realm to visit yours."

I shook my head vehemently, because Matty didn't know the first thing about summoning demons or casting spells. He was just a teenage boy. But Hook pushed on.

"The demon's mission right now is to make your brother feel at home. There will be fun and games, lots of food, maybe a little adventure. The demon and the lost boys—I like that name for them, by the way, though they aren't exactly kids anymore—they will do everything in their power to convince your brother it's safe to let his guard down."

I grabbed his arm and pulled him to a stop. "And then?"

His gaze flicked down to where my hand was wrapped around his forearm. "Then they'll set to work separating the boy from his shadow."

"How long?"

"It depends on the boy. Wendy's brothers let their guard down after two days, but they were young, not yet in their teens. How old is your brother?"

"Seventeen."

"We may have more time." He motioned to a narrow path snaking into the woods up ahead. "Stay close. The trail is less treacherous than attempting to traverse straight through, but it is by no means safe."

The warning did exactly nothing to ease the tension growing inside me as I followed him into the trees.

"His age will likely work in his favor. Is he the trusting sort or is he more like you?"

I snorted at that. "Like me?"

"I distinctly recall having to earn your trust over the threat of a slit throat." He was an arm's length ahead of me and I still heard the smile in his voice, even though he didn't turn to face me.

"Right. I did say that."

He hummed appreciatively and the vibration of it seemed to carry through the air and sink into my core. Had that promise of violence impressed him?

A vision of me straddling Hook on his bed, with my blade pressed to his neck, seared its way through my mind, and that seductive hum rippled through my body.

Holy hell.

I shoved my hand through my hair and hissed when my fingers caught on a spiky tangle. That should have pulled me right out of my dark little fantasy, but when Hook snapped back to check on me, a delicious smirk graced his lips.

"Here," he said, humor lacing his gruff voice. "Don't yank. It looks like you picked up a nightshade thistle." His long fingers wrapped around my wrists and pulled them down, pressing them to my chest. "Keep those there, please."

"Nightshade? Is it poisonous?"

"If it breaks the skin, yes. Now, hold still."

I could barely breathe as he set to work untangling the knot. Each gentle tug and pull sent a new flare of arousal through my body.

"Will you tell me more about him?" he asked softly.

It took me a solid five seconds to figure out just what he was talking about, because all my lust-addled brain wanted to focus on was him. His teasing touch, his scent. The man smelled like a god, and I closed my eyes, breathing him in deep.

What had he asked me?

Right. About my brother. About my baby brother, who was the whole reason I was there in the first place. You know, the one who was in danger from a soul stealing demon.

A blood red thistle landed just off the path in front of me. I blinked rapidly and reached up, interfering with his ministrations. "You know, that's probably good enough. It's not like I'm here to win any beauty contests."

He lingered as he was, his amber eyes burning into me, then he dropped his hands with a little frown. "As you wish."

I stared for a second. Hadn't his eyes been light brown before?

Man, this place was already doing a number on me.

I shook off my confusion and motioned for us to continue walking, letting him take the lead again without another word. Once his back was turned, I ran a tentative hand through the tangled mass of my hair, but there were only one or two little snags left, easy enough to break loose with a little coaxing.

"Matty is more trusting than me, but he's no dummy. Except with girls. The poor kid is a blubbering idiot around a pretty girl."

"Ah." His response was barely audible and carried with it a tinge of worry.

"That's a good thing, right? I never read anything about Pan kidnapping girls." Then again, the information from Wendy's journal was proving to be only partially accurate. "There aren't any lost girls roaming the island, are there?"

Even if there were, Matty was a good kid. I knew that better than anyone. There was no way some dickhead demon with a gang of soulless kids was going to trick him into giving up his soul in the space of a day or two. I still had time.

"The demon has never shown an interest in females, at least in my experience." His confirmation was bland, emotionless. Suspicious.

"What am I missing?"

He glanced over his shoulder. "What was the Pan in your stories like? Was it the same as in the journal?"

"Oh, no. Complete opposites in fact. According to Wendy's account, Pan is some super powerful demon thing. I don't know that she ever actually saw him though. Her descriptions were always second-hand. And she never actually called him Peter, so I don't know where that name came from. Probably artistic license."

"And the story?"

I thought back through the different versions I'd seen and heard. "It's one of those stories that has been told and retold so many times. For the most part though, he's just a magical little boy who wants to have fun. He wants friends to play with and endless adventures, but Wendy and her brothers want to go home." My memories of the story stung a little. It'd been so long since I'd let myself really think about it. "I always kind of felt sorry for that version of him."

I fell silent, listening to the chirp of birds and whistle of something

I couldn't identify as I waited for a response. The woods on either side of the trail were open, like they'd been pulled back by some great magical net just so the relentless sun could beat down on us from above.

"What is he really like?" I asked, hoping to spur him into conversation. He was, after all, the only one of us who knew the truth about the asshole demon that had spirited my brother away.

"For starters, the demon is not the kind of creature you should ever make the mistake of having sympathy for." He paused and turned, pinning me with a serious look. "That creature is a monster, wicked and dangerous beyond measure, and prevented from wreaking havoc in the universe only because a handful of powerful ancients sacrificed their power to create this prison."

"What kind of demon is he?"

Hook shook his head and turned back to the trail, continuing forward without checking to see if I was following. "The original kind."

"What does that mean?" I asked, putting on a little burst of speed to catch up. As much as I wanted him to slow down so I didn't feel like a toddler running to keep up with an adult, the need to find my brother was growing stronger by the minute. Original demons and ancient protectors? "None of what you just said was in Wendy's journal."

"Wendy changed while she was here. I've told you that. Perhaps the stories she brought back with her, the stories she shared in her writings, were how she wanted to remember things. Or maybe she just couldn't bring herself to record the truth."

"What can you tell me that *is* true?" I didn't know what else to ask. I felt like he was talking in circles, deliberately avoiding giving me real answers. And he was starting to piss me off again.

He sliced with his blade, severing heavy fronds from an encroaching bush. "We have a very long day ahead of us."

I waited, and waited, and fucking waited. But that was all he gave me.

HOOK

CHAPTER 19

Another bead of sweat rolled down my spine and I pulled at the front of my shirt, peeling it away from my heated skin. The afternoon sun was a brutal thing on the island, especially when there was no shade to break it.

When I looked back, Never was a few paces behind me, eyes trained on the trail as she trudged along. Her face and neck were flushed pink with effort and her own shirt was damp with sweat. The way the fabric clung emphasized her curves, and my hands itched to wrap around her waist and strip that thin layer off her.

She glanced up at me, freezing mid-step, her eyes growing wide. "What the fuck?" Her gaze turned fiery, and she rocked backward. "Don't tell me you're a fucking demon too."

Oh hell.

I slammed my eyes shut and shook my head. "No." I heard the rustle of clothes and knew without looking that she had her dagger in her hand. "I am not a demon."

"Cool, cool. Except, and pardon my ignorance here, I've never met a *human* whose eyes glow. Shit. I thought that was a trick of the light last night."

The heat inside me receded a little and I latched onto that feeling, shoving it the rest of the way down. When I dared a look, she had her blade out but down at her side in a deceptively casual grip. To someone who'd been in countless knife and sword fights, that grip told me she meant business. But she didn't need the blade to slice me open on the inside. The betrayal on her face did that all on its own.

"I never said I was human." It was the only response I could think of. Never couldn't know that I was a disgraced demigod. Not yet. Maybe not ever.

Her lips pressed into a thin line and her eyes narrowed to slits. "What are you then? Incubus? That would certainly explain a few things." Her attitude was back in full force and honestly, it eased a little of my tension. At least until my mind processed her words.

"What would my being an incubus explain for you?" Arousal thickened my voice because I already knew, but now I desperately wanted to hear her say the words. An incubus was a creature who fed on lust, capable of using his magic to bring others, men and women alike, to such a state of erotic titillation that they would be compelled, desperate, to engage sexually with the creature. If even a small part of her thought I had that ability—

Her half-naked form flashed through my mind again. It hadn't occurred to me that she might have been thinking about me while she touched herself the night before. My cock rose to attention at the possibility. Had she been imagining me the same way I'd envisioned joining her in my room?

She raised the blade and pointed it at me, taking a step back. Her eyes were locked on mine, and I knew she saw the glow there. I tried to will it away, to shove it down where I'd kept my powers locked up for eons. I hadn't lost control in a very long time, and I certainly was not going to start with her.

I turned away, knowing full well I was risking a knife in the back, but I needed to break the connection. The forest stretched out in front of me, and I drew in a breath, letting it out on a slow count.

"I am not an incubus either," I finally said. She remained silent behind me. "What I am doesn't matter, as long as you know I mean you no harm. My job is to keep the demon imprisoned here. It is something I was tasked with long ago. I have, admittedly, grown a bit lax in recent years because it seemed as though it gave up the fight. But that doesn't change my duty to this realm. It is my job to protect it, and as you are a visitor here, I will protect you as well."

Even if that meant protecting her from me.

Her clothing rustled softly, and she let out a resigned huff. "Let's get something straight." She waited until I turned to face her to continue, looking both fierce and disappointed in a way that tugged painfully at my cold heart. "I'm willing to admit that I might need your help to get to my brother." She focused her attention on her hands as she adjusted her jacket around her waist. "But if you make me regret trusting you, I swear on all that shimmers in this world that I will repay that regret tenfold."

When she met my gaze again, all I saw was stony resolve. Never had erected a wall between us in her mind, one she clearly intended to defend.

I didn't know why I was hoping for more from the woman but being shut out like that was decidedly unpleasant. Would it have been worth it to tell her the truth about who and what I was?

Memories of the last time I'd let someone in darkened my mind and before I realized it, my fingertips were tracing the ragged edge of the scar on my chest.

Never watched me silently, her gaze locked on my scar. I adjusted my shirt to cover it. "We should be going. There is still quite a lot of ground to cover."

She looked up, searching for something in my face, as if a question was dancing on the tip of her sharp tongue. With a little shake of her head, she dismissed the notion. What was she thinking? I would have given the world to know in that moment. The world, but not the truth.

I scanned our surroundings in case any sneaking spies had overheard our conversation. The demon had eyes all over the island,

and if that wretched creature caught even a hint of the effect Never had on me—

I shoved the thought from my mind. There was no point in tempting fate by imagining the worst.

We walked for another few hours in relative silence, aside from her mumbled "thank you" each time I held a branch out of her way. I hadn't dared to touch her again, not with my self-control on the fritz. Even when she slipped on a steep incline and scraped her knee badly enough to tear her jeans and draw blood.

No, coward that I was, I just stood there watching, flexing my hands to keep from reaching out. I had asked if she was okay, but I hadn't even helped her to her feet. The fact that she didn't seem to expect my help, that she just picked herself up and dusted herself off with a little murmur of "I'm fine," grated on me almost as much.

A woman like her should have been used to being taken care of.

After another hour, when the sun was beginning its afternoon descent and shade finally began to stretch across the trail, I stopped. She hadn't said as much, but she looked like she needed a break.

"This island is a lot bigger than it looks from the beach." Her voice was tired, but not breathless.

"Aye." I checked the sky. "We're over halfway now. Should be there before the sun sets if all goes well." I plucked two bright purple bulbs from a nearby tree and sat on a boulder, motioning for Never to join me. Then I split the first of the spiky fruits with my dagger and handed her half.

She took it warily, giving it a little sniff. "What is it?"

"Wikali." I took a small bite of the rich purple interior. "The rind is bitter, but the inside is sweet and safe to eat."

She sniffed it again, did an adorable little shrug, then pulled out her own dagger and cut off a little slice. When she bit down, her eyes fluttered shut and a moan escaped her lips. Even watching her eat was an erotic experience. As if she could track my thoughts, her eyes flew open and she covered her mouth with her hand.

"Sorry," she mumbled through a mouthful of the fruit.

I pressed my lips together to smother a laugh. "Nothing to apologize for, love. I should have thought to grab us something to eat before we left the ship this morning."

She cut off another small slice and brought it to her lips.

"No need to stand on ceremony. I'm hungry too." I held my half up and took a large bite. She watched me chew and her gaze dropped to my throat when I swallowed. Even with the juiciness of the wikali coating my tongue, I felt suddenly parched under that gaze.

It did unspeakable things to my resolve when she looked at me like that.

When she realized I was watching her watch me, with the fruit still hovering at her lips, she turned her eyes abruptly away and chomped down.

"It tastes a little like kiwi," she said as I handed her half of the second piece. "Kiwi but with the consistency of a ripe strawberry maybe? It's a little confusing, but it's good."

We ate in silence as the forest came alive around us. The longer we sat and watched, the bolder the native creatures grew, chirping and clicking and venturing out from the safety of their hiding places. When had it become so easy to forget the beauty of the place?

Before the demon's recent foray away from the island, it had been decades since I'd stepped foot on it. The other islands, sure, but not this one.

Never finished her fruit and wiped the blade on her pants, leaving a bright purple smear across her thigh. She frowned when she saw it, then shook her head. "Of course."

"It'll wash," I offered, hoping to head off the inevitable meltdown that seemed to accompany most women when they'd potentially ruined an item of clothing. "The juice of the wikali is colorful, but it comes out easy enough."

Her half-shrug was a tad anticlimactic. "Thanks, but they're just jeans." She turned to study the forest. "Kind of small potatoes on the scale of things I need to be worrying about." One second she was talking calmly, and the next she was on her feet launching herself at me.

We hit the ground in a thump with her body crashing on top of mine, and the strangest feeling of rightness invaded my senses. "What's all this now?" My voice was gruff as I fought to keep my power firmly leashed.

Never shifted her weight, pressing one palm to my chest to get a better look around. "Did you seriously not see that shimmery ball that just tried to attack you? It was headed right for you."

Damn.

Something whizzed by overhead, and I wrapped my arms around Never, rolling until her taut body was pinned safely beneath me. She writhed under my weight and at any other moment I would have taken the time to revel in that feeling.

I leaned my head close, pressing my lips to her ear and keeping my voice low. "Quiet."

Thank the goddess, she stilled beneath me at the command. When I pulled back to look at her, fully aware of the effect her proximity was having on my control, she met my glowing gaze head on.

Good. I couldn't have her running scared from me.

Our lips were just inches apart, so my barely whispered, "Trust me," was more of a caress than actual words. It was a long shot. The woman was a willful creature with the heart of a warrior, but I had to try. "Please."

Her gaze searched mine. I braced for a rebuff or some smartass remark, but her only reaction was a barely perceptible nod.

"Follow my lead." I managed to get the words out without sounding like a blubbering fool. Then I pushed up and got to my feet, leaving her in the dirt. It went against every instinct I had, all my training, and I felt slimy doing it, just like I had all damn day. I turned my back on her without another word, as though she wasn't the most captivating soul I'd ever encountered.

A familiar sound, long lost in my ocean of memories but not

forgotten, filled the space around us, like tiny shards of glass falling delicately on a marble floor.

"Hello, Anya."

"My dear, sweet Hook." The pixie's sing-song voice was an instant irritation across my nerves, and hearing that cruel name on her lips sent a flurry of fire through my chest and back that made my scars tingle. It brought with it a maddening urge to reach up and press my hand to the irritated flesh. To claw at it and rip it apart just to make it stop.

If I could have seen the normally faded, puckered scars, now many centuries healed, I knew I would find those lingering reminders of her viciousness flushing a bright, angry pink. As though the injuries she'd inflicted with her magic and malice had only just happened.

I stopped myself before I reached up to touch my chest, anchoring my restless palm to the hilt of my cutlass. "Careful, pixie."

There was a rustle behind me, and I felt more than heard Never get to her feet. She kept a few feet of space between us and, thankfully, kept her mouth closed.

The pixie's tiny form was unassuming, at least until her wings agitated the air around her. In a swirl of brilliant turquoise dust that made the ferns and palm fronds nearby shiver, she grew to nearly match my size.

Her green eyes danced between me and Never. "Does this mean our arrangement has come to an end?"

Our arrangement. She made it sound so civilized.

I forced a casual stance, feigning calm. "The arrangement stands."

Her wings fluttered in pulses as she circled us, no doubt trying to glean something useful about Never. She turned up her nose with a little huff. "Taking in humans now? I knew you'd changed, but this is bottom of the barrel, even for you." She raised her glittery hand and tapped her lips with her index finger. "But I'm curious, what is a human girl doing in this realm in the first place?"

Tension rolled off Never, and she stiffened behind me.

Anya's face lit up. She almost looked like the sweet pixie I'd made the mistake of trusting all those years ago, save for the malevolent gleam in her green eyes. She touched down, her bare toes settling lightly on the rich soil, but her translucent wings never stopped moving.

"Aw." She pressed a hand over her heart, or the place a heart would have been if she'd actually had one. "This is the big sister, isn't it? Come to rescue the new kid?" She looked Never up and down and clucked her tongue. "Too bad you decided to shack up with a pirate."

"I didn't shack up with anyone," Never hissed from behind me. "I came here looking for my brother when this asshole kidnapped me off the island and detained me on his ship. Now he's trying to make amends by playing tour guide." The venom in her voice sounded real enough.

Was she just playing along, or was some of that ire truly meant for me?

Anya shook her head. "Nice try, girl. I saw you protect him."

She laughed mischievously. "You saw me tackle him. That was not protection. In case you haven't noticed, he's kind of a dick."

Anya hummed thoughtfully and gave me a seductive once over. It was almost enough to make me physically ill. "He is many things." She spread her wings and shook them gently, releasing a cascade of fine turquoise dust that shimmered in the light.

"Don't." I tapped the handle of my cutlass in warning, but she just shrugged innocently. As if she hadn't just been releasing pixie dust around her for some malicious purpose. I wasn't sure the maniacal creature had ever actually possessed innocence.

Her eyes glittered knowingly. "Don't what, pirate?"

Before I could respond, Never stepped in front of me. "Where is he? Where is my brother?"

Anya folded her arms over her chest and grinned. "What's in it for me?"

CHAPTER 20

My mind raced trying to think of anything I could offer the pixie in exchange for my brother's location. What could she possibly ask for? According to the stories, her kind loved collecting shiny things, little trinkets. Yeah, the only two things I had that met that description were my dagger and the pendant.

No and no.

She stood just shy of six-feet tall, and her wingspan, or what I could see of it when she stretched them out until they looked like iridescent gossamer pulled tight over a fine silver frame, was nearly twice that. It made perfect sense why she would need the ability to shrink down to the size of a softball. There was no way she could fly through the forest otherwise.

"You work with Pan, correct?" I asked, eying her and those gently fluttering wings. Not going to lie, she made me a little nervous.

"We often find our interests are aligned." Anya gave me a smug look that burned away the nervousness and left me scrambling not to slap that smile clean off her stupid, glittery face.

"What do you want in exchange for information? What would you consider a fair price?" I asked, doing my damnedest to put on a civil front.

"Never, she cannot be trusted." Hook's quiet voice was weirdly insistent, pleading even, but I blocked him out.

She gave me another searing assessment, raking me from head to toe with her dark gaze. "A kiss."

Huh?

Before I could respond, Anya turned those dark eyes on Hook. "From him."

Something powerful flared in me, a feeling so completely out of place I couldn't fully admit I'd felt it. Everything in me wanted to shake my head and tell her to go to hell, but he held up a hand.

"One," he said with a voice so gruff it sounded like a threat. His entire body had gone rigid and the muscles in his neck flexed. In another situation, that would have been undeniably hot. "One kiss and then you tell her everything she wants to know."

I didn't like it. Not one bit. I reached out for him, but he pulled away, taking a step toward the pixie as my fingertips brushed his retreating shirt.

"Do you accept, pixie?" he asked.

Realistically, it was a small ask. A kiss? Come on. Who was I to stop a pirate captain from making out with a smoking hot pixie if it meant she would tell me how to find my brother?

The pixie's wings quivered as he took another step toward her. "Mmm." She bit her bottom lip and threw me a knowing look. A vindictive look. The little bitch moved around him, tugging at his shirt so I could see his face over her shoulder. "I accept."

His expression was unreadable, and he kept his gaze focused on her right up until she grabbed him by the back of the neck and pulled him in for a passionate kiss. She flattened her body against his, putting her all into the moment.

My stomach knotted painfully and when his gaze met mine, I shut my eyes and turned away. I couldn't watch.

"Nev—" Hook's voice cut out just before invisible hands cinched around my limbs, my waist, my neck. They tangled in my hair and yanked me off my feet, ripping me backward into the shadows.

The feeling was gone in the next instance, disappearing as quickly as it'd come, and I stumbled fighting to keep my balance. The humid, salty breeze of the forest was replaced by a mustiness that reminded me vaguely of an abandoned basement. Outlines of shapes slowly morphed into focus as my eyes adjusted to the shock of darkness.

I squeezed them shut, trying to force my pupils to react more quickly. When I opened them again, swirling sandstone walls rose up around me, close enough that I could stretch out my arms and touch both sides of the narrow corridor at once. Apparently, that little insect had the power to transport people.

"Awesome," I muttered.

Even in the dim light I could make out the brilliant streaks of color layering the cave walls, as though the passage was carved through the inside of a petrified rainbow. I reached a hand out to touch the nearest jut of stone, but a muted tinkle of broken glass stopped me and I spun to face Anya. A special kind of hate lit her eyes, the kind that implied she wanted to see me skinned alive and slow-roasted over a pit of coals.

"Where am I?" I gave her back my best hard stare, struggling against the urge to clutch the pendant protectively. "And what did you do with Hook?"

She held a finger to her glittery lips. "Unless you want them all to know we're here, pipe down, human." She snuck around a massive boulder and crooked that same finger for me to follow. Her voice was barely a whisper when she spoke again, but still crystal clear in the hushed air. "And Atlas is fine. On his way back to his ship as we speak."

His name. She'd used his first name. Granted, she'd called him Hook at first, but hadn't he said only his dearest friends called him Atlas? My stomach flip-flopped for some foolish, idiotic reason that I definitely didn't want to examine. Then her words sank in.

"He left?"

The gentle light emanating from the pixie dimmed and she tucked her wings behind her back with a smirk. "He *is* a pirate, girl. It's every man for himself in his world."

I shouldn't have been surprised, right? It wasn't like I actually knew the man, not the way Anya clearly did.

"Come along. We shouldn't tarry here for long."

She tiptoed down the curved path and I hesitated to follow. I wanted to find Matty. I did. But Hook's words were still ringing through my mind. What if she was leading me to a trap?

Barely audible footsteps padded through the dirt until the pixie's irritated frame appeared in front of me again. She jerked her head in the direction she'd come from. "Are you coming or not?"

"Yeah, just give me a minute," I said quietly. She let out a little huff and a few specks of blue-green glitter drifted from her folded wings. I knelt, pretending to tighten the laces of my boots as I discreetly slid my blade from its leathery hiding place, palming it so the blade rested flat against my wrist. "All better," I said, getting to my feet.

She pursed her plump lips and headed off again. I gave her a head start, keeping a safe distance between us in case she decided to turn on me in the confines of the passage.

The path led us to an outcropping of sandstone overlooking a yawning cavern. The hollow space was only dimly lit by a smattering of lanterns that all seemed to pulse unnaturally. Far beneath us, dozens of boys lay on the ground. Some appeared to be sleeping peacefully, while others talked or played quietly. They ranged in age from about ten-years-old to probably sixteen or seventeen. It was tough to tell from that distance.

My heart leapt at the thought of seeing Matty, but a quick scan of those faces revealed nothing familiar. "Are these the lost boys?"

The pixie wrinkled her nose, but her treacherous eyes lit up in a way that made my anger flare. Everything she did seemed to piss me off.

"No." She held her hand up, palm out, and the scene in front of me shimmered. The playful giggles and boyish snoring morphed into moans and groans and muted cries of misery. Those healthy, happy boys withered, losing their mass and shrinking, some to little more than flesh coated skeletons.

The first threads of panic tightened my throat and I swallowed hard. "What the hell is this? What are you doing to them?"

Anya brought that silencing finger to her lips again and I wanted to break it. The word "trap" pounded through my awareness with my rising heartbeat. My fingers loosened on the handle of my blade, preparing to flip it around so I could take her out if I needed to.

But could I?

It wasn't a moral question, not a question of right or wrong. I was more than willing to end her existence if it came down to it. She wasn't fooling me with that gorgeous, glittering façade. Anya was a predator through and through, and killing her wouldn't cost me a wink of sleep.

But was it even a possibility?

Hook's injuries back on the ship should have been life threatening. Hell, if someone I knew had sustained that kind of injury back home, I would have been on the phone with 911 in a heartbeat or hotwiring a car to speed them to the nearest hospital.

What if his ability to heal quickly was tied to this place? And if it was, who was to say Anya didn't benefit from the same magic? I tightened my grip on the blade again, feeling the cool metal press against the skin of my wrist.

"Whatever you're doing to them, stop now."

The pixie's eyes gleamed in the dim light. "This isn't my doing. All I've done is lift the glamour." She shook her head, but the look on her face as she smiled down at the misery below us was one of twisted reverence mixed with pleasure. "You see, you naïve little girl, there is no escaping this realm, not for boys who summon demons. The ones who play the game are granted the freedom to roam this island, to play and dance and do whatever they wish with their endless youth, so long as their loyalty is true." She motioned to the moaning, writhing bodies below us. "This is the fate that awaits your brother if he doesn't give her what she wants."

The sing-song tone of her voice grated against my already fraying nerves, but I didn't miss that little slip, if it was a slip. I narrowed my eyes. "She?"

CHAPTER 21

Anya tilted her head like she was listening for something, then her wings fluttered rapidly and we were back outside.

Except we weren't just outside the caves or back on the trail where we'd met. I squinted against the sudden brightness. That pixie-shaped monster had taken me all the way back to the beach.

"What the hell?" I spotted two sets of footprints moving toward the tree line and my heart sank. It was the same place where Hook and I had started that morning.

"Please, I just want to find my brother and get him home." I dropped my blade in the sand and held my hands up.

She was perched on a thick branch in a tree a few yards away, examining her nails without a care in the world.

"What do you want?" It was a challenge to keep the venom from my voice.

Her gaze dropped to my hips, and she licked her lips.

Um, no. Hard pass on that one.

She must have read my mind, or maybe the look on my face, since I probably didn't do the best job of hiding what I was thinking.

"That is mine," she said, pointing one glimmering finger at my right hip. At the pendant.

It suddenly felt like a twenty-pound weight pressed against my body. How had she even known it was there?

"This old thing?" I reached down and pulled the necklace free, letting it dangle from my middle finger. Her gaze followed the soft swing of the pendant greedily as I held it up and examined it. "This is yours?"

Her eyes narrowed. "Do you have any idea what that is, child?"

I chewed on the inside of my lip, considering my options. Really, I didn't have much to work with, so I shook my head. "No."

She sniffed like a debutant faced with the task of addressing someone below her station, wrinkling her nose. A wave of rage tore through me, setting my skin alight and making my extremities tingle. What was it about her that triggered that response in me?

Was this what it felt like to have a mortal enemy? A nemesis?

"If you tell me what it is, I'll think about trading it."

Her grin turned into a snarl. I hadn't ever considered what a snarling pixie might look like, and I definitely wasn't ready for the shock of terror it sent through my body. I stumbled backward, tripping over something in the sand and almost falling on my ass before I managed to stabilize. I shoved the necklace in my pocket and flicked my gaze over the ground, checking for any more potential hazards.

"Give it to me," Anya hissed, except she didn't sound like a sweet, adorable pixie. No, her voice was like a dozen dark, dangerous voices twisted around each other.

I knelt slowly, trying to appear non-threatening, but she saw right through me.

And shit, she was fast.

I dodged her mid-air charge by the skin of my teeth and whirled around, wielding the piece of driftwood I'd snagged from the sand like a bat. Under no circumstance was I letting that little glitter bitch get behind me, or in my pants.

In the blink of an eye, she shrank to the size of a grapefruit and disappeared into the trees.

Yeah, I definitely wanted to cut the little bitch. Maybe, before everything was said and done, I'd carve those pretty wings from her back when she was in her creepy bug-sized form and string them up on a delicate silver chain.

It would make a lovely necklace.

A high-pitched battle cry pierced the air, like an angry hummingbird on the warpath, and she barreled at me. Her charge through the trees was jagged, but I squared up and swung that gnarled chunk of wood like I was Babe Ruth aiming for a home run.

The crack when it connected reverberated up my arm and into my shoulder, and it sent her screeching ass tumbling into the shadows in a giant puff of turquoise glitter.

I waited for a breath. Then another. "Want to try again?" I yelled. I scanned the darkness as my chest rose and fell with quick, shallow breaths.

Part of me wanted to pull the pendant from my pocket and examine it, but I knew better. She was probably out there waiting for another shot at me.

Anya appeared out of nowhere, hovering just inside the tree line. "That was a mistake, girl." Her lips twisted. "You'll never find him in time." A blinding flash of turquoise light illuminated the darkness beyond the trees and in a blink, she was gone.

"Wait!" I lunged forward then spun in a circle, making sure the glitter bitch hadn't rematerialized somewhere nearby. A quick scan of the beach told me what I already knew; I was alone.

The skiff was gone too, and the pirate ship that had been anchored offshore was nowhere to be seen.

A rollercoaster of emotions twisted inside me, all battling for dominance as an invisible vice slowly clamped around my heart again. I'd expected that wretched little bug to pull something, but to have Hook ditch me like that, to see the evidence that he'd bailed. Ouch.

"Classic Never," I grumped at myself, bending down to pick up my knife. I stared out across the open water, frustration bubbling in my chest. "And to hell with you too!"

The gently rolling waves gave me nothing in return, no hint that I might have been wrong about him. Why did any part of me *want* to be wrong about him anyway? Even if the man wasn't a pirate, which he most definitely was, he was also snarky and cocky and a giant pain in my ass. I drew in a deep breath and held it for a count of four.

When I let it out, I didn't feel any better.

"Fuck it." I slid my knife between my belt and my jeans, wedging it in place at my hip, and marched back toward the tree line. "Fuck it all."

The rest of the day crawled by. Even the sun barely inched across the afternoon sky. And it felt like I was making stunningly slow progress finding my way through the woods. I was on the same trail Hook and I had followed earlier, I was sure of that much, but the vines and palms were already creeping back into the path, reaching ever closer as the minutes ticked by and the shadows slowly stretched longer across the ground.

Eventually, I reached the spot where we'd gone our separate ways. At least, I thought that was it. The fruit rinds were gone, and everything looked just different enough in the waning daylight to make me question myself. Being on the right trail meant nothing if I didn't know where I needed to go.

I took a minute to rest, sitting on a boulder and closing my eyes, trying to conjure the sounds that had surrounded me when I'd had my run in with the glitter bitch.

How close had Hook and I been to Pan's lair when she'd intervened?

Close enough to get her attention.

The sandstone walls of the cave had buffered the outside world, absorbing most of the sounds that dared intrude from the dim openings. I squeezed my eyes shut and focused on the memory. Water.

I remembered the dull roar of running water, but none of that babbling brook nonsense. No, this water was headed somewhere, fast.

The cave had been cool, uncomfortably so in comparison to the heat outside. The chill was even worse standing on the outcropping in the cavern. My mind flashed back to the boys trapped there, caught in some eternal hell all because they'd refused to play some twisted demon's soul-sucking game.

A shiver wracked me, and I rubbed my arms despite the sweltering afternoon heat. I was not a sissy, not about a lot of things, but I truly hated being cold. Give me sunshine and sweat over shivers and snow any day of the week.

Then my woefully urban-bound brain struck gold, and I nearly slapped my own forehead for my stupidity. It was just like my first day in that goddess-forsaken place.

"I need higher ground." A quick glance around me made it clear the place I was sitting wasn't the place to search.

I scanned the woods as I walked, finally landing on a palm tree with ringed bark that looked like it wouldn't be too difficult to scale. Assuming it wasn't crawling with biting bugs like the last one. I was a kid the last time I'd successfully climbed a tree, but I still remembered how, especially with a mature palm. I walked over to the base of it and sat down to unlace my boots. I peeled out of my sweaty socks and laid them over the top, careful to keep the balls of my feet balanced on the toes of my boots so they didn't pick up a bunch of dirt and crud.

I didn't mind getting dirty, but when a girl needed to climb a palm tree barefoot, dirt was the enemy. Craning my neck back to look up, the tree seemed to double in height. My stomach sank. What was I thinking?

"Maybe it's like riding a bike," I said to myself, without nearly enough confidence. I stood on the base of the tree, wrapped my arms tight around it, and planted the soles of my feet against the bark, just like I remembered doing as a younger, much lighter, and much more agile child. Then I squinched upward little by little, pushing with my feet and holding myself steady with my arms as I lifted my legs and repositioned for the next push.

The whole process got both easier and harder as I went. I found a rhythm, but it wasn't long before my muscles were shaking from the exertion.

Slow and steady.

I inched up the tree until I was finally, blessedly, high enough to see above most of the canopy. "What does a girl need to do to find some cursed caves in a magical realm?" I grinned victoriously, despite the rapidly waning daylight. "Find a mountain."

I studied the rise of the peak against the darkening sky and spotted a jumble of amber lights flickering toward the base, winding their way lazily up the mountainside until they coalesced into one large, pulsing ball of light.

"A bonfire," I whispered to myself, though I had no idea why I was whispering.

Excitement rippled through me and a new sense of urgency pulsed in my veins. All I'd needed was a target and now I had it. Now, I could find Matty.

I glanced down to plan my descent and sucked in a pinched breath as the ground, which logically shouldn't have been more than fifty or sixty feet below, seemed to pull further and further away the longer I looked. Thanks to that momentary jolt of panic, my feet slipped, and I slid down the tree, scrambling with my bare feet as I fought for any kind of hold.

The sound my clothes made scraping down the smooth, ringed bark only ratcheted up my panic and I gave up trying to get my now scraped and battered feet to hold me up. I wrapped my legs around the trunk like a drunk stripper on a very large pole and squeezed as tight as I could.

I slid another foot or so, but much slower, until I came to a complete stop. When I sucked in a ragged breath, my throat was so raw I had to squeeze my eyes shut against the burn.

Did I scream?

The bark was cool against my cheek when I pressed it to the rippled surface. I drew in another shaky breath, forcing myself to inhale slowly rather than sucking the great lungfuls of air my body demanded.

"Panic is the enemy," I whispered in a raspy voice. "Panic gets people killed."

When I finally worked up the nerve to crack one eye open, the sun was disappearing behind the horizon and the ground was still entirely too far away. The soles of my feet throbbed painfully, and I was pretty sure I had about a thousand tiny scratches and scrapes bloodying them up.

Stupid, stupid girl. Why did I think I could do this?

"Fuckity fuck," I hissed. It wasn't like I could hold myself up there all night. And even if I could have, I would still have to find a way to the ground in the morning.

I tightened my grip on the tree and ventured another glance down. The trunk of the palm was slightly curved, which meant I wasn't looking at a straight down descent. "Thank the goddess for small miracles."

I wiggled my butt a little, loosening my thighs just enough for my body to slip a few inches, then I clamped down tight again.

"Okay," I let out in a little huff. "I can do this."

I closed my eyes and repeated the process, sliding in short, jerky bouts, until the trunk of the palm was too large for my quaking legs. My muscles vibrated with effort and fatigue, and I knew it was coming before it happened.

"No! No, no, no," I pleaded with any power that would listen. "Pleas—"

My battered muscles gave up the fight, top and bottom, legs and arms, and I slid way too fast for comfort. The ridges of the bark scraped against my chest, thighs, and arms. Even my cheeks caught some of the friction because I was still leaning in, trying desperately to slow myself down. Then I hit a large hump in the trunk and lost my grip entirely, tumbling the rest of the way down like a discarded ragdoll.

HOOK

CHAPTER 22

"Have you seen the girl?" I barked the question at the two men working to maneuver the skiff closer to where I was standing on an outcropping of weathered boulders.

"No sign of her yet, Captain," Linus said, his normally confident voice more brittle than usual. He worked the oars cautiously, clearly attempting to keep from damaging the small craft on the rocks.

"Oh, for crying out loud." I stepped down into the water and yanked the skiff toward me, then hopped over the edge. "We need to get back to the ship as quickly as possible." I held out my hands for the oars, but Linus only stared at me like I'd grown a second head.

"Sir?" he asked. I had to forgive him for questioning me because even I knew it was an unusual request. My men handled the rowing, just like I handled the sirens during a storm. We each had our duties, but I didn't have the patience for their caution.

"Hand me the oars and move aside."

He did as he was told, and I was fairly certain he was trying to be quick about it, but I still found myself grinding my teeth impatiently.

Anya was up to her old games, and the last thing I wanted was for Never to pay the price for my mistakes. I had my suspicions with the wicked pixie's none-too-subtle barter for a kiss, but I hadn't expected her to use her magic to hurl me into the sea.

I paused rowing long enough to wipe my sleeve across my lips for probably the thousandth time since I'd made the swim to the rocks. Kissing Anya had always felt a little off, even when we were in the throes of our forever-ago fling, but kissing her in front of Never had felt unequivocally wrong.

The look in her eyes, that scorching flash of betrayal I'd seen just before the sea had swallowed me out of thin air, clawed at my conscience.

Why? It was one of a thousand questions I had been asking myself since I'd laid eyes on her. Why did her feelings matter to me in the slightest?

But that look... it wasn't betrayal, not exactly. I replayed the moment in my head again, as if it hadn't been on a constant, torturous loop in my mind since it had happened. The look on her alluring face was a mix of disappointment and resignation, like she'd been waiting for me to hurt her, and I'd just met her expectations to a T.

Except it wasn't a betrayal. For starters, I didn't owe the girl anything. I might not have had complete control over my cock when she was around, but it wasn't like we meant anything to each other. We were essentially strangers.

Secondly, there wasn't a sliver of my being that had actually wanted to kiss Anya. I would have been perfectly content to never set eyes on the monstrous pixie again. The kiss was the price she'd demanded for the information Never needed to find her brother and I'd paid it, simple as that.

I looked over at the island as I rowed, checking for anything out of place. When I turned back around, both of my men were watching me.

"What is it?" My mind was already jumping ahead, imagining the worst things they could tell me.

They shared a look, then Linus gave me a resolute nod. "We'll find her, sir."

The scar on my chest tingled, reminding me again of just how heartless Anya was and how creative she could be when she didn't get her way. If my men could see through me so easily, maybe she could too.

Was that why she'd bartered for a kiss, to see how I would react? Or was she testing Never?

The haunted look on Never's face filled my mind again, and I rowed harder.

CHAPTER 23

I had officially lost track of how long I'd been laying there. My plan had been to rest for a minute or two, to just take a moment to bask in the fact that I'd survived my harrowing trip down the palm tree. At least, I was pretty sure I'd survived, except for the tiny fact that it was pitch black and dead quiet. A thread of unease wound an icy trail up my spine.

What if I was dead? Was that what it was like to die in Neverland? What if I was alive but I hit my head so hard I went blind?

That could happen. I knew it could. Well, I thought it could. I was pretty sure I'd read it somewhere.

I rolled my neck gently and winced, then my other injuries overrode my fear and adrenaline. When it finally dawned on me to open my eyes, I realized my throbbing head was resting on my boots and the rest of my body was splayed awkwardly on the ground.

So, I was actually alive. One point for me.

I tried to move each of my limbs, cataloging potential injuries as I went. My feet were a little worse for wear, along with my ribs, but nothing felt broken. I sat up cautiously but still moaned out a self-serving "ow" as I examined the damage. There wasn't much to see, what with the sun little more than a memory and the remnants of light fading from the shielded sky. I wasn't sure if that was a blessing or a curse.

Using my raw fingertips, I prodded gently along the soles of my feet, finding a series of fine cuts and scrapes. My arches were covered in a thin sheen of blood, but it wasn't anything serious. Nothing a few days of rest and watching movies curled up on the couch couldn't fix.

"I just have to find Matty," I said into the inky woods.

When I did find him, and I would, his obnoxious teenage ass would be the one bringing me popcorn and iced tea while I was laid up. And veggie stir fry from the Thai restaurant down the street from our apartment.

My stomach grumbled at the thought. For one fleeting second, I could almost smell the savory mix of hot, crisp vegetables and steaming jasmine rice.

And now I'm hallucinating. Excellent.

I pressed my hand gently to the knot forming on my head. It was a small thing, certainly not concussion/hallucination worthy by any measure. The mouthwatering scent faded, but my stomach continued making its displeasure about being empty known, audibly.

Nothing I could do about that in the short-term.

I felt around for my boots and found them within arm's reach, but my socks were another issue. In a place with magical beings who could zap people from place to place, you would think I could figure out how to conjure a firebug or something to lend a hand.

Out of nowhere, a soothing warmth spread through my hips and a dull yellow glow pulsed from my pocket. I blinked down at it a few times, then pulled it free. The light wrapped around me, beating back the darkness.

Holy shit. Had I made that happen?

I glanced over my shoulder but only shadows stretched out behind me until they melded with the darkness.

Turning my attention back to the pendant, I reached up to touch the glowing stone but pulled my fingers away at the last second.

"First things first." I needed to take advantage of the light while I could. There was no telling how long the magical batteries in that little rock would hold out.

I spotted my socks and snagged them, keeping an eye on my surroundings just in case something decided I was easy prey. Which I totally was at that moment. Barefoot and sitting on the ground like a preschooler wasn't exactly prime positioning in terms of self-defense.

I fastened the necklace around my neck and did my best to brush the dirt off the soles of my feet before pulling my socks on. When I reached for my first boot, the light flickered weakly.

"Stay with me, little light," I said quietly. Grabbing at my boots like a drowning girl flailing for one of those bright orange floating rings, I yanked them on and laced them as quickly as I could. The light, bless the stars, didn't falter again.

Then I checked for my knife. It was still there, wedged safely between my jeans and my belt. "It's a freaking saturnalia miracle," I muttered, letting a wave of relief wash over me. I could find another weapon if I needed to. Hell, a sharp stick was better than nothing, but I was good with my blade, my Stabina. I knew how to handle it, how to move with it. Knowing I had it with me gave me a sense of control over the carnival ride my life had become in the last forty-eight hours.

It felt like weeks had passed since I'd stumbled upon Clint with the slutty cop riding him like one of those spring-loaded plastic animals toddlers bounced on in the playground, and it occurred to me that it was the first time since all that shit had gone down that I'd thought of him.

To be fair, the last two days had been a fuckstorm of weird, but still. I should've felt something when I thought about him, right? Love, loss, hate. Anything.

But I didn't. I was indifferent.

Two days after my boyfriend of six months cheated on me and I was over it. Just like that.

"Yeah," I muttered, getting to my feet. "I'm definitely broken."

As if my luck for the day weren't already total shit, the light from the pendant snuffed out.

"No. Shit. No, no, no." I tapped the pendant gently. "Come on, magical necklace night light thingy, don't fail me now."

It didn't respond. The thing was now just a cold, dead weight around my neck. I leaned my back against the tree and sank down until I was crouched against it. Then I rested my head in my hands and I wallowed. A full on, pathetic wallow. All the mean, hateful things I had to say about myself? Yeah, I let myself stew in them for a solid sixty seconds.

But that was all I would give myself. I could kick myself and call myself stupid for sixty seconds, but then it was back to business.

After my designated minute of hard-core self-loathing, I drew in a deep breath and let as much of it go on the exhale as I could manage. In my book, it was okay to feel like crap from time to time, but it wasn't okay to carry it around with me. Life was too damned short for that bullshit.

"So, what do I do next?" I asked the darkness. There was no answer, thank the stars. If someone had answered me right then, I might have pissed myself. At least my options were simple: stumble through the darkness and try to find Matty or stumble through the darkness until I could find a safe-ish place to hole up until the sun was up.

"Choices, choices." I slapped my thighs and stood. If I was going to be fumbling around in the dark either way, I might as well use the time to my advantage.

And with that, the pendant started to glow again.

"Seriously, what the hell is up with this thing?" I asked, not bothering to keep my voice low anymore.

That time, when I reached up to touch it, I followed through. Cautiously. It was radiating this incredible, reassuring warmth into my chest, but when I took it in my fingers and rolled it gently, it felt like it was the same temperature as my skin.

I set it carefully back against my chest and waited. When the light didn't flicker or fade, I let out the breath I'd only just realized I'd been holding.

There was a secret to the thing. It was magical, sure, obviously. But it felt like there was more to it than that. Whatever it was, it was enough to make the wicked witch of pixies salivate at the thought of getting her hands on it.

She'd said it was hers. Screeched it at me, actually. Which meant in order for me to find it in my mom's box of junk, someone from my world must have taken it from her.

Wendy.

As far as I knew, she was the only person who'd ever made the adventure to my realm a round trip affair. My mind raced back through memories of the journals and stories, but I didn't remember anything about a pendant. No trinkets. No amulets. Pixie dust was a thing in the storybook version, but the pendant was stone, not dust.

I was missing something. Probably something painfully obvious, but what? I mulled that over as the pendant lit my path while I moved through the trees. It was surprisingly easy to navigate with my eyes finally adjusted to the dim, but it hardly felt like progress.

Time passed the way it always did in the dark, at whatever goddess-forsaken pace it wanted to. Either it went crazy fast when you were sleeping well, or it inched by, one second-hand tick at a time. I couldn't tell which was the case, but it definitely felt like the latter.

After a while, every muscle in my body began to stage a weak revolt. My thighs were bruised, that much was evident from the aching tenderness between them as I walked. Even my back and shoulders jumped into the fray eventually. Full-body fatigue bled through my system like a slow-moving sedative and the familiar cold that inevitably came after every harrowing situation sank in.

The adrenaline had finally burned off and the recovery crash was coming on fast. I gave myself a good, hard slap across the cheek. Sometimes that worked, sometimes it didn't.

Better luck next time, Never.

I wrapped my arms around myself and checked my surroundings, spotting a hollow carved in the base of a tree that looked like it was born from some maniac's twisted nightmare. "Not a chance," I muttered.

Out of the blue, the fine hairs at the back of my neck came alive and I froze.

The forest had gone dead quiet around me.

I slid my hand to the hilt of my blade and waited, watching and listening for whatever threat was scary enough to shut the whole damned forest up.

A hint of laughter floated through the night air. Boyish, playful laughter, but not like elementary-age children tumbling around a jungle gym. It sounded more like a bunch of high school, or maybe young college kids having a tailgate party.

And it was getting closer.

My instincts told me to run or at the very least hide, which was confusing as all get out when the whole reason I was even in that psychotic realm was to find my teenage, junior-in-high-school brother. I glared at my surroundings, knowing full well my best option was the creepy black maw of the nightmare tree.

Nope. Still not happening.

I'd rather face the lost boys en masse than crawl in that hell hole. As if the thought had summoned them, three forms came crashing down the trail like drunk frat boys on their way back to their dorm after a night of heavy drinking.

Except I couldn't tell if they really were boys.

Ducking behind a massive fern like the coward I was, or like a genius, depending on who asked later, I slapped my hand over the pendant and tried to block out the light. For a magical amulet, or whatever it was, it wasn't very intuitive. "Could you please go dark again?" I whispered harshly. The words were barely out of my mouth before it winked out.

I sucked in a relieved breath, quietly, and kept my gaze trained on the path, not that I could see shit now. But wait, what the hell was that coming toward me in the darkness? My hackles hit high alert at the sight of the inhuman greenish-yellow eyes glowing in the black. It was just one set, but they were looking right at me.

CHAPTER 24

Shit, shit. Stay or run?

Every cell in my body voted for running.

I turned and took off through the woods as fast as I could, stumbling over shallow roots and rocks. "Light!" I hissed, without glancing down at the pendant. It bounced darkly against my chest without giving off so much as a spark.

Of course.

Branches slapped at my face and scraped against my skin, and I prayed to any god that would listen not to let whatever razor-sharp thorny shrubs were in my path take out my eyes. I squinted, keeping my hands up protectively and my lids narrowed to slits. I moved through the woods like a blindfolded kid doing a trust walk at camp. Except without the partner for guidance.

The boys' hyena-like laughter faded, at least from what I could hear above my own hammering heartbeat, and I let myself slow for a moment.

Epically, stupid mistake, Never.

"Hello, lady." The voice was male and sounded about as old as I'd figured, college-aged maybe.

When I whirled to face him, I was greeted by a smiling Adonis with predator's eyes. A torch flickered in his right hand, and he had a hungry look that made my stomach do a weird little somersault.

His deeply tanned skin gleamed in the orange fire light, highlighting the thick muscle layering his bare chest. Save for the battered board shorts he was wearing that looked vaguely homemade, he could have stepped right out of a magazine.

Drool-worthy—I think that was the right term—like he'd been plucked from a college swim team and dropped in that magical forest to play out all my darkest sexual fantasies. If not for that gleam in his eyes.

I could get on board with shirtless and shoeless, but I drew the line at soulless.

I squared my shoulders. "Are you one of the lost boys?"

He didn't say anything in response, only stared at me like I was a plate of warm chocolate chip cookies and he'd been neck deep in a keto diet for three months.

Maybe he hadn't heard me?

I kicked my voice up a notch. "Where is my brother?"

His eyes flickered at that. It was a tiny, almost imperceptible twitch of the lids, but I saw it.

My system was in overdrive, caught between running and fighting, while that base, primitive part of my stupid brain seemed perfectly happy focusing on the last of the four F's: fight, flight, freeze, or fuc—

He took a slow, measured step toward me before I could finish the thought. Finally, the part of my brain that wasn't trapped in my panties took over. It was only then that I realized I was clutching the pendant again. I dropped my hand and reached for my blade, but at the sight of the temperamental trinket around my neck, he stilled.

His voice was low and dark, rumbling through the air. "Where did you get that?"

I glanced down at the shiny stone resting against my breastbone. "A friend."

He nodded slowly, shifting his grip on the torch and running his tongue over his bottom lip. "Give it to me and I'll let you go." His voice had a sensual, conspiratorial edge to it, but I knew better.

"Take me to my brother," I demanded, sliding the blade from my belt and bringing it into view.

His gaze flicked to it, his lips curling in a half-smile, half-snarl. "Give it to me now."

I lifted one eyebrow at him. "Have you ever heard of the art of negotiation? I'm thinking not, because you clearly suck at it."

The soulless Adonis tilted his head to one side, then gave it a little shake. "Have it your way." He cupped his free hand and held it beside his mouth. The sound that left those plump lips turned my blood cold. He didn't just look like a predator; he sounded like one too.

Run.

I spun and took off through the trees again, but the light his torch threw from behind me created strange, living shadows in my path, making it harder to navigate than if I were just moving in the dark. There was no noise behind me, no cracking branches or heavy footfalls, and when I glanced over my shoulder to see if I'd lost him, I swear to the gods, he was silently pacing me.

"Boo!" Another boy leapt into my path, and a squeak escaped me as I whipped back around.

A fucking squeak, like I was a mouse and the big bad cat of the house just caught me by the tail. That was about how it felt too. They were playing with me.

The universe apparently took their side, sending all the shitty karma I'd ever put out in the world back to bite me in the ass with a single step. Literally.

The ground fell away beneath me, and my stomach floated up to my throat for a split second before gravity took hold and wrenched me down. I couldn't tell how far I fell, but I sure wasn't ready for the ground when it rushed up to meet me.

The collision was bone-rattling, and my ankle gave out on the uneven ground, sending a jolt of white-hot pain up my leg. I collapsed in a big, pathetic heap and rolled onto my back, slamming my eyes shut and clenching my teeth. My upper lip curled involuntarily as I let out a silent snarl.

I dug my fingers into the ground, anchoring myself to the cool, damp earth until the first searing wave of pain passed. Pain like that always passed. The human body was weird like that. It would fire off the message up to the brain, pulsing and relaying the pain and damage, but eventually the brain numbed to the feedback. The damage was still there, but it was like the brain was already over it. It got the message, took the notes, and now it had other shit to do.

Yeah, I was an old pro at twisting my ankle. It was one of the benefits of earning a severe sprain as a teenager, and then not actually doing the exercises my doctor gave me to strengthen the joint. Why? Because I was a stupid kid, and the doctor seemed a little too nice to be trusted.

For a fleeting moment, I wondered if I would have followed through with the exercises if I'd had some drill sergeant hard ass giving me the instructions. Probably. Even back then, naïve as I was, I'd learned the hard way that kindness was a currency, and the cost wasn't always worth the benefit.

Vicious laughter filled the air above me, pulling me out of my thoughts. My breath was coming in shallow pants as I worked through the pain, but it caught in my chest at the sound. I opened my eyes and gripped the ground beneath me harder, digging my nails in until I could feel the soil packing in beneath them. Three sets of inhuman eyes peered down at me from the mouth of the hole. The very unnatural, obviously planned, hole.

Awesome. Those assholes had driven me right into a trap.

I didn't give a fuck what Adonis's real name was at that point, because whoever he was, he was officially on my shit list and quickly rising to the top.

Not that it mattered. I was stuck where I was, at least for the moment. The sharp pain in my ankle started to fade into more of a throb, but there was no way I was climbing out of that hole without getting mauled by the feral frat boys leering at me. So, I sat up and examined the primitive trap. It was probably seven feet deep, but the sides were just dirt and rock. It might take a few tries, but I could pull myself out if they decided to leave me there to die.

Except, I was ninety-seven-percent sure that wasn't happening. The other two frat boys argued over something, but I wasn't tracking the details of their bickering because all my senses were hyper-focused on Adonis. He was taller than the other two by nearly a foot, and broader across the shoulders. If I'd seen either of the others first, I might have thought they were attractive too, but next to him, they were downright homely.

And his eyes were different. Still not human, but maybe not soulless, exactly.

Even without looking directly at him, I knew he was watching me, cataloging my every move as his hot gaze slid over my skin. Rather than let that feeling eat away at my nerves, I turned my attention to dealing with my ankle. If I was going to stand any chance of getting to my feet, it would need support and stability around the joint.

I untied my boot and pulled the lace as tight as the battered leather, and the already impressive swelling, would allow. That was phase one.

Phase two involved scooting to the nearest wall and rolling to my knees, which went smoothly enough. I pulled in a deep breath and held it as I rolled back onto my feet, doing my best to keep most of my weight off the injured side. I had to brace my hand against the crumbling dirt wall to keep from wobbling as I pulled myself upright, but after a few shaky seconds I was standing, albeit on one leg.

I let out a slow breath, counting to four on the exhale while I let myself do a little victory dance in my head. If a person couldn't learn to celebrate the little things in life, what was the point of it all?

My moment of triumph faded quickly though, because phase three was next and I so wasn't looking forward to it. Taking that first step after twisting my ankle was always a bitch and I hesitated for a second, holding my foot up off the ground, letting it hover there while I sucked in a breath and held it firmly in place.

No time like the fucking present, Nev. The thought came through in my snarkiest inner bitch voice.

"I should be an inspirational speaker when I grow up." I almost snorted a laugh at my own stupid joke, but the notion made me smile and gave me a much-needed boost of confidence. I would be fine. I stepped gingerly, testing how much weight my ankle could actually support.

Survey says: Not much.

Pain lanced down my foot and up my calf, turning my normally reliable knee to jelly. I lost my grip on the dirt wall beside me and spun awkwardly, trying desperately to regain my balance.

Total failure. My ass collided with the ground so hard the air whooshed out of me.

"For fuck's sake," I gasped, looking down at the useless pendant/amulet thing. "Would it kill you to lend a girl a hand? A little pick-me-up would go a long way toward making me like you more." To my surprise, the damned thing flickered. But that was it.

"Stop talking." Adonis's voice sent an icy shiver through me.

Did that stop me from glaring up at him? Nope.

"Make me." The challenge was out of my mouth before my common sense had time to catch up.

The pendant flickered again, and a muscle in his beautifully sculpted jaw slid. The other two boys fell silent beside him. My stomach sank a little lower in my abdomen, like it was trying to hide from the shit storm my mouth was stirring up. Of all the things Adonis could have done, dropping quietly into the hole beside me hadn't been especially high on my list of possibilities.

I scrambled back to put some distance between us, freezing when my back hit the dirt barrier behind me. Not far enough, but it'd have to do. I threw him my best *fuck off* look, complete with the obligatory chin jut, while I oh-so-discreetly reached for my knife.

"Stop." The single word warning stopped me dead. He crouched beside me, dwarfing my five-foot-six-inch frame. His shoulders and chest were a wall of solid muscle, and the way he positioned himself, that wall blocked my view of the other boys entirely.

My anxiety ratcheted up a few hundred notches, sending a fresh surge of adrenaline coursing through me. He leaned in and I flinched back, but instead of grabbing or hitting me, he inhaled deeply. His eyelids fluttered closed and when he opened them, the yellow-green shimmer was gone, replaced by breathtakingly haunted, hazel eyes. It wasn't the color so much as the longing that called to me, so raw it made my chest tighten painfully. With the next blink, the shimmer was back.

Was I losing my mind? Because it sure as hell felt like it.

He leaned in close enough that I could feel the heat radiating from his body. Keeping his voice so low I could barely make out the words, he said, "If you value your life, hide that necklace. Let no one else on this island or in this realm lay eyes on it. And keep your dagger hidden. If the others see it, they will take it."

Wait. What?

CHAPTER 25

Adonis's moment of kindness—or was it comradery? I didn't know. Whatever it was, it was short-lived. He gave me just enough time to hide my necklace and blade before pulling me to my feet. He spun me around and hoisted me up to the ledge of the hole so quickly I felt like he might launch me into space. He didn't, obviously, but the boost left me sprawled half in and half out of the hole, with my ribs screaming and my legs and feet dangling over the edge. I had to claw at the soft ground to pull myself the rest of the way up.

The other two, true to their asshole frat boy forms, just stood back and laughed while they watched my struggle. When I finally got to my feet, holding most of my weight on my uninjured side, I flipped them both the bird.

It was downhill from there.

The laughing stopped abruptly, and they both came at me at once. I probably should have gone along quietly, since Adonis had gone to the trouble of helping me, but that wasn't my style. I caught one on the side of the head with a rock I'd managed to pick up on my way to standing and shoved the other prick into the hole with Adonis.

I took off running. Well, more like hobbling, and I made it all of ten steps before the kid I'd hit with the rock caught me by my jacket and yanked me back, tossing me to the ground. He was just cranking his leg back to kick me in the ribs when Adonis stepped in.

Which was how I ended up slung over the shoulder of a shirtless, confusingly helpful frat boy, being carried goddess only knew where. It would have been great if any one of them would have bothered to clue me in as to our destination, but they refused to even acknowledge my questions, let alone answer them.

"Are you three lost boys?" I asked, trying to keep my voice sweet and curious rather than bitchy and demanding. It was a challenge.

And what did I get for my efforts? Jack all.

"Okay, let's try something else. Are you taking me to meet the great and powerful Pan?"

That at least got a reaction, even if it was only a warning growl from Adonis and a tightening of his grip on my thighs.

"Look, cocksuckers, I can't see where you're taking me, so maybe you can talk me through it?"

"Does she ever shut up?" one of the boys asked.

"Like you have room to complain," the other one snapped back. I was pretty sure he was the one I hit with the rock, but since I couldn't see them, it was hard to say.

I tried to crane around to look, but my ribs were still a little tender from my tumble down the palm tree. I straightened back out, bracing my hands against Adonis's lower back so my head didn't bounce off his fine round ass with every step.

The man really did look like a Greek god, the kind of gorgeous that would make most women swoon, regardless of their age.

That, at least, explained my reaction to him.

Yeah, he'd chased me through the woods, lured me into a trap, and now was carrying me like a neanderthal against my will, but how was that any different from how Hook had treated me?

The thought of the feisty pirate tossing me over his shoulder and carrying me to his bed like that sent a hot little thrill through me, and for once, I rolled with it. It was better than focusing on the pain radiating from my ankle, not to mention the throbbing headache that only seemed to be getting worse.

It didn't take much to imagine it was Hook's arm wrapped around my thighs. And it certainly didn't hurt that I already knew he was the kind of guy who wouldn't hesitate to smack my ass to make his point.

Delicious heat coiled inside me, and I dug my fingers a little harder into Adonis's back, letting myself sink into the feeling.

"Whatever you're thinking about, stop," he said in a harsh whisper. "Now."

My whole body went rigid for a beat, but I recovered quickly. "If I want to spend my time plotting your demise, I don't see how it's any of your business."

"Does envisioning death and destruction always arouse you so much?" His voice carried a dark warning.

"What?" I sputtered. "You can't—"

His hand squeezed the back of my thigh and he nearly growled, "I can smell it."

He could what?

"Ew." I shoved at his back and wiggled my hips, trying to move them as far away from his face as humanly possible. "Are you some hot fucking pervert?"

I was expecting laughter or some snide comment, but he just shook his head. "If I can scent your arousal, others will be able to pick up on it too. That won't go well for you when we get where we're going."

A series of snarky comments flicked through my mind, but I kept them to myself. He was still trying to help me, or at least it seemed like he was, even if I couldn't work out his motive.

"Where are you taking me?" I asked.

He said nothing.

"Back to the silent treatment, huh? I guess you won't mind if I start singing then, right?" I tried to think of the most annoying song I'd ever heard, but the only thing I could think of was that eighties song by Starship, "We Built This City". The thought of it dredged up long forgotten memories of riding in my mom's shitty old Chrysler LeBaron convertible, listening to that song on repeat and belting it out at the top of our lungs.

Ah, the good old days, back before she bailed on life. And me.

Deep, rumbling drumming filled the woods around us, and Adonis stiffened beneath me, as if I wasn't already riding on a shoulder carved from marble. His fingers dug into my thigh in warning. "Sorry about this," he whispered.

The next thing I knew, he grabbed me by the waist and basically tossed me to the ground. Part of me was fully enraged at the treatment, but the fact that he managed to unload me without hurting my ankle didn't escape my notice. Again with the weird kindness.

I still glowered up at him though, partly because I was a little miffed at being dropped on my ass and partly because he clearly didn't want anyone to know he had a soft spot for me.

"What do we have here?"

A trickle of dread worked its way through me at the sultry sound, and Adonis's gaze flicked to mine for a nanosecond before it snapped back to the owner of that voice. I clambered to my feet as best I could and turned to see something so wholly unexpected my brain refused to process it for a solid three seconds. My mouth worked like a fish out of water before I regained enough sense to slam it shut.

How had I managed to miss so much of my surroundings on the trip up there?

Oh right, my view was limited to the ground or a Greek god's ass.

An intricate network of bridges spanned overhead, creating a web of rope and board walkways. Each suspended path was lit end to end with glowing turquoise orbs that bobbed and swayed in the gentle breeze. I craned my head back and followed the interconnected paths to at least two dozen shed-sized structures built right there into the trees.

Three main highwire paths stretched out from the courtyard my new buddy had dropped me in. Perched in the center, sprawled lazily across a throne made entirely of interwoven vines, was a woman. A drop-dead gorgeous woman, whose only visible flaw from where I was standing was the pure fucking evil glistening in her black eyes.

"We found her wandering out by the boar pit," Adonis said stiffly.

"Is that why she's lame on the one side?" the woman asked. "Or did you forget my orders?" The question came out dangerously polite, and the look she gave the kid I'd cracked over the head with the rock almost made me feel sorry for him. He stumbled over his words, yipping like a panicked puppy when one of her perfect eyebrows winged up impatiently.

As much as I wanted to kick that particular frat boy in the nuts for being an insufferable dick, his reaction to the woman triggered something protective in me.

I hobbled forward a step and held up my hands. "They didn't hurt me. They just caught me off guard and I fell in a big ass hole trying to get away." I motioned to my right foot. "Twisted my ankle a little, but it's nothing serious."

That perfectly manicured brow ticked up a little higher, and her plump pink lips quirked up on one side. "Is that so?"

The two dickhead frat boys were quick to agree, but Adonis didn't move a muscle.

"Leo." She said his name on a soft sigh, then swung her long legs off the throne and stood in one fluid movement. Her hips swayed gently as she prowled toward him. "My sweet Leo. I can always trust you to tell me the truth." When she reached him, she ran a finger down the side of his face. "Is that what happened?"

So, Leo was Adonis's real name? I studied his features as he stared back at the woman, his expression blank. He didn't look like a Leo.

He nodded once.

She turned her attention to the bleeding boy. "And what happened to you?" She tipped her chin down and watched him like a wolf stalking its prey.

The boy pressed a hand to his head.

"I hit him with a rock," I offered.

Her head swiveled slowly toward me. It was a weird, creepy

movement, like the way a possessed doll's head spins in exaggerated slow motion in a horror movie. "Why would you do that?"

"I'm kind of a bitch that way." I gave her a half-shrug. "I mean, these three did sneak up on me in the woods, in the dark. So, it's kind of on them if they got hurt in the process of taking me hostage. Don't you think?"

The woman bit her bottom lip and tipped her head with a smile. "Feisty. I can see why he's so taken with you."

My stomach churned uneasily, and it was all I could do not to look at Adonis-Leo. There was no way she could possibly know he'd helped me. The other boys were oblivious to it. At least, I thought they were. Shit.

Maybe it was a test. Maybe she was fishing for information.

She shook her head and turned, tossing one hand in the air dismissively. "He always was a foolish creature, even before he started playing the role of surly pirate captain," she said coolly, sashaying back to her throne and summoning two more frat boys with the snap of her fingers.

Surly pirate captain. She was talking about Hook, not Leo.

I let out the breath I hadn't realized I was holding on a silent huff, refusing to let any of them see my relief. That brought me back to Earth, so to speak, and a fresh wave of anger tingled across my scalp.

"Why did you have your goons bring me here?"

She draped her long, shapely body back over the throne and motioned for one of the new frat boys. He hustled to her side with a large bowl of fresh fruit, and she picked through it as she answered.

"I wanted to get a look at you. When the offspring of your enemy lands on your doorstep, it's only natural to be curious. Don't you agree, Moira?"

CHAPTER 26

I stiffened at the sound of my real name coming from her lips, and only barely managed to keep my tongue in check by balling my hands into fists and digging my fingernails into my palms.

"Oh, wait." She glanced up at me through impossibly long lashes. "You don't like that name, do you? Shoot. What is it you call yourself again?" She tilted her head to the sky and tapped a finger against her lips like she was thinking.

It was a show, of course. She was stalling for effect, which only pissed me off more.

"Never," I snapped.

A knowing smile spread across her face. I wanted to slap it off.

"Yes." She drew the word out like a hiss. Her tongue flicked out and ran along the edges of her teeth, which were straight, white, and vaguely threatening.

The only person, reasonably, who could have told her my real name was Matty.

"Where is he? Where is my brother?"

The sultry brunette with skin the color of warm bronze flashed a wicked grin and plucked a piece of fruit from the bowl. It was similar to a peach in size and shape, but the coloring was off, so pale it was almost ivory.

"Not entirely unintelligent, I see," she said, adding insult to injury by sounding genuinely impressed.

"I'm so glad you approve."

She ignored the sarcasm layering my words and looked at the college-aged kid kneeling beside her with the bowl, motioning for him to set it down. When he did, looking up at her like a puppy desperate for praise, she leaned in and kissed him deeply, passionately. After a moment, she pushed him away just enough to whisper in his ear, and he began kissing his way down her chin and her neck.

I felt like a pervert for watching, but a quick glance at the others told me I wasn't the only one caught in the trance. Was that good or bad?

The frat boy's tongue traced a line over her collar bone, and I shivered imagining the sensation. He kept going, dipping his tongue into the hollow of her throat before licking and sucking his way gently down one breast and circling her tight nipple.

It was unlike anything I'd ever seen before, at least in person. I wasn't a prude, I'd seen a little porn and worn out more than my fair share of battery-powered toys, but this was different. Wickedly erotic in a way that had my body coiling with liquid desire.

Oh shit. Was I a closet voyeur?

It was then that I realized she was watching me. Intently. My cheeks flared with heat, and I tried to turn away, but Adonis—Leo—grabbed me by the arm and forced me to stay put.

It was another show and she wanted me to watch.

So many thoughts tried to rush forward at once that my brain felt like there was a pile up inside, jamming up the flow of traffic and bringing everything to a slow, brutal crawl. Dots were connecting and puzzle pieces were coming together, but it was all happening too slow. It didn't help my focus in the slightest when she brought the fleshy fruit to her lips and bit down, closing her eyes and moaning at the taste.

The juice dribbled down her chin, thick and red, like blood.

She opened her eyes and smiled suggestively at me, but her face changed from the kind of beauty that would make a straight woman question her sexuality to something else entirely. Her eyes took on a deep, green glow, and her movie star teeth sharpened to small, tightly packed points. Recognition hit me like a bus.

The demon that had attacked me in the park, the one that left its thick, black, stinking blood smeared on my windowsill; it was her.

I replayed my interaction with Anya, remembering that one word that tripped me up before she transported us from the cave. Those three, crucial little letters. She.

"Pan."

"In the flesh." The demon's grotesque face shimmered, replaced again by the breathtaking beauty, except she wasn't so breathtaking anymore. "Though people here call me Petra."

My mind couldn't unsee the truth beneath the glamour. The frat boy laving at her demon flesh, though, he hadn't missed a beat. He was too busy kissing down her stomach that he didn't even seem to notice the change.

My stomach rolled dangerously, and I swallowed hard, fighting back the bile rising in the back of my throat. Leo's strong fingers squeezed my arm tighter, hard enough to hurt. I'd definitely have bruises after that, but at least they'd blend nicely with the others I'd acquired over the last few days.

I yanked my arm, breaking free of his grip. I had no doubt that was only because he let me go, but that wasn't my main concern at that moment.

"Give me my brother," I demanded, keeping my voice surprisingly even.

Before she could respond, a familiar chime filled the air and the devil pixie appeared at her side.

"Anya, so nice of you to join us," Petra said, not bothering with so much as a glance in her direction. She flicked her fingers toward me. "I thought you took care of this." Her voice had a playful edge to it, but the underlying threat was unmistakable.

The pixie's gaze darted between us. "I did. I sent her back to the beach." Confusion twisted her features and her wings ticked erratically. "How did you get here?" She turned to Petra. "There's no way she made it this far without help."

I cocked an eyebrow at her and tilted my head. "There's no way I survived a little nature walk? Please. I've been to petting zoos that are more dangerous than this place."

Anya whirled on me, snarling like a rabid ferret.

"Come at me, glitter bitch. I've had hours to imagine all the different things I can do to those pretty wings of yours after I rip them off your back."

Was it smart to taunt a vicious pixie who had an immortal demon as a bestie? Probably not, but I couldn't help taking a twisted kind of pleasure in how easy it was to get a rise out of her.

Petra raised a hand, stopping the angry little bug from flying at me. "As much as I would enjoy watching you two battle it out, I'm afraid time is of the essence."

"Give me my brother."

"No." Petra's response was immediate and curt, leaving no room for negotiation.

Luckily, I was prepared for something like that. "Then let him go and take me instead." Leo stiffened beside me, but I ignored him. "If all you need is a soul, you can take mine, but only if you send him home unharmed."

Her black eyes narrowed, and she studied me, like she was measuring me up to see if I would make an acceptable replacement. "That is quite an offer. So selfless."

"Do we have a deal?" I asked firmly. I didn't want to make the deal. Who would? But if it was the price I had to pay to keep Matty safe, I'd pay it.

Her alluring chuckle sent a chill through me. "I'm afraid you're not really my type." She motioned to the frat boy pressing wet kisses down her leg, as if that explained everything.

Which, with a minute to consider the situation, it did. What that meant for my brother though, the implication, set my blood to boiling. "He's just a kid."

Petra smiled knowingly. "Not to worry. It takes time to cultivate the young men who come here into these strapping specimens." She threaded her fingers through the guy's hair and tugged, pulling him up to look in his eyes. "It'll be years before I…" She licked her lips like she wanted to devour the guy whole. "Take him."

Her phrasing made me recoil. Bile threatened again, searing the back of my throat with its bitter fire. The weight of my blade, neatly tucked in my jeans at my hip, grew heavier with each passing second. Maybe if I stabbed her when she was in human form like that it would do some damage. I had managed to hurt her in my world, after all. But then how would I find Matty? I hadn't seen him anywhere, hadn't even heard his voice.

I swallowed hard and recentered my focus. "Can I at least see him?" I held out my hands. "I just want to see that he's okay."

"Of course," she said, catching me off guard with the ease of her acquiescence. She let go of the frat boy's hair and he dipped his head automatically, resuming his oral exploration of the demon in goddess form. She motioned to Leo. "Fetch the boy."

He turned and stalked off without a word. When he was out of sight, Petra flicked her wrist and a great round table appeared, stacked high with more trays of food than I could count, each more fragrant and delectable than the next. I recognized a few of the dishes, sort of: roasted, stuffed bird of some kind, freshly seared fish, a rainbow-colored selection of every fruit and vegetable imaginable, and four trays fully dedicated to sweets that looked like they'd come from the snooty bakery across town.

My stomach grumbled when the mixture of mouthwatering scents hit me, loud enough for Petra to hear, apparently.

"Please, have some." She motioned to the table.

Yes, I was starving, but I wasn't born yesterday. "No thanks. I'm on a pretty strict diet. No sugar, no caffeine, and nothing conjured from thin air by a demon."

She ignored my rebuttal because Leo was coming back through the trees with my brother close on his heels. My heart leapt at the sight of him. He was walking with another boy who looked a few years older, laughing and smiling, until his gaze landed on the food.

He started for the table, then paused and glanced around. His eyes skated right over me like I wasn't even there and settled on Petra. "Can I?" he asked, motioning to the table.

Her eyes had changed at some point, lightening to a stunning shade of teal. "Of course, handsome. That's what it's there for." She waved a hand at the others. "Everyone, dig in."

"Matty, no!" The desperation in my voice startled me, but only because I wasn't used to hearing it. He acted like he hadn't heard me. "Matthew!"

He paused in the middle of grabbing for a tin plate and looked around. Confusion wrinkled his brow for a moment, then a flicker of something else. Maybe sadness?

One of the boys bumped his shoulder. "Come on, new kid. Get your grub. We've got something fun planned for after dinner."

"Matty!" The air around me shook with the force of my scream, but the other boys had all joined in the conversation, talking over each other and growing louder by the second.

Shaking with fury, I wheeled on Petra. "What did you do to him?"

"To him? Nothing." She traced the tips of her fingers down her thigh and smiled salaciously at me. "Yet."

I was so going to cut that psycho bitch, slice her gut open, wrap her toxic intestines around her neck and hang her from a tree until the last little twitches of existence drained from her body. I reached for my blade, but both my arms were wrenched painfully behind my back before I got my fingers around the hilt.

"Do not provoke her." Leo's warning was so low I barely heard it, but the intent was clear.

Her silken voice was eerily polite when she responded. "Thank you, Leo. I'm afraid our delightful new guest has just about worn out her welcome." She leveled me with a condescending scowl that would have made a bitter old nun proud. "You asked to see him and there he is. Happy and healthy."

"Why can't he see or hear me?" I snapped back, pulling against Leo's grip.

"That wasn't part of your request. Though, even if it were, I wouldn't have agreed to it. This is a delicate time in the boy's, hmm, we'll call it a transition. Interference from someone like you, from his old life..." She narrowed her eyes, dropping the charade long enough to let the deadly black shimmer shine through again. "That could be devastating."

The threat came through loud and clear, bringing my blood to a boil in the space of a heartbeat. "Fuck you!"

I wrenched and twisted my upper body, trying to break free, but Leo's hands shifted higher and became hot vices on my upper arms, pinning them in place. I glanced down, saw his bare feet, and acted without an ounce of mercy. Bones broke with a sickening crunch beneath the sole of my boot as I stomped down with all my force.

Leo let out a muffled "humph", but instead of letting me go, he pushed me away from his body, holding me at arms' length. I twisted and kicked and bucked, but after a while it became painfully clear that all my fighting was getting me exactly nowhere.

When I finally stopped, Petra looked less than impressed.

"Well, that was unnecessary." She motioned to Anya and whispered something in her ear.

The wicked pixie sneered gleefully, her wings fluttering with a new, excited energy. The vibration released a fresh puff of turquoise dust that swirled around her. When she straightened and held out a hand, that colorful dust pulled together, creating a concentrated, shimmering mist in her palm.

Petra snapped her fingers once and Leo's grip fell away, then the glitter bitch rushed forward and blew that shimmering cloud right in my face.

    I took a swing at her but hit only air as her body became translucent. Everything around me took on an iridescent hue, and it was only when I looked at my own hand that I realized it wasn't the pixie that was disappearing. It was me.

CHAPTER 27

"Anything yet?" I yelled, tilting my head back to look up at William.

He was leaned far out over the edge of the ship's railing watching the water. Every man still on my ship was on deck, all spread around the rim, with three of them crammed into the little crow's nest atop the main mast. We were all waiting for the same thing.

"Nothing so far, sir," he hollered back.

The oar handles were warm in my hands as I fought for a calm I didn't feel thanks to the heady flow of adrenaline coursing through me.

Please, let me be wrong. That or let me get to her in time.

No matter what else had happened on that island, Never didn't deserve a fate as cruel as the one that awaited her if Anya did what I thought she would. The pixie might have been creative with her punishment back when, but she'd become predictable in so many ways since. Maybe it was because she'd experimented enough. How else could a malicious creature like her discover her favorite methods for torturing those who crossed her.

I'd seen all of them, but this was the cruelest, even by my standards.

Night had fallen over the island well over an hour earlier and with every second that dragged by, the muscles in my back and neck grew tighter. I was wound so tight I might just snap if I couldn't get there in time.

No. There was no might about it. No maybe. I'd go on a rampage, slaughter every living thing on that island, and spend the rest of my endless life pulling the demon apart piece by piece, over and over again.

"We have incoming, sir!" William's voice carried an edge of panic as he leaned out and hollered down to me.

I scanned the choppy water around the skiff but saw nothing. "Location!" I shouted back up.

"Starboard quarter, roughly five hundred yards out!"

I plunged the wooden paddles into the water and heaved backward. As I drew closer to the area where William was pointing, an eerie, ivory glow formed deep beneath the surface.

"Goddammit, Anya," I muttered under my breath, trying to get control of the adrenaline coursing through me. My only saving grace was that I hadn't seen any sign of the nocturnal sirens that usually prowled those waters.

Then, as if I'd conjured them with the thought, a heart-wrenching wail sounded in the not-too-far distance. Then another. And another.

The clock was ticking.

CHAPTER 28

Déjà vu. It was that feeling you got when you were pretty sure you'd seen or done or heard something before and it was happening all over again. Like that movie *Groundhog Day*, with Bill Murray and Andie MacDowell, except what I was experiencing wasn't an endless loop of the same colorful local holiday set to playful music.

Chilly saltwater crushed in around me, filling my ears and nose, threatening to breach the lock I had on my lips if I opened them so much as a crack. The magical glow receded with the current, leaving me swirling in the darkness of the sea, flailing with fatigued arms and legs to find a surface that refused to reveal itself.

My boots were too heavy, dragging me down just like they had when I'd first arrived in this wretched place. I remembered the feeling all too well.

I scissor kicked with as much force as I could manage, trying to propel myself in what I thought was an upward direction as I fought to strip out of the leather death shroud of my jacket.

The sea had other ideas.

It was rougher than before, tossing me about like I weighed nothing, meant nothing, was nothing.

My last breath burned dangerously in my lungs, and I squeezed my eyes shut for just a beat. I absolutely would not panic. Would not. Would not fucking panic.

When I opened them again, a brilliant yellow flicker of movement was streaking through the water, coming straight for me. My oxygen-deprived brain tried to convince myself it was help coming, that the calvary was on the way. I almost believed it too, until I remembered precisely which creatures prowled the waters at night in this stupid realm.

Siren. No, wait… the single yellow streak split into three distinct forms.

Make that sirens, as in plural. Awesome.

That was the moment the panic got the better of me and I did what any sane person would do. I screamed. The tang of liquid salt and seaweed filled my mouth, shoving into me faster than I could scream it out, filling the void left by my moment of weakness. I flailed backward but they were coming too fast.

This is how I die?

I'd really been hoping to at least make it to thirty. I would have owned that shit. And forty, well, that was my stretch goal. Dying in my twenties was such a cliché, the kind reserved for overdosing rock stars and tragically suicidal starlets.

Not me.

The saltwater finally stopped stinging my lungs as it replaced the last of the air, and a weird calm washed over me. If I was lucky, the universe would let me die before I felt the siren's teeth tear into my flesh.

That's it, Never, keep thinking those happy thoughts.

Then everything started the inevitable slow fade to black. The water turned cloudy around me, filling with an inky darkness as a soothing warmth wrapped around my body like a glove. And before I knew it, I was flying.

It wasn't at all what I'd expected my death to feel like.

"Never, can you hear me?" Hook's worried face filled my vision. "Stay with me." His voice was like gravity, pulling me in until the burning orange rings around his blown pupils were all I could see. Until those deep black pools swallowed me whole.

My body shook. He was telling me to look at him, begging me to stay.

Goddess, how I wanted to, but when I tried to speak, pain bloomed in my chest, a searing, crushing torment that dragged me deeper into the darkness.

CHAPTER 29

I shook her limp body again, but there was no response.

"Not like this." I reached inside myself, searching for the reservoir of power I knew was there. All I needed was the tiniest thread to guide me.

What if I really had lost my connection to it entirely?

That wasn't possible, was it? Power like that didn't just evaporate. Yes, it had lain dormant for centuries. At least. But it couldn't just be gone.

Something in my chest twisted painfully and I tried again, digging deeper. I clawed through the endless years I'd spent wandering these waters, finding my way back to the last time I'd used it.

Nothing.

"Come on," I whispered, pulling Never's body closer, holding her head against my chest. "Come back to me."

It was just a twinge, a tiny, fleeting thing, like a word you couldn't remember dancing on the tip of your tongue, but I was sure I felt… something. When her hand twitched at her side, I forgot how to breathe.

Had she felt it too?

Leaning down so my lips barely brushed her ear, I tried again, silently pleading with the universe as I did. "Come back, Never."

I was rewarded with another tiny surge and another barely perceptible twitch.

She *could* hear me, or sense me. I didn't really care which, so long as she kept fighting. I gathered her up in my arms and when her eyelids fluttered weakly, my heart swelled. It was a familiar sensation, like a growing warmth that started deep in my chest and radiated out, seeping into my bones and coursing through my veins until every cell in my body was filled with it.

Her neck was soft against my lips, her skin delicate and sweet even with the sheen of saltwater. I kissed her gently just below her jaw and channeled every ounce of power I could dredge to the surface into the command. "Wake up."

Seconds tick by and nothing happened. No reaction at all. I was nowhere near full power, but no ordinary mortal had ever possessed the will strong enough to disobey that kind of command, even in my diminished state.

But Never was far from ordinary.

She wasn't the kind of woman who responded to orders, even when it was in her best interest. Did that rebelliousness extend even to her unconscious mind? The woman had a will of iron, if that iron had been forged in the fires of hell and quenched in the blood of gods. So yes, it probably did travel with her in every state of her being.

I kissed her neck again and tried to coax her with a whisper, "Please, you frustratingly stubborn woman, please come back to me."

When I pulled back, a soft moan slipped through her lips. Her hand found my arm around her waist and her cold fingers wrapped around my forearm. The contact, her response, only made the warmth in my chest burn hotter. Her sweet lips twisted into a grimace and her whole body vibrated against me.

Heat built on itself, compounding until my skin stretched uncomfortably tight across my muscles and it felt like flames were crackling across the surface. It'd been too long. I counted myself lucky to reconnect with my source power at all, given everything, but I felt another small issue developing.

I wasn't entirely sure I remembered how to control it.

Which meant this could go very badly, very quickly.

I pushed her away, trying to put some distance between us, but it was already too late. A surge of power pulsed from me and slammed into her. Her back arched and her body twisted. It was all I could do not to lose my grip and send her tumbling to the concave floor of the skiff. I had about one second of terror wondering if that blast had succeeded where the wretched pixie had failed before Never's eyes snapped open and locked on mine.

Relief flooded her features, but in a blink, it was replaced by a fury so raw it was devastating.

She shoved at my smoldering chest with such force that I actually did let her go that time. She fell backward, landing on her butt in the bottom of the boat with a defiant little thump, and a sound I'd never heard before rode the night air to me.

"Did you just growl at me?" It was nothing short of adorable, and I clenched my jaw to hide the smile threatening to curl my lips, despite everything.

She opened her mouth, no doubt to fire off some feisty retort, but before she uttered a single syllable, her eyes flew wide. She scrambled sideways, wrenching herself up and leaning out over the edge. Her body heaved and bowed violently as her system purged the seawater she'd inhaled.

Gods, it looked painful. I inched over and reached out to run a reassuring hand down her back, wincing as another silent retch contorted her torso. When it passed, she batted my hand away. It was a weak effort, and I disregarded her protest, pressing my palm between her shoulder blades instead and letting a wisp of my power pulse gently into her.

After a few seconds, the tension drained from her body and she turned, sinking back against the side of the skiff with her eyes closed. She let out a bone-tired sigh and laid her cheek against the sealed wood.

"Better?" I asked, keeping my voice gentle.

Her lips pressed into a thin line that morphed into a grimace when the skiff knocked noisily against the hull of the Jolly Roger. She jerked up, but I held out a hand to still her, not quite touching her when she pulled back.

A glance up showed me William standing at the railing flanked by two more of my crew. With a quick nod, he dropped the rope ladder, letting it unfurl along the curve of the hull until it landed on the bench beside me.

I didn't even want to ask the question, given her state, but I suspected reaching out and touching her right then wouldn't win me any points. "Are you well enough to climb?"

She was leaned back with her eyes closed, the faint rise and fall of her chest offering me the only sign of life. A cold strand of worry wormed through me. "Never?"

Her eyes popped open and, though it was muted by exhaustion, the fury was still there. Whatever I'd done to earn her ire, I didn't care. I was just relieved to see she still had some fight in her, even if it was a shadow of the pluck I knew she possessed.

"If you're not feeling up to it, I can carry you."

She narrowed her eyes to determined slits and pushed away from the edge, lumbering uneasily to her knees as the boat tilted and swayed. "I'm fine." Her voice had a gravelly edge to it that begged to differ.

She grabbed the ladder and gingerly hauled herself up to standing. When the skiff bounced off the ship she stumbled awkwardly, biting back a wince as she steadied herself. The woman was clearly injured, though I couldn't tell exactly where. The second I opened my mouth again she pinned me with another furious glare.

"I said I'm fine."

Stubborn wasn't a strong enough word for her particular level of bullheadedness. She was lying, any fool could see it, but if she insisted on refusing my help, what was the harm in testing just how far she'd push it?

"Very well." I leaned down to tie off the skiff then motioned to the ladder. "It's all yours, miss."

Did she just flinch?

I knew she wasn't fond of the 'miss' moniker, but she didn't seem particularly fond of anything to do with me, so it was anybody's guess.

Her fingers wrapped so tightly around the wooden rung of the ladder her knuckles were nearly white in the moonlight. When she tilted her head back and looked up, her whole body deflated a tiny bit. She clearly didn't want to make the climb, but there was clearly no way in hell she was going to say the words out loud.

Instead of shifting her weight to step up onto the ladder, she reached a little higher with her hands and kind of hopped while pulling herself up, until she found the lowest rung with her left foot. She let out a shaky breath and waited for several beats. When she repeated the process, keeping her weight almost entirely off her right foot, I understood at least part of the problem.

I was tempted to toss her over my shoulder and haul her up the ladder myself. It certainly would have sped things along, but I let the temptation go. The woman seemed entirely too young to already have such an overdeveloped need to do everything on her own.

That kind of rigid independence usually only came with experience, and not just a few instances of being let down by others. That kind of independence took years. And for some infuriating reason, she thought I was one of those people.

HOOK

CHAPTER 30

Rather than waiting and letting her continue that torturous climb, I stepped up behind her and took hold of the ladder. Her body stiffened against mine, but she didn't try to pull away or fight me off. Just more proof that she wasn't feeling tip top.

"Hold on tight," I said quietly.

She clutched the rung in a death grip as I gave William the signal to pull. After a second, the rope ladder began a slow, steady slide up the side of the ship.

"I could have made it." She somehow managed to sound both irritated and relieved at the same time.

"I have no doubt, but it's only a matter of time before more sirens catch your scent in the water. So, it was this or me throwing you over my shoulder and carrying you up."

She barked out a jagged laugh, then coughed painfully into her arm. Her whole body shuddered with the force of it, and I wanted nothing more than to wrap my arm around her waist and tuck her safely into me, letting my heat and my power heal what injuries it could.

When she found her breath, there was no shortage of snark in her response. "I've had enough of being lugged around like a sack of flour for one day, thank you very much."

My mood shifted swiftly, starting with a shock of anger so damning I had to consciously lock every joint in place just so I didn't jostle her. The thought of another man touching her in such a way set something dangerous alight in me. When the urge to put words to those thoughts hit, all I could do was clench my jaw and will myself to keep my reckless mouth shut.

The anger, however, was quickly replaced by pure, unadulterated lust when my mind finally processed the hint of longing in her statement. Breathtaking images seared my mind like an unstoppable flow of lava down the side of a sputtering volcano; her taut body draped over my shoulder as I carried her to my bed, my hand gripping her bottom and giving it a firm smack, her little cry of pleasure and all the things that would follow.

My brain had truly horrible timing.

My cock grew hard, pressing against the seam of my pants in a matter of seconds. The feel of her body against mine only drove my desire higher and I gripped the wooden rung so tightly it cracked under the strain.

Distance. I desperately needed to put some space between our bodies so she couldn't feel the effect she was having on me.

I leaned back, still close enough to keep her from falling if she lost her grip, but at least the evidence of my arousal wasn't throbbing against her backside the rest of the way up. At the top, William was there waiting, quick to help Never as I steadied her from the back. When I wrapped my hands around her waist to help hoist her up, she sucked in a sharp breath, and I loosened my grip, sliding my hands down to her hips and lifting from there. Her lack of protest at the hip contact told me that sharp inhale had nothing to do with my touch being suggestive and everything to do with pain.

"Tell me what happened." I'd intended to make it a gentle request as I hoisted myself over the railing, but it came out as a gruff command. It was the wrong tactic.

She said nothing, offering me a little shake of her head instead, which did precisely nothing to help my impatience.

"Would it help if I said please?"

Her huff was nearly silent. "As if you care."

"I wouldn't have asked if I didn't care. If someone touched you…" I reached for her instinctively, acting on the need to keep her close and keep her safe, without taking the time to think it through. The way she pulled back was like a slap across the face, leaving my outstretched hand hovering uneasily in the space between us. After a second, I brought it slowly down to my side, fighting the urge to ball the offending appendage into a fist.

I closed my eyes and drew a breath. Why couldn't I seem to do anything right with her?

"I saw my brother," she finally said in a small and unsteady voice.

When I opened my eyes, she was staring out toward the island. There was no way to tell from the declaration whether seeing him had been good or bad.

"How was he?"

She hesitated, and her body lost some of its rigidness. "Happy, I guess." Her brow furrowed when she looked down at her hands. "He couldn't see me. Or hear me. Petra did something to block me. I don't know. It was strange though. He looked like he was having fun, the time of his life." When her gaze met mine, her blue eyes were filled with doubt.

"That's how it works, love. The demon will try to earn his trust by offering him whatever his heart desires. For many boys his age, that amounts to fun, adventure, and acceptance."

She nodded, then shook her head. "Why didn't you tell me she was, well, a she?"

I lifted an eyebrow. "It didn't seem relevant. Whether it takes a male or female form, a demon is still a demon."

"Yeah? Well, you could have at least warned me she was a total perv. She's going to try to mold Matty into one of her lost boys, right?

I mean, she said as much. But how? And why? He's scrawny compared to Adonis, and he's only seventeen."

"Adonis?" I knew the name of every lost boy who had ever wandered the island and not one possessed the name of that particular god.

Never closed her eyes, pinched the bridge of her nose, and gave me a weak, dismissive wave. "He was one of the guys. I didn't know his name, but he fit the description well enough, so I just named him Adonis in my head."

He fit the description. Why did that rankle? Adonis was an incredibly attractive being, bordering on truly undeniable when he set his sights on someone. Did that mean she was attracted to the man she was referencing?

Petty, jealous thoughts poisoned my train of thought before I pulled myself together and shoved them down deep.

She is not mine.

I had no claim on the woman, and no matter how much some archaic part of me wanted to lay that claim, I had no right to place those shackles on anyone, let alone someone like her.

So, why did I keep throwing myself into the human's orbit? If I had left her on the beach, she would have been dead by now. The same went for leaving her in the water.

Why did I keep gravitating to her?

"You're injured," I said, keeping my tone matter-of-fact.

She didn't bother looking at me. "I'm fine."

"At least let me help you to my quarters so you can rest." That way I could lock her in there, keep her from wandering about the ship, and put some space between us until morning. When my brain brought it to my attention that she would also be safe in my room, I blocked it out. I didn't need to concern myself with her safety right then.

Never pinned me with a glare so fierce I had to fight the urge to take a step back. "Are you deaf or just stupid? I said I'm fine."

Was she *trying* to make me angry? Because it was working. If she wanted to play that fiercely independent card with me, I'd call her bluff.

"Aye?" Before I gave it another thought, I reached out and nudged her shoulder. I didn't push hard, just enough to knock her off balance and force her to put weight on her injured side. Just enough to make my point.

Her jaw clenched and unclenched as she balanced herself, eyes squeezed tightly shut. She managed to hold herself up, barely. The hiss that escaped her lips hit me like a punch to the gut, but it was the fine tremble in her bottom lip that cut to the core of me.

What the devil had gotten into me?

"Never, I—"

Her eyes snapped open with a sheen of furious tears reflecting the yellow glow of the torches behind me. "Fuck you." Her voice was little more than a whisper, but the hate swirling in it could rival a tornado.

She blinked the tears back and stared me down, issuing me an open challenge. The message was clear. If I didn't take a step back, she'd make me, no matter how much she hurt herself in the process.

I let a mask of cold detachment fall over my face, hiding the guilt that was ripping me apart inside. Living in this wretched realm truly had turned me into a monster. "William, please escort Never to my quarters. Get her a change of clothes." I couldn't meet her fiery gaze when I finished. "She is not to have access to the rest of the ship tonight."

His bushy eyebrows popped up. "Sir?"

"Lock her in and bring me the key when she's settled. I'll have Cook make her something to eat and deliver it in short order."

He hesitated for a breath, then nodded quickly. "Yes, sir." He turned to Never, reaching out gentle, concerned hands. "Miss?"

"I need off this ship," she said, yanking her arm clear of the other man's reach.

"No, you don't. We had this same conversation last night, and I will not have it again." I turned on my heel and walked away, leaving my trusty first mate to handle the furious human. As much as I didn't envy him the task of dealing with her after the mood I'd put her in, the tug to go back and try to smooth things over was undeniable.

"Is he always this much of a raging dick?" she asked, pitching her voice loud enough for me to hear.

Instead of getting under my skin and pricking my anger the way it should have, that little dig brought a smile to my lips. She still had plenty of fight left in her, and just the fact that she was trying to rile me up meant we were nowhere near done with each other.

CHAPTER 31

William was kind enough to guide me as I hobbled my way into the asshole of a captain's quarters, refraining from laying even a gentlemanly hand on me. He then floated about the room like a seasoned butler, choosing clothes and laying them out on the bed before beating a quick, albeit polite, retreat.

"You're still an asshole!" I doubted Hook could hear me yelling at him through the thick wooden door, but a girl could dream.

It was adorable that either man thought there was a chance in hell I would strip down and wear that backstabbing pirate's clothes. No and thank you. All I had to do now was ignore the fact that the fabric of the deep blue, pinstripe sleep set looked impossibly soft, while my own clothes still clung to my gritty skin like fleece to sandpaper.

I pounded my fist against the door once for good measure, but immediately sucked a sharp breath through my teeth. Only I would think beating on something like that when I had injured ribs was a good idea.

"Yep, that's me: Never Darling, genius extraordinaire."

I limped back toward the bed, not so silently cursing Hook and William and everyone on the ship as I went. Not that the others had done anything to earn my irritation. In truth, Hook was the only one I had a problem with at that moment. You know, if I completely dismissed that tiny little thing where they were all working together to hold me hostage on his ship.

Okay, so, I knew I was being petty. Yes, he could have left me in the water and didn't. And yeah, he could have tossed me overboard and left me to the sirens if he'd wanted to. Heck, he still could.

Running a finger over the clothes William had so kindly set out for me, I couldn't think of a single good reason why I was still being so stubborn.

And damn, those fine pajamas really were soft.

My skin itched against my rough, saltwater-soaked clothes. It didn't make sense to slip into clean clothes when I was fifteen levels of filthy, and William *had* mentioned the basin was warm.

I hobbled my tired butt over to the tiny door tucked back in the corner and peeked through the cracked opening. A single lantern lit the small space, highlighting an ancient copper tub half-filled with water. Moving carefully, I sat on the edge of the basin and dipped my hand in.

Of all the things in the universe that could make a girl cry, why did a hot bath after a long day have to be a trigger for me?

I blinked back the stupid, girlish tears as I stripped out of my clothes and slipped into the liquid heat. The tub was small, barely big enough for me to stretch my legs out straight while sitting up, but it felt like heaven. The unique warmth quickly got to work, loosening the knots in my chest and smoothing over the worries in my head the moment I sank down into it.

Closing my eyes, I bent my legs and slid forward until just my chin and knees were above water. Then I leaned my head back against the smooth copper and finally let the tears fall.

I made it about five minutes like that before my inner bitch demanded I get my shit together. It was okay to breakdown, but it wasn't okay to stay broken.

After a quick wash with a rough cloth and soap that smelled like a mountain forest—pine needles and cold rain—I forced myself out of the tub. I dried off with the surprisingly feminine fluffy towel and wrapped it around myself before heading back to the bed.

Every independent instinct in me told me not to touch the clothes, not to accept any offer of kindness from the crooked captain and his cronies, but who was I kidding? I'd caved the moment I dipped a toe in the bath.

"Down the rabbit hole we go," I muttered, letting the towel drop to the floor.

The sleep shirt and pants weren't just comfortable, they were next level divine. A little big, yeah, but I'd never owned anything so silky soft. I ran my hands over the fabric slinking down my hips and moaned. If I made it back home, I was so saving my money and buying something like that to sleep in.

Home. The thought was a shot of cold water, stealing my moment of luxury from beneath my tired feet. I wouldn't leave without Matty, but I had no idea how I could convince him to come with me if he couldn't see or hear me. I wanted to pace and try to work out a plan, but my ankle was swollen to the size of a freaking grapefruit and demanding elevation.

I situated myself on the bed, which took forever with the vicious knot on the back of my head, my definitely bruised and possibly cracked ribs, and my throbbing ankle. In the end, I settled for laying on my side with my leg propped up by all but one of Hook's pillows. Once I was reasonably comfortable, I realized I was still on top of the covers.

"Fuck it." I was too tired to go through all that again just so I could slip under the blanket. If I got cold in the middle of the night, I'd deal with it then. It was officially a future-Never problem.

The clock, the one I had yet to see resting on a shelf or hanging on a wall, ticked away quietly, marking each and every second of wasted time. I knew I couldn't do much to rescue Matty right then, not in the dark and not in the state I was in, but that didn't stop a bolt of guilt from sinking into my chest.

Goddess, I couldn't cry again. I would not let myself cry again. One breakdown, that was all I got.

I pinched my eyes closed and buried my face in the pillow, holding my breath until my lungs ached and screamed for air. When I let it out in a huff and drew in another, Hook's masculine scent filled my senses. It was a mix of his foresty soap and him, saltwater and sunshine. Without thinking about it, I sank deeper into his pillow and his scent, breathing it in, letting it warm me from the inside and soothe my frayed edges.

After a few more breaths, most of the tension drained from my tired body, and after a few more, I was floating on a blissfully soft black cloud in an ocean of darkness.

HOOK

CHAPTER 32

Impatience nearly got the better of me as I all but snatched the tray of food from Cook's hands. "Thank you," I said, trying for a grateful tone even though I was feeling less than generous. The way he took a step back and nodded told me I'd failed in that attempt.

The man was one hell of a cook and loyal as they came, but some days his perfectionism in the kitchen went too far. He wanted to create a memorable meal for Never, which was a wonderful notion, but tonight was not the night for finery. She was injured and tired, and I just wanted to make sure she got something in her system before she fell asleep.

She already thought I was an asshole. A fact every man on my ship now knew based on the muffled laughter that echoed across the deck in the wake of Never's earlier rant. Dinner wouldn't make up for my misstep when we'd made it back here, and that was fine. I was just hoping it would at least get me a foot in the door.

Hope.

I hesitated outside my own bedroom, tripping over the thought. I hadn't hoped for anything in so long. It was a strange feeling to experience again, like a flurry of tiny butterflies dancing across my skin, willing me to take flight with them.

"This woman is going to ruin me," I muttered under my breath before I balanced the tray on one hand, slipped the key in the lock, and opened the door.

Remembering how it had gone the last time I'd locked her in, I let the door swing open but kept my feet firmly planted. No matter how repentant I felt, I had no interest in taking a shot to the head with another piece of furniture.

When I spotted her curled on her side on my bed, a mixture of pleasure and disappointment seeped through my veins. I'd been hoping to talk with her, to explain my earlier actions, but it looked like that apology would need to wait. Along with her dinner.

I set the tray on the table and moved closer, taking in the sight of her in my bed. There was no logical reason why seeing her in my clothes should have brought me anything resembling joy, let alone have an erotic effect on me. Oh, but it did.

Her bright red hair was mostly hidden, swept up in the towel wrapped loosely around her head. She looked peaceful. Beautiful. It wasn't until my gaze trailed along her body, tracing the curve of her hips and thighs down, that I saw the reason for the array of pillows scattered on the floor at the foot of the bed.

A twinge of guilt burrowed in my chest at the sight of her ankle. The joint was an ugly, swollen mess of discolored flesh that blended sickeningly into the scarlet duvet.

No wonder she thought I was an asshole.

I circled around to the end of the bed, sinking to my knees so I could examine the damage more closely. Eggplant-tinted pools of trapped blood darkened the sole and outer edge of her foot, lightening in color as the bruising moved up her leg. I carefully plucked the edge of the soft pant leg and slid it up. The visible damage tapered and faded as I pulled the fabric past her calf, thankfully, but it still stretched to mid-shin.

It was the kind of injury that would hobble a human for weeks, maybe months if they didn't care for it properly. And all she'd done was wince and glare at me when I'd so callously forced her to put weight on it.

Drawing in a deep breath, in a useless effort to relieve the tightness in my chest, I laid my hand gently over the worst of the puffy, mottled joint and searched internally for that guiding thread of my power. Less than a heartbeat. It wasn't just there, it was waiting, reaching back out and demanding to be put to use.

I let it melt out of my palm and into her skin, bleeding deep into her flesh, fanning out around the torn and inflamed connective tissue below. After a moment, tension crept into my hand in a familiar warning—recently familiar and long forgotten all at the same time—and I pulled back, taking a minute to breathe and control the flow.

Was I really just out of practice?

I'd rarely used my power to heal in the past, so maybe what I was doing was different in some way. I also didn't remember controlling it being so demanding. It was as if something inside Never was calling to it, coaxing it out. When I lowered my hand back down, I honed my focus to what I wanted my power to do and where I wanted it to go. Without knowing the extent of her injuries, I couldn't just send a wild pulse of power through her. What had happened in the skiff earlier had about as much chance of saving her as it did of finishing her off.

I'd gotten lucky.

There was no way in hell I was letting it get away from me again. So, I gave her a slow, steady wisp of it, keeping my eyes locked on the colors of the bruises as they faded and the swelling as it diminished slowly beneath my fingers, until the joint felt normal to my touch. Normal but surprisingly dainty for a woman who stomped about in heavy boots. The thought nearly brought a smile to my lips, but my foul mood smothered it quickly.

That mood, however, didn't stop me from giving in to the urge to trace the lines of ink twisting around the delicate joint with my index finger. It was similar in style to the artwork radiating down her arms. Judging by the coloring, it was newer, though a few faded lines in the background hinted at something that had been recently covered.

What would a woman like her want to hide? And just how far up did those fine black swirls go?

The thought sent a hot spike through my middle, and I tried to shake it off. This was certainly not the time to imagine what mysteries the woman hid beneath her clothes, and not just because she hated me. Her ankle wasn't the only source of pain when she'd tried to climb the ladder. I thought back, remembering the way she'd held her arm to her side and hesitated to reach up and grab the rungs.

I sat quietly on the bed next to her, studying her serene, sleep-softened features. The steady rise and fall of her chest was strangely soothing to watch, and I stayed as I was for gods only knew how long before I made another move. There was no sign of injury to her hands and forearms, aside from a few scrapes that healed quickly with a gentle pass of my fingers.

She hadn't moved an inch. Her breathing was steady, like the soft rolling tide on a still night, but noticeably shallow. When I lifted the bottom of the shirt, I cursed inwardly. The bruising on her side wasn't as severe as her ankle, but that was little consolation. Bruised ribs could be unbelievably painful.

And to think I'd been turned on by the thought of throwing her over my shoulder.

Disgust wormed its way through my guilt, complicating my already unacceptable reactions to the woman. Then her earlier words came back to me; someone *had* carried her.

Whoever her Adonis was, I would uncover the miscreant's true identity and find a way to remove him from existence. I hadn't accessed the power needed to end a life in my enchanted realm in a very long time, but for her, I saw no problem using it.

Never shifted in her sleep and a barely audible wince interrupted my internal rant. Her eyes were pinched shut, and the hand curled beneath her head became a claw digging into the pillow. The fact that she'd managed to sleep through the pain up to that point spoke volumes about how worn out she must have been, and I wanted to keep her there, resting. Sleep was healing in ways even my magic wasn't.

Using both hands, I slid the shirt up to just beneath her breasts, then laid my palms against her heated flesh. My power tried again to surge into her, but I managed to rein it back to a semi-controlled pulse, letting enough through to get the job done. When she moaned and tried to shift again, I kept my hands on her, holding her in place so I could wholly focus on healing the physical damage.

The next sound she made was nothing like the one before it. There was no thread of pain in it, not unless longing counted as pain. My cock reacted instantly, coming alive at the thought that she was finding pleasure in my hands on her.

"Never?" Her name was a whisper on my lips. A whisper that elicited no reaction. I let a little more power pulse into her, in part to speed the healing and in part because when it came to her, I was clearly no gentleman. If I'd imagined that sensual reaction, pumping a little more power into her was the easiest way to find out.

Never moaned again, turning her face into the pillow and clenching her thighs, but not trying to pull away.

I knew I should stop. Healing her shouldn't have had that kind of effect. At least, I didn't think it should have. I'd seen plenty of humans receive healing magic from others like me back in the old days and it had never had an erotic effect.

A good man would have put an end to it. Even a halfway decent man would have taken his hands off her, at least until she settled. Apparently, I was neither. It might not have been the morally right choice to continue, but I wanted her healed. If that earned me a slap to the face when all was said and done, so be it.

When I felt the last of the injury repair itself beneath my touch, I pulled my hands away slowly, hesitantly. Part of me rebelled at the act, demanding to feel her skin against mine again. She twisted on the bed and a tiny mewl of displeasure speared me, at least until she rolled her head back on the pillow and her eyes pinched tight again.

Another injury? I should just throw myself on my cutlass and be done with it.

Forgiveness had always been a challenge for me, especially when dealing with my own shortcomings, and the grudge I was building against myself on Never's behalf was one I was unlikely to let go of anytime in this century. Or the next.

I leaned forward and slipped my hand behind her neck, sliding it up until I found the source of her wince. The knot was half the circumference of my palm and raised at least half an inch. Honestly, if the woman was this prone to injury in her normal life, it was a miracle she'd survived to adulthood.

Again, I loosened my grip on my power and let it trickle out, giving her body what it needed to heal. When the crinkle at the corner of her eyes smoothed out, I let out a silent sigh and closed my eyes. I could have watched her, could have studied every tiny curve and fine wrinkle of her unique beauty, but her features were already seared into my memory.

Her image hadn't left my mind since that very first moment on the beach.

I opened my eyes when my power pushed back at me, only to find her wide awake and staring up at me with an intensity that sent all the blood from my brain rushing to my groin.

HOOK

CHAPTER 33

Fury and desire warred in that heated gaze and my body responded to both, coiling tightly around the heat building inside. The urge to kiss her, to taste her, was like nothing I'd ever felt. A pull that was nearly undeniable.

Nearly.

The confusion in her gaze was the only thing that stopped me. I was no stranger to a good, old-fashioned hate fuck, and I would have been one-hundred-percent on board if she'd made that move, but there was too much uncertainty shining through those stone blue eyes.

She didn't say a word when I moved my hand, maintaining gentle contact as I slid it down her shoulder and arm to her wrist. Her muscles tensed when I lifted her hand and turned her palm up, but she didn't pull away. I kept my gaze locked on hers and leaned down, pressing a kiss to the inside of her wrist.

Her pulse raced against my lips and suspicion flickered dangerously in her gaze. "What is happening? Am I dead?" She glared down at her wrist. "I'm dead and this is my hell, right?"

Ouch.

I straightened a little and brushed my thumb over the spot I'd just kissed. "You're very much alive, Never, and this…" I shook my head. "This is my feeble attempt at an apology."

"For being the kind of asshole who would leave me in the forest to deal with that little glitter bitch on my own, or for being the kind of prick who hurts a woman to make his point?"

It took me a minute to process that retort. Once I did, I had to make a real effort not to smile at the ill-tempered reference to the villainous pixie.

"First, I'm glad to see you're feeling better. And my apology is for the second part. I was out of line and I am deeply ashamed by my behavior."

She tugged her hand free and looked away. "Yeah well, that actually hurt less than the first part."

"I didn't leave by choice." I could have said more, could have tried to convince her of my sincerity, but I was finally realizing the seemingly fearless woman used words as armor, hiding her real feelings behind a wall of snark and sass. It probably worked well for keeping the wrong kind of people from getting too close but, in some ways, it made her even more vulnerable.

The first sign of hope flickered in her gaze when she looked at me. "Anya?"

I nodded once. "She wanted to deal with you one-on-one, so she sent me to the sea, the same as she did with you later."

"She sent me back to the beach the first time." Never scooted back on the bed, propping herself against the headboard. She pulled her knees up and wrapped her arms around them. "I think it was a test, you know, to see if she could break me that easily."

"That sounds about right. Her powers to transport are limited, with only a few locations holding enough of their own magic for her to link to. The four compass points in the sea surrounding the island, the beach, her tree, and two or three others. My crew was prepared in case she tried something like that. I wanted to go back for you, but—"

"You didn't." She let out a tired sigh and closed her eyes. Silence filled the space between us, creating a void that made me want to reach out and touch her just so she didn't slip away from me entirely. Only a second passed before those gorgeous eyes snapped back open, filled with an emotion I couldn't quite put a name to but that had my full attention.

"How did you find me? How did you know where she would send me?"

"Luck, more or less. I had a team waiting on the beach, and I called in a favor to make sure there were friendly faces patrolling the other points surrounding the island. I figured if she did the same to you, she would make sure there was as much distance between us as possible. The pixie is vicious that way, vicious but predictable in her pettiness."

"You know all her tricks, don't you?"

I stretched out on my side in front of her and propped my head on my fist. "No, but when you've been enemies for as long as we have, you start to notice the other side's habits and tendencies."

"So, it wasn't luck. You were waiting for me."

It wasn't a question.

"There was a chance she might try something else, or that something would go sideways on the island."

I couldn't bring myself to tell her how I'd paced the deck endlessly until the sun set or how I'd doubted every decision I was making. She didn't need to know that I'd called in a favor I'd held onto for over a century to make sure there was someone there waiting for her, just in case Anya surprised me. No doubt the shifters were all too happy to clear that particular debt from their books.

"But you were waiting for me. And you saved me."

"I think you can chalk your survival up to your own stubbornness more than anything."

Her lips quirked up in a smirk. "Funny."

I gave her a little shrug. "You *are* stubborn."

She unwound her arms from around her knees and leaned back, pressing a hand to her side. After a second, she stretched her leg out and rolled her ankle. "I suppose you had nothing to do with that either. Has my stubbornness given me the ability to heal at superhuman speeds?" The sarcasm in her voice was at odds with the heat in her gaze, and when she bit her bottom lip, I had to sit up to disguise the reaction that tiny move had on me.

"How are you feeling now?" My voice rumbled lower than I'd intended, but there was nothing I could do about it. My body was responding to her heated glances and her movements without any guidance from my brain. It refused to heed the warnings flashing through my mind.

Instead of recoiling from the roughness, she swung her legs beneath her, climbed to her hands and knees, and closed the distance between us without a hint of concern for her own safety. When she pressed a hand to my chest, the fire in her touch was undeniable.

Is this what it feels like to be a moth circling a flame?

"So, it's not just me." Her lips curled into a wickedly sensual smile.

"Careful, Never." I was a dangerous man, and she knew it. Instinctively, she knew. It was obvious from the very first moment, and with her touching me like that, looking at me like that, my self-control was hanging by a thread.

Challenge darkened her gaze, but she didn't move. "Do you want to hurt me?"

Good gods.

I leaned into her touch and growled the truth. "Yes."

Her hand twitched at the response. Finally, a sane reaction. So, I took it a step farther.

"I want to rip those clothes off of you, throw you back on my bed, and fuck you so hard the memory of how it feels to have me slamming into you will be permanently seared into your mind."

Her chest hitched.

I had just enough time to think I'd gone too far before her hand clenched around the fabric of my shirt and she yanked me toward her, crushing her lips to mine. She tasted like fresh gingerbread and warm milk on a cold night, luscious and rich. Her kiss was a drug I only had to try once to know just how mindlessly addictive it was.

With my chest heaving, I broke the kiss and leaned back, searching her gaze. All I needed was a hint of doubt, just one sliver of hesitation, and I would back off. What I saw was a flame that matched my own.

I slipped my hand around the back of her head and kissed her again, forcing myself to be gentle. She melted into me, meeting my every cautious move with her own barely contained energy.

When I slid my hand to her shoulder and tried to pull back, she took over, pressing me back into the plush mattress, straddling me and grinding down like she was as desperate to claim me as I was to claim her.

Gentle. I replayed the silent warning in my head over and over until I had to close my eyes, throwing all my focus into not digging my fingers into her hips and grinding back up against her. I wanted to flip her over, pin her down, and have my way with her so badly my hands were trembling.

The woman was clearly no novice, but I didn't know what she was used to in a lover, or what kind of experience she had. And I didn't do sweet and tender.

Part of me wanted to try to give her gentle and sweet, but I could barely hold myself back as it was. Everything about her unraveled my resolve by the second, and it didn't help at all that her kiss was the mirror image of mine. Hungry. Like she was afraid she'd never feel that way again, and she was dying to hold onto it.

Her fingers tangled in my hair and she tugged at the ends, sending a delicious sting through my scalp that had me groaning into the kiss.

"Never," I warned, but she pulled again, harder, and when I looked up, she was right there with me, not giving in.

"I can see it in your eyes." The huskiness in her voice sent another surge of lust through me. "You want this as much as I do."

She was challenging me, intentionally riling me up. Only she didn't know the kind of fire she was playing with. I hadn't been with anyone in ages, and I'd never felt a need like I felt with her. It was all-consuming, and absolutely, without a doubt, dangerous.

I would tear her apart.

As if she could read my thoughts, she ground her hips down,

pressing her softness against the hard length of me with a throaty moan. The fabric of the silk pants was so thin I felt her heat beckoning. She leaned in and pressed her lips to my neck, and when her teeth nipped at the sensitive skin there, I nearly lost it.

I can't do this. Not with my newly rediscovered power roiling inside me, pressing and swelling just beneath the surface.

I grabbed her waist and forced her to still. "Stop." I didn't recognize my own voice. I could barely breathe as I dragged in a ragged lungful of air, but it did nothing to soothe the burn. She would probably never forgive me, but I couldn't risk hurting her. "I can't do this with you."

Hurt flared in her irises a split second before she slammed her eyes shut and twisted out of my grip. She lurched off the bed and stumbled toward the curtained windows.

"If you won't let me out of this room and off your ship, then you need to leave." She wouldn't look at me, wouldn't even turn my direction. Even with the distance between us I could see the tremble in her shoulders.

Never folded her arms over her chest and drew in a bracing breath. "Now."

I dragged my idiot self off the bed and took a step toward her. "It's not that I don't—"

She cut me off with a wave of her hand and all but spit her reply. "I get it."

CHAPTER 34

For Pete's-fucking-sake. Just once could I have feelings for a guy who wasn't intent on playing games with me? Once? Not that I had feelings. No, that would be so incredibly stupid of me.

Sexual attraction? Yeah, I felt that. But definitely not *feelings*.

I'd just met the man, what, like two days ago? I honestly had no idea how long I'd been in his world, because it had all felt like one, long energy suck.

I felt Hook's presence behind me, the heat of his body sending a shiver through me. Why? Because my body was stupid, and my brain was stupid, and apparently, I had no clue how to handle rejection. I ground my teeth so hard I could swear I heard the enamel wearing.

His hand gripped my upper arm, and he spun me around to face him. "You *don't* get it. This." He motioned between us. "This is dangerous. *I* am dangerous. I don't want to hurt you, but I will. You…" The word faded on his lips, and he shook his head like he was debating something. Without another word, he grabbed me roughly by the back of my neck and pulled me into a bruising kiss.

I'd read about kisses like that, the kind that left you breathless and panting and desperate for more. I'd always believed that kind of passion was nothing more than romantic fantasy.

But when he pulled back, he took all the air in the room with him, leaving me reeling inside. That unearthly orange glow created fiery rings around his irises, and it did nothing to calm the drum of my heart hammering in my chest, keeping time with the pulse beating out a rapid rhythm in his neck.

I should have been terrified. I *was* terrified, but I was not letting fear stop me.

Fear of getting hurt had kept me from letting anyone in since I was a kid, since my mom had ditched me to go live her own life. I was not letting my stupid, misplaced fear rob me of this moment.

Because that's all it will be. A moment. A night. One time.

"You are playing hell with my self-control," he said, his voice filled with barely contained fury. Was it fury or desire? Or maybe a bit of both?

One hand was still wrapped firmly around the back of my neck while the other was braced on my hip. It felt like every inch of him was filled with heat and tension. He wasn't exaggerating. He was riding the edge, and that realization was like throwing gasoline on a fire.

"Don't move," I said darkly, putting as much confidence into the command as I could muster. I slid my hand down his abdomen, loving the feel of his taut muscles even with the soft fabric of his shirt in the way.

His eyes stayed locked to mine, that rich glow pulsing hotly. When I explored further down and wrapped my palm against his bulge, giving it a gentle squeeze, a low warning rumbled through his chest.

Hottest fucking thing ever. You know, besides his cock pressing and stretching against his pants, like it was desperate to come out and play. It was bigger than I'd expected, much bigger, and I legit salivated at the thought of tasting him.

I was Pavlov's dog, and this fucker was my dinner bell.

Except I'd never been a fan of blow jobs. They were always a one-sided venture for me. I was pretty sure the guys I was with were more than happy to be on the receiving end, but they always lacked in the reciprocation department.

But Hook? I licked my lips. I was thirsty for him in every way.

His chest stilled for one beat, then another. It was a tiny little hiccup in the steady flow of his heated breath, but it told me what I needed to know.

I brought my hand back up and tugged at his shirt. "Off."

He was not used to taking orders. It was obvious in the way a muscle in his jaw ticked and his eyes flared. He was the captain of a ship after all. Men like him were the masters of their worlds. But if he was worried he'd lose control with me, then I'd take away that option.

He couldn't lose what he didn't have.

Seconds ticked by as I waited. I would have paid damn good money to know what he was thinking just then. On a heavy breath, he untangled his hand from my hair and reached behind him. He pulled the soft fabric over his head in one smooth movement, then let it dangle from his fingers, waiting for my next move.

"Good." I let that one whispered word speak everything I was feeling, even when I was barely sorting through the flood of emotions myself.

I worked slowly, unbuttoning his pants at a pace that tested even my patience, giving him every opportunity to end it if he really wanted to. When the last button popped free, I waited, holding my breath. I let three full seconds tick by, marked by the incessant and yet to be seen clock, then I dipped my hand inside and a new jolt of excitement spiked through me. I wouldn't have pegged him for the kind of guy to go commando, but the evidence was right there.

I wrapped my fingers around his length, giving him a firm squeeze. He was hard, so deliciously hard. I slid my hand up and brushed my thumb over the tip, spreading the warm bead of precum over the swollen head. I'd never wanted something in my mouth so badly.

I brought my thumb up and licked, and Goddess save me, his flavor was divine.

Lust blazed in that orange glow when his gaze locked on mine.

"Keep your eyes on me," I said, tracing the index finger of my other hand down his bare chest, enjoying the ripples of goosebumps I left in my wake.

His whole body stilled. Even the rise and fall of his chest ceased, like he was afraid to breathe, afraid I might take that as a sign to stop. I gave his cock another firm pump as a reward.

When I looked up at him again, his pupils were so dilated they were just pools of darkness surrounded by a ring of flames, and that fire branded me where I stood.

It took me a moment to find my voice. Fortunately, when I did, it came out sounding far more sultry and confident than I felt. "Good." I released my grip on him and stepped back. "Now drop the shirt and take off your pants."

He did as he was told, slowly toeing off his boots and sliding the rough fabric of his black pants down his thighs until they were a puddle of cloth on the floor. It wasn't exactly a strip tease, but with the way his eyes never left mine, it sure as hell felt like it was.

Don't drool. Do not fucking drool.

Adonis was gorgeous in that heavily muscled, bulky kind of way, but Hook's chiseled physique won the sexy competition, hands down. Every line of muscle from his shoulders to his calves was clearly delineated, giving him the look of a wicked sex god. The only visible imperfection—not that it took anything away from his beauty—was a scar on the left side of his chest, jagged and puckered, like a chunk of his flesh and the muscle beneath had been cut out with something too dull to do the job cleanly.

I reached up and ran a finger over it, memorizing the soft, uneven skin. I wanted to see more of him. Letting the pads of my fingers trail across his chest and over his shoulder, I moved slowly around, drinking in the sight of him like a woman dying of thirst and loving every minute of it.

He shifted uneasily on his feet, and I paused, giving him a moment. Was he shy about being nude? He hardly seemed like the kind of man who would be self-conscious, but you never could tell what wounds people were hiding under their skin.

When he settled, I started moving again until I saw the source of his discomfort. A thick, ragged scar in the shape of a cross marked his otherwise perfect back. I bit my tongue against an involuntary wince at the sight of it.

"Someone did this to you," I said, not really meaning to say anything at all. I let my touch drift over the long-healed wound.

"Yes." His voice was harsh, just this side of a whisper, but he didn't move.

I leaned down and pressed a gentle kiss to the bottom of the scar, then traced a line with my tongue over the length of it. His whole body shuddered.

"Should I stop?"

His response was instantaneous and just as coarse. "No."

I did it again, pressing another firm kiss to the apex of that torn flesh before I moved on. When I came around the other side, some of the tension drained from his body. That scar bothered him deeply and I wanted to know why, but this wasn't the time.

I might have been dangerously curious, but I wasn't a total moron.

CHAPTER 35

He was staring at me with a raw heat that I'd never seen in another man, and as much as it frightened me, it called to me. Something torrid and wild inside me ached to answer. I raised up on my toes and pressed my lips to his, tasting him again.

Our tongues tangled in slow, lazy movements. Sensual and sweet. His hands moved to my waist, anchoring me in place. The warmth of his palms bled through my clothing, soaking into my skin, but he didn't push for more.

I pulled back just a little. "Is it challenging keeping your hands where they are?"

A smirk lifted the side of his mouth, and he gave me a single slow nod.

"Good." I was starting to love that word. Leaning into his chest, I brought my lips to his ear. "For this next part, I'll show you where I want them."

His breathing picked up a little, the pulse in his neck hammering in response. I pressed my lips to that rapid thrum, then nipped at it gently. A warning hiss slipped through his teeth and his fingers jerked on my hips, sending a shot of excitement straight to my core.

How on earth had I gone my entire life without experiencing this kind of power? I'd been in control of every sexual encounter I'd ever had, and the guys were always happy to hand over the reins and let me lead. But it had never felt like this. Not even close.

The power pulsing through me was heady, and lovely, and oh-so-dangerous.

I tugged Hook's hands away from my hips, and sank slowly to the floor, letting my fingernails rake lightly down his abdomen as I did.

"Never, what are you doing?"

I slid my hands around to his hips and dug my nails in enough to bite. "If you're not telling me to stop, then stay quiet."

His mouth snapped shut on a snarl that liquified my insides.

Holy Mother of Pearl.

I'd purposely kept my eyes locked on his face, because, frankly, I was a little scared to get up close and personal with the thing that had lured me down to my knees. When I finally looked at his cock, curving beautifully up into his abdomen with the perfectly formed tip glistening, the heat pooling in me became almost painful.

That was one of the things about most guys that always left me shaking my head. They complained about blue balls like women had no clue what they were talking about, when we absolutely did. At least, I did. I'd been there more times than I would ever admit, taking care of myself after my "lover" had left me wanting.

I took hold of him gently and licked up the length of him. The rumble in his chest vibrated through me, and his hands clenched into fists at his side. I paused to make sure he was still looking at me, then grabbed his wrist with my free hand and moved it to the back of my head. The look on his face when I pulled my own hand away was fierce.

And a little terrifying.

Come on, Nev. This is not the time to chicken out.

I traced my tongue around the rim of his cock, testing his resolve, but aside from his fingers tangling in my hair, he didn't move. He didn't push or pull, and it was then that I was fully convinced I'd been wrong before; *this* was the hottest fucking thing ever.

It was also torture. I knew, without a doubt, taking the kind of pleasure I wanted to take was also going to leave me wallowing in that special kind of agony. I could feel it in my bones. But I still wanted to give him that pleasure, or take it from him, whichever way it worked.

That was the last thought that flickered through my mind before I wet my lips and took him in, reveling in the feel of my lips stretching around his girth. His hips twitched as I backed off and did it again, and again, pulling him in a little deeper each time, until he hit the barrier at the back of my throat.

His tortured moan sent another sharp thrill through me. How could I possibly feel so powerful when I was the one on my knees?

I moved slowly, alternating between sucking and licking, with one hand wrapped around the base of him, loving the way his abdominal muscles tensed when I pressed my tongue flat against the head and licked. It was a delicious reaction that sent my confidence soaring.

I glanced up, expecting to find him standing with his eyes closed and his head rolled back, but I was met with his fiery gaze still locked on me.

It was intoxicating to have him watching me like that, to see his reactions to the different swirls and flicks of my tongue. But after a few minutes of exploring and building him up, I was done playing. As much as I was enjoying the show, I wanted to take him over the edge.

I shifted a little higher on my knees and braced a hand on his hip, taking him in deep, and deeper, past my gag reflex until his cock filled my throat. There wasn't a chance in hell I'd be able to breathe if he lost control and decided to hold me there. The strain of it made my eyes water and I backed off, digging my nails into his hip to keep myself anchored.

He was a lot to take in, in so many ways.

His fingers in my hair were tense and trembling, but he hadn't made a single move to try to take over. He was fighting hard to let me have the control, and I felt the need to reward him for it. Or torture him with it.

Drunk with power. I finally understood that reference because I definitely felt more than a little tipsy.

Did he have some crazy, magical pheromones he hadn't told me about? It would certainly be a great explanation for me acting the way I was, so utterly unlike myself.

Even if he did, I was enjoying the moment far too much to care.

I pulled back and covered his hand with mine, pressing it gently to the back of my head. "Show me." I wanted to know what pace he wanted, what he needed to take him to the edge of ecstasy so I could send him tumbling over.

When I took him back into my mouth, tilting my head and opening my throat so I could swallow him almost to the base, his hand pressed ever-so-gently, nudging his cock deeper. The first little flutter of panic filled me, and fresh tears sprang to my eyes at the effort it took not to gag.

That was when it finally hit me just how stupid I was being.

What woman in her right mind would hand over that kind of trust to someone she'd only known a few days?

I pressed my head back, bracing for the resistance my suddenly panicked mind was sure I would find, but the pressure disappeared. His hand was still there, strong fingers still tangled in my hair, but he wasn't forcing. I closed my eyes for a second, chest heaving, trying to temper the jolt of adrenaline that shot through me.

Way to pick the worst moment in the history of sex to have a little freak out.

I dared another look up, bracing myself for the disappointment I knew I would find staring back down at me. Instead, I was met with something closer to... admiration? Hook's breathing was labored, coming in heavy, jagged bursts, but there wasn't a hint of displeasure in sight.

Good lord, he is loving the shit out of this.

The fact that he was so clearly trying to give me what I wanted without hurting me was just one more point in his favor.

Gathering my courage, I sat up a little taller on my knees and licked the head of his cock lovingly before sucking him deep. Again, when I got nearly to the base, when my own natural limit had me pausing, he pressed gently. This time, I forced myself not to panic. I pulled back all the way to the tip and did it again.

The pressure on the back of my head increased a little, but not in a threatening way. If I wanted to pull away, I knew he wouldn't try to stop me. That was all the incentive I needed to keep going.

After a few more seconds, his hips pumped forward when he pressed into me, causing those involuntary tears pooling in my eyes to spill down my cheeks. When I looked up again, his eyes were still firmly locked on mine, and his low growl of approval became my new favorite sound.

His cock swelled impossibly and the salty tang of precum hit the back of my throat.

"Never." His voice was thick and hot, barely recognizable, and his fingers tensed in my hair.

A chill raced across my skin when he tugged gently, trying to pull me back, warning me that he was right there on the edge. It was sweet and thoughtful, and my heart did a little flip flop in my chest, but I didn't let it break my rhythm. Instead, I slid both my hands around to his smooth, hard ass and dug my nails in, anchoring myself as I swallowed him deep.

It only took a few more beats before his whole body went rigid and his fingers fisted so tight in my hair that I felt the sting at the roots. His eyes finally squeezed shut and a ragged groan ripped out of him. I held my head perfectly still, taking him in and swallowing him down as his hips pulsed in a shuddering orgasm.

Gooseflesh streaked across his body in a wave, and I pulled away slowly, sucking all the way to tip. I couldn't remember a time in my past when I'd enjoyed giving head that much. Ever.

I swiped the back of my hand across my lips and looked up, but instead of seeing a languid, relaxed, and utterly satisfied man looking down at me, the fire in his eyes seemed to burn hotter.

He hauled me up roughly, pulling me close as he pressed his lips to my ear. "My turn."

HOOK

CHAPTER 36

Never startled in my arms and I drew in a deep breath, inhaling her scent to ground myself. I had to be gentle. As gentle as I could manage, anyway.

I pressed my lips to hers, softer this time, enjoying the taste of her sweetness mingled with my pleasure. It was an addictive flavor. Passion spiced with trust. Heat tinged with hope.

I wanted her so badly I felt as though I might just vibrate out of my skin.

She said nothing when I picked her up and carried her to the bed, setting her on her feet beside the nightstand. Not even a peep escaped her lips as I pressed gentle kisses to her neck, working my way down. I fought a brief, losing battle with the tiny buttons of the silk nightshirt.

Whoever thought that many buttons on a sleep garment was a good idea should have been hanged. Or at the very least flogged.

And not in the fun way.

After the fourth button eluded me, again, my patience slipped. I yanked the smooth fabric apart, sending tiny, iridescent buttons flying through the room. Still, all she did was watch with a look on her face like she was caught halfway between desire and fear.

I peeled the fabric back slowly, keeping my eyes locked on hers even as the shirt dropped to the floor at our feet.

Every inch of her I'd seen up to that point had been breathtaking, and as much as I wanted to lay her back and drink her in, I needed her to know that she could trust me.

She sucked in a little breath when my knuckles brushed the sensitive skin of her stomach and my fingers hooked into the waistband of the silk pajama bottoms. I raised a brow in question, giving her the chance to stop me. Her eyes narrowed slightly, and she gave me a quick nod.

Another little victory that sent a rush of excitement through me.

I dragged the pants down, sinking to my knees in front of her as I did.

She blinked a few times rapidly. "I thought you were worried you would hurt me."

A dark chuckle slipped through my lips as I reached up and traced a finger down her breastbone. I'd been absolutely terrified when she'd dropped to her knees in front of me, and again when I'd tried to pull away and she'd stopped me. Terrified and then utterly lost in her.

I trailed my hands down her sides, loving the way her body trembled. "I still am."

Her head fell back, and she stared up at the ceiling. "I must be out of my goddamned mind."

I froze where I was, holding my breath. I was desperate to taste her, to have her unique flavor on my tongue, but I needed to know she was on board. If she told me to stop, it might take a few lifetimes to get over missing this chance with her, but I would. One word from her was all it would take, and I would end it then and there.

When she finally looked at me, my heart leapt. "All right, pirate, show me what you're working with."

Foolish girl.

I couldn't help the growl that rumbled out of me. It was instinctual, a byproduct of my breeding. She was playing with fire issuing a challenge like that, and I was made of flames that wanted nothing more in the universe than to consume her.

I grabbed her by the waist and tossed her onto the bed, enjoying the surprised little squeak that escaped her lips. She was bold and mouthy and endlessly obnoxious, but somehow also gorgeous and sweet and completely enchanting. She scrambled back a few inches, losing some of her bravado, and I took the opportunity to drink her in as I followed, crawling slowly across the mattress.

She was magnificent. The lines of her body were the perfect balance of curvy and muscular. A strong woman who clearly put in the work to keep herself that way. But even with all that natural beauty, my eyes were drawn to the artwork sprawling across her skin.

An intricate, ancient tree twisted its way up one leg, starting with the roots fanning out across the top of her foot. Its gnarled trunk hooked over her hip before it disappeared around her back. A matching branch peeked out over the opposite shoulder where it twisted and wound its way out to her wrist.

Her other leg was covered in a delicate series of black whorls and swirls interlaced with colorless flowers unlike any I'd ever seen. The artwork was nothing short of masterful, creating a markedly feminine pattern across her flesh, save for the middle of her thigh. The graceful blooms and swirls peeled away from the area, forced out by the intense stare of a black wolf with vivid green eyes. Eyes that looked all too real glaring out from their charcoal depths.

The effect was startling, a stark contrast between danger and beauty.

And now I had so many more questions about the woman who called herself Never. Not just why someone as stunning as her would choose to cover herself with art, but why she would choose those images.

She shifted on the mattress. "The staring thing was kind of hot for a minute, but you're veering into creep territory now, pirate."

When I looked back up at her face, she had her sarcastic mask in place, but I could still see the vulnerability she was trying to keep hidden.

"I'm not going to apologize," I said, running my hands up her calves and the inside of her thighs before I shoved them roughly apart. "You are breathtaking."

Her eyes narrowed like she didn't believe me. Maybe she didn't. For all her brash and bluster, maybe there was still a woman in there who wanted to be wanted. I could work with that.

I ignored her little squeal as I kissed my way up her inner thigh. When I reached her apex, the smell of her arousal made the muscles in my abdomen clench, and I couldn't wait a second longer. Running my fingers along her lips, I gathered her silky wetness before I dipped my head down to taste her.

Heaven.

She tasted decadent. Irresistible. Another low growl escaped my throat before I could stop it.

She tried to scurry back, but I hooked my hands under her legs and pulled her to me. "Tell me to stop if you want me to stop, otherwise I'm going to keep dragging this hot little pussy of yours right back to my mouth."

She stared at me wide-eyed, but when I lowered and licked again, her head fell back. The moan that followed was the stuff of dreams.

One of her hands tangled in my hair and the other fisted the bedding as I worked her with my mouth. Her flavor was a delicacy I wasn't sure I could ever get enough of, and the little noises she made had my cock throbbing painfully despite my recent release.

I spread her wider, running a finger down her folds before pressing it inside her. She was soaked and swollen with arousal, and so deliciously tight. I slid a second in and set a brutally slow rhythm of licking and sucking at her clit as I worked my fingers, finding the sensitive spots inside her and stroking gently.

Her hips moved with me, matching the rhythm of my fingers.

"More," she said on a desperate whisper. "I need more."

I pulled away for a moment and her frustrated mewl was

wonderfully satisfying. I grabbed her wrist and pulled her hand away from my head, guiding it to the bed. "Keep your hands there."

She looked like she wanted to murder me but did as I said, crumpling the duvet in a death grip. I dipped my head again, keeping that same, maddening rhythm, until her hand fisted in my hair again and she tried to pull me closer. I shoved her hand away and gave her swollen pussy a single, flat smack.

"Fuck!" Her cry was shocked and loud, and from the way she was squirming, she was right on the edge. Right where I wanted her.

"Hands on the bed, Never."

She kept her eyes squeezed shut and slapped her palms against the mattress before balling the crisp fabric in frustrated fists.

"Good girl," I said in a low whisper, dipping my head. Another shudder ran through her, and I paused for a beat. Was she reacting to my praise or was it something else?

I ran my tongue along her wet heat, returning to that sensual rhythm that had her winding back up. It felt like only seconds passed before she was riding the line again. Her hand tangled in my hair for the third time, and I froze.

She dropped it back to the bed and shook her head wildly. "I didn't—"

"Too late now." I dragged my fingers out of her and gave her pussy a quick, firm smack.

Her hips bucked violently, and her thighs tried to snap together. She was so close.

Seeing her like that, spread across my bed and writhing for me, was a special kind of pleasure. Part of me wanted to draw it out, to bring her to the edge again and again before finally letting her come, but not tonight. She'd already given me far more trust than I deserved, than I had any right to even dream of, and edging her was a sure-fire way to lose it.

I spread her wide again and gave her sensitive pussy one more firm smack before diving back down to savor every second as she unraveled for me.

Her breathless cries and heavenly taste nearly tore me apart, even as they spurred my craving for her higher. I needed to be inside her, driving into her, making her mine.

A tremor racked her body as I rose, climbing my way up and settling myself between her legs. Her deep blue eyes fluttered at first, then snapped open when I slid the head of my cock along her wet, swollen slit. Just that short bit of contact was almost unbearable.

"I'll try to be gentle," I said, trying to maintain some semblance of civility. "But I need you to stop me if it's too much."

She was staring up at me, all the languid pleasure washing away, and I hated myself for not having better control. Then her focus snapped, and she shook her head. "Whoa, back up a beat, cowboy. What about protection?"

I tensed, glancing around the room. "From what?" I sensed no threats looming, and my ship was one of the safest places in the realm.

"As in a condom. You know, to prevent the spread of sexually transmitted diseases."

Ah. I bit my tongue before my immediate reaction got away from me. I'd just had my mouth all over her, and hers had been all over me. It was a little late in the game for this conversation, but at least I could set her mind at ease on one point.

"This is a magical realm, Never. There is no sickness here. No disease." And even if we did suddenly find ourselves somewhere other than this nothing of a place, I still couldn't catch or transmit any illness. Those kinds of ailments were purely mortal concerns.

She studied me closely, as if she couldn't fully bring herself to believe what I was saying. And why would she? The two of us were little more than strangers in my bed. Strangers with an undeniable connection, but strangers all the same.

That fire inside me wavered. There was still time to stop this. We *should* stop it.

"Give me your word," she said, her gaze dancing across my face.

"You have it." I gave it without thinking, without hesitation, and waited with my breath lodged in my chest, listening to the endless tick of that incessant clock as she stared back at me. Would she put her faith in me? Trust me with her body and her pleasure?

More to the point, *could* I be trusted with her?

She nodded. "You won't hurt me?" Her bottom lip slipped between her teeth, and the unspoken part of that question, the "unless I ask you to", ignited a flare so strong within me it threatened to burn my world to ash.

"I will try." I leaned in and inhaled her scent, sliding the head of my cock through her folds again. A groan slipped out. Her slick heat battered my restraint. "But you have to tell me if I do."

Gods, my muscles were already shaking from the tension.

"I told you, this is dangerous. It's been a very long time since I've shared my bed, and you're unlike anyone I have ever met." Because I didn't just want to fuck her, I wanted to own her. That deep, primal, powerful part of me wanted to lay my claim and leave my mark so no one ever dared touch her. It was an irrational desire, there was no doubt in my lust-addled brain about that, but that didn't change the barely contained urge to make her mine.

I pressed a soft kiss to her jaw, then cupped her face in my hand. "I need your word, Never. Promise me you'll tell me to stop."

She searched my eyes for something, then nodded once.

"Give me the words." I pulsed my hips, letting my cock slide up and down her slick folds, loving the jerk of her hips when the head nudged her sensitive bud.

"I promise."

Those two breathy words were barely out of her mouth before I slid my swollen head to her tight opening and pushed in. I tried for slow and easy, but the second I felt her wet heat envelop me, my control slipped. The animal inside me reared its feral head, and I slammed into her, driving deep.

She cried out in surprise. Or was that pain? I stilled, my chest heaving and fear chasing through me. Christ. She was already clenching and spasming around me.

Slow. Slow and easy.

"Talk to me, Never."

Her eyes opened and she pinned me with a glare. That wasn't enough. I needed to know what she was thinking, what she was feeling. I was bracing for the worst, forcing myself to pull back, when her legs came up and wrapped around my hips, stopping my retreat.

"Where do you think you're going?" Her words were every inch a challenge and the animal inside me rose to meet it. "That's not all you've got, is it?"

On the last word, I drove back into her, deeper but still not all the way. She didn't cry out again, but she bit her lip hard enough to turn the pink flesh white.

She tilted her hips up and anchored her hands to my biceps, digging her nails in. "Again," she said in a hoarse whisper.

The bite of pain as her nails raked across my skin only ratcheted my own need higher, and I plunged into her, driving deeper into her pulsing pussy, until she accepted every last inch of me.

It was blissful agony. The best kind of unbearable. And I felt my control slipping away, with every moan and every buck of her hips tearing it to tiny, useless shreds.

"Never." I growled her name because I couldn't manage to get even my voice under control. Her head snapped up at the sound.

I knew what she saw when she looked up. A monster. A wild animal with eyes like fire. My heart was hammering in my chest, and there wasn't enough air in the world to make me feel like I could breathe normally.

Her eyes widened, but only for a second before they narrowed dangerously on a low, husky warning. "I swear to all the gods, pirate, if you stop again before I come, I'm going to slit your throat in your sleep."

The last of my control was ripped away. All hope of sweet and gentle disappeared. I grabbed her wrists, pinning them beside her head, and slammed into her, over and over, driving us both higher. Her cries filled the air around us, bouncing off the walls and echoing back, until her breath caught in her chest and her body bowed beneath me.

"That's it, Never," I whispered darkly. "Come for me." I threw all my weight behind the command and bit down on her shoulder hard enough to leave a mark.

The scream that erupted from her throat was perfection. Her orgasm tore through her, spilling her sweet heat over my cock while her body clenched and spasmed around me. It was hell trying to hold back, to keep moving and drawing out her pleasure with her tight body milking me.

The best kind of torture.

And when I followed her over the cliff a moment later, crashing into oblivion, everything else in the universe disappeared, until all that was left was her body tangled up with mine.

HOOK

CHAPTER 37

The aftermath should have been awkward. It always had been in the past. When the heat of the moment drifted away, and I was left trying to figure out what to say and how to move. It was always that way the first time.

Except it wasn't. Not with her. I lifted my spent body off her and rolled to my back, pulling her into my side. Where I expected resistance, I found only soft, languid, compliance. She curled into me, draping one leg over mine and resting her head on my shoulder. It felt... right.

I wanted nothing more in the universe than to stay just like that for an eternity. Wrapped up with her, feeling the beat of her heart against my chest and the gentle, almost ticklish wandering of her fingertips over my skin. But moments like that weren't designed to last, even in a place where time barely existed.

Never patted my chest with a sleepy smile. "I'll be right back." She sat up and slipped off the bed, padding across the room with absolutely no concern for her own nakedness before she disappeared into my bathroom.

Her confidence was definitely one of those things that made her so undeniably attractive. It wasn't cocky or shallow. The woman knew who she was and wasn't afraid to show it. No, that wasn't quite right. Sometimes she hid behind her snarky attitude and snide comments.

When the door opened and she reappeared, she hesitated a step.

"I won't bite," I said, keeping my tone light. Maybe she wasn't as confident as she pretended to be.

She pursed her lips and stalked back to the bed, running her fingers gently over the puffy pink marks on her shoulder. "Again, you mean?"

Heat rushed up my neck in a torrent, filling my cheeks like I was a man a thousand years younger. "Right, yes." I had let myself get carried away. Hell, I'd lost control. It was a miracle I'd had enough sense left in me not to break the skin and stake my claim for real. I had wanted to, with every fiber of my being.

Never's skin was cool against mine as she laid down, resting her cheek on my shoulder. I waited for her to say something else. Anything else. And when I couldn't take the silence any longer, I whispered, "Are you okay?"

Her hand twitched against my chest, and I glanced down to find her eyes closed. Her breaths were coming in slow and heavy. She was sleeping. The woman had actually fallen asleep in my arms, willingly.

She must have been beyond exhausted.

A twinge of guilt dug into me. Had I taken advantage of her? Fatigue could play tricks on the mind.

I lifted my head, careful not to move her, and scanned the room. The tray of food was still on the table, completely untouched. I cursed inwardly. How was it that I didn't even have the decency to feed her?

I scrubbed my free hand over my face and pulled in a steadying breath. I wanted to stay with her, desperately, but she clearly needed sleep. The kindest thing I could do was give her space to rest.

Untangling myself from her as carefully as I could, I tugged the covers over from the other side of the bed to drape over her gorgeous, naked body. She woke just enough to pull the duvet around her, curling into it with a satisfied sigh before her breathing settled back into that slow, steady rhythm.

Was it a creepy thing to do, to stand at the edge of my own bed watching her? Possibly. But I didn't want to move. Everything inside me longed to crawl back into bed with her, like she was calling me to her even in her sleep.

I let myself stay there for a few more beats, feeling my own body relax as hers settled deeper into unconsciousness. Then I finally pulled myself away and set to work quietly cleaning up the mess of clothes scattered across the floor.

Her own clothes, the ones she'd been wearing when I had pulled her from the water, were draped haphazardly across the back of the small loveseat, still damp to the touch. They'd never dry by morning like that, so I gathered them up to hang them properly. Halfway across the room to the closet, something slipped from the pocket of her pants and clattered across the floor.

I paused, eyes darting to her sleeping form to see if I'd woken her, but she hadn't moved an inch. In fact, if I focused, I could just detect the hint of a feminine snore. I smiled at the sound.

That smile faltered when I knelt to pick up the thing I'd dropped. I recognized it before my fingers ever touched it, and a wave of cold dread washed over me. Every muscle in my body went taut.

It can't be.

My fingers were shaking as I picked the necklace up off the floor by the chain, careful not to touch the gruesome pendant.

What the hell was Never doing with it? I glared over at the bed, feeling all at once like the whole evening had been a set up.

Gods, what if it wasn't just tonight. What if everything had been, from the moment my men had found her on the beach. Was she working with Anya? Or Petra?

I resisted the rising urge to stalk over to the bed and shake her awake, but only because I needed to be certain the necklace was what I thought it was before I made another move. I left her sodden clothes in a pile on the floor and got dressed quietly, then I slipped out into the night with the necklace.

The moment the door shut behind me, I lifted the pendant up to the nearest torch and sucked in a sharp breath. It glowed orange in the light, the same color as my eyes. The same color as the source of my power.

Damn.

I let it fall into my other hand and hissed when it came more alive, glowing brightly and pulsing rapidly, in time with my heartbeat. Balling my hand into a fist, I squeezed my eyes shut. For the first time in centuries, I was whole. The part of me that Anya had ripped from my chest all those long years ago was finally back in my possession.

So why did it feel like I was being torn open in the slowest and most agonizing way possible?

"Everything all right, sir?"

I jumped at William's whispered question, a testament to just how lost I was feeling. I wasn't the kind to startle easily.

"No, I don't believe it is." I held my hand out and showed him the necklace, still glowing brightly.

His eyes flew wide, and he rushed forward, cupping his hands around mine protectively without actually touching. "Is this what I think it is?"

I nodded.

"Where did you find it?"

That was the kicker, wasn't it? I pressed my lips into a thin line and jerked my head toward my bedroom door. "She had it."

"What?" His shocked gaze shifted to the door, then back to me. "You don't think…"

I shook my head and pulled my hand away, tucking the pendant safely in my pocket. "I don't know what to think."

"Oh, Atlas, I'm so sorry."

I let out my breath in a short huff, trying to dismiss his concern. "Like I said, I don't know. I have no idea how she got it or why she had it, but I have every intention of finding out once she wakes up."

He nodded slowly. His voice shifted seamlessly from the concerned friend to the stalwart first mate. "In the meantime, we do have some business to attend to." He was an amazing first mate, but he was an even better friend for knowing how to handle me in a situation like this.

"What's happened?" I asked, rolling my shoulders back and shoving thoughts of Never from my head. Not that I had much luck with that. I could smell her on me, all over me.

"Leo is here to see you."

My eyebrows nearly hit my hairline and I glanced up, just to make sure I hadn't missed the rising of the sun. The deck was still cloaked in darkness, save for the eternal torches scattering their flickering light across the dark wood, and the sky was exactly as it always was that time of night, with its ancient stars glittering in the distance.

"He did come alone, correct?"

William nodded once. "Yes, sir. He's waiting in the war room."

I pulled in a deep breath and let it out on a heavy sigh. "Very well."

The night was just chock full of surprises.

CHAPTER 38

The ornate handle turned smoothly in my angry grip, and I had to force myself not to rip the door open and tear the ship apart looking for that asshole.

He was gone when I woke up, which shouldn't have been a big deal. He was a captain, and probably busy doing captain-y things.

That was what I'd tried to tell myself, anyway, until I'd spotted my clothes in a pile on the floor and found my necklace was missing.

When I get my hands on him, I'm going to kill him.

The light ocean breeze cut right through my still damp clothes as I slipped out of the room, but I was too pissed to give a fuck about being cold. As long as it didn't make me shiver uncontrollably and drop my blade, I was golden.

Did it strike me as odd that the man took the pendant and not my knife? Yeah.

The pendant was my way home, Matty's way home, and that sonofabitch had stolen it from me. I knew it had some kind of nifty magic, but it wasn't like the damned thing worked with any level of consistency.

So why take it? This place was straight up his home, his realm.

Unless he took it just because he was a royal dick. That could easily be why. Or maybe it was worth something. Or maybe he was just a misogynistic bastard who liked to trick women into thinking he was all wounded and damaged.

"Fucking pirates," I muttered under my breath. The words were barely out of my mouth when I caught the sound of his irritated voice coming from around the corner. He sounded like he was in the middle of a heated argument.

Should I wait or just barge the fuck in?

Yeah, I slammed the door open and spotted him behind a large desk, hands pressed flat to the surface and an intense look on his face.

"Give it back." I had no idea what kind of reaction I was expecting, but the way he narrowed his eyes and curled his lip wasn't it.

"No."

"It's not yours." I demanded, doing my very best to sound authoritative. "Give it back."

The orange ring around his irises glowed threateningly. "No." He said it slowly, drawing out the single syllable like I was too stupid to understand it any other way.

"You fucking asshole! That's my ticket home. It's the way to get my brother home. Which, yeah, I don't have him yet, but I will. And when I do, I have to be able to get us both back." I shoved my hand out, palm open, and gritted my teeth. "Please."

Some of the anger drained from his face and he leaned back, narrowing his eyes. His gaze darted to my left, and that was when my genius brain remembered I'd barged into the middle of another argument.

I snapped my head around to see which of his pirate buddies he was quibbling with and nearly stopped breathing. "Adonis?"

Hook snarled something under his breath and Adonis took a step back, dipping his head to hide his smile. "Leo."

I knew that. Shit. But that didn't mean I wasn't still pissed. "Leo, cool. Fucking wonderful. Are you two in this together?" I motioned between the two men. "Is this some kind of twisted game you two like to play?"

He flinched at the venom in my voice, and his gaze flicked to Hook. "What is she talking about?"

He ignored the question, keeping his eyes pinned on me. "*This* is Adonis?" His voice was low and ominous, and I felt something tug a warning in my chest.

Was he *jealous*?

I licked my lips, my heartbeat thrumming in my chest. "Just give me the necklace."

"Oh," Leo said. "I forgot to mention that, didn't I?"

We both turned to glare at him.

"You knew?" Hook asked.

"She had it on her when we captured her." Then he laughed. Actually laughed, like any part of my rage and confusion was funny. "She was using it like a torch to light her way."

Hook's eyes widened. "What?" His gaze volleyed between us. "How?"

I shrugged stiffly and adjusted my grip on my knife. "I don't know how. Half the time the damned thing doesn't work, but it lit up in the woods and I used it to see. Then this big, pretty jerk told me to hide it." I turned to Leo. "Thanks for your help and all, but I'm just a touch confused right now. Are you on Team Slutty Demon or Team Asshole Pirate?"

Leo's lips twitched like he was trying to hold back another smile. "I'm glad to see you're feeling better." His eyes traced a path down and back up my body before he continued. "The answer to your question is neither, though the demon does believe she has my loyalty. That's why I'm here."

"Things have changed on the island, Never," Hook said. His whole demeanor shifted with that sentence, from menacing and possessive to something that could have been mistaken for concern. You know, assuming he wasn't a conniving, thieving bastard.

"Could you be any more vague?" I snapped.

"Not long after you were… uh, sent away, your brother started talking about going home," Leo said. "Which means Petra's chances of winning him over are dwindling. She knows it and she's not happy."

I'd gotten through to him? Hope surged, but I reined it in fast. That might not have been the best development for him. Not if Petra was the vindictive type, and she definitely seemed like the type.

"Is she going to throw him down in the caves?" That could work out. It would give me more time to find him and get him out of this god forsaken realm.

Leo leaned back in the plush leather chair and laced his finger behind his head. "Normally, yes. But now, she knows you're here. And with how much your brother has been talking about you, she knows how much you mean to him."

Shit. I didn't like where this was going. "What's going to happen?"

Leo's eyes narrowed a bit, studying me. "She plans to use you as leverage."

"For what?" I knew the answer even before the question slipped through my lips.

"Your brother's shadow for your life," Hook said flatly.

He meant his soul. My brother's soul for my life. And what better way to manipulate a seventeen-year-old kid than by threatening the last real family he had left? Matty wouldn't hesitate to make that trade.

I shook my head. "Not happening."

"She's not planning on giving *you* the choice," Leo said.

"No shit. But she needs me to make that threat. If she can't get to me, she can't have his soul. Right? And she can only get to me if she knows…" A sick feeling washed over me.

She would need to know I was on Hook's ship.

I held up a hand. "How did you know I was here, Leo?"

"Anya." When I just raised my eyebrows at him in response, he drew in a deep breath. "Anya told us Atlas had been in contact with you, and that she'd spotted him fishing you out of the sea after she'd sent you away. I came here to warn him, and you."

"You two are on a first name basis, huh? No captain or sir for you?"

Leo and Hook shared an infuriating look, but neither felt the need to expound on their relationship dynamics, which made them both even bigger assholes in my book. I leveled Hook with a glare. "What's your price?"

"I beg your pardon?" The look he gave me told me he didn't misunderstand my question in the slightest. But hey, I could break it down for him third grade style if that was what he needed.

"The slutty demon wants me, and now she knows exactly where to find me. Since you're obviously not above manipulating me into bed so you can steal from me, what's your price? What is she going to offer you in exchange for me?"

Hook's expression had turned dangerously dark, but Leo's bark of laughter tore my attention away from the brooding pirate. The sound echoed off the walls.

"I knew you were full of fire on the island, but I thought some of that attitude you were hauling around was for show." He dropped his arms and leaned forward, eyes softening as he took me in. He made zero effort to hide the way he cataloged every visible inch of me. "Clearly, I was wrong."

He was like a different person compared to the intense, borderline terrifying man I'd met in the woods. The intensity was still there, but he was more laid back in that little office, comfortable, like he knew he didn't need to be on his guard.

They're friends. Real friends, the kind who trusted each other implicitly, not just allies. That was the only reasonable explanation for his relaxed demeanor.

"What is she planning?" I asked, trying to ignore the way his heated stare seemed to warm me from the inside. "The demon, what is she going to do?"

"She plans to take you by force."

CHAPTER 39

Hook straightened, pressing his lips into a thin line as his nostrils flared. "Leo, I appreciate you coming to me with this."

"Can't that little bitch pixie just fly her glittery ass out here and zap me back to the island herself?" It was a valid question. She had wings, after all.

I got another tandem head shake from the two men, but it was Hook who filled me in. "She can't come near the ship. I have it warded against her magic and her presence."

Interesting. "Are you afraid of her?" I asked, genuinely interested to hear his answer.

They certainly had a connection when I'd seen them together on the island, but to go as far as warding his home against her? That meant something.

Hook let out a long breath and sank into his chair, leaning back and kicking his feet up on the desk before he deigned to grant me an answer. "No."

Just no? Nothing else? Did he have to make a conscious effort to be that difficult or did it come naturally to him?

"Whatever. I don't actually care. Give me back my necklace. I'll go meet with her in the morning and find some way to get close enough to my brother to make the damned thing work." That was assuming I had any fucking clue how to make that happen, which I didn't. But I had plenty of time to figure it out, right?

I held out my hand again. "And you'll never have to see me again."

He flinched just the tiniest bit at that, but it could have just been one of his many, super annoying quirks. Like making me feel—

I tried to shut down the thought before it filled my head, but it didn't work. He'd betrayed me. When I'd curled up next to him and drifted off to sleep, I'd actually let myself think he was something other than an asshole pirate.

It was so much worse than seeing Clint with the girl in the park. I didn't even really care about that, because, let's be honest, I didn't really care about him. I wanted to care, or maybe I wanted to want to care, but the feelings weren't there. The feelings were never there with other guys. But with Hook…

Fuck it. Whatever.

"Hand it over, pirate." I made a 'gimme' motion with my hand, fully expecting another flat refusal and bracing for an argument. I wanted to fight with him, to tear him down and try to hurt him the way he'd hurt me. Not that I could, necessarily, but that vicious, vindictive little part of me wanted to take him down a notch.

He dropped his feet to the floor and leaned his elbows on the desk, watching me intently. "You're sure it was the pendant that brought you here?"

My growing anger pulled up short. "Yes, I'm sure."

"Where did you get it?"

The glimmer of hope that had just started to shine in my chest fizzled out. I was not in the mood to play twenty questions, so I gave him everything: finding Clint with the slutty cop, the demon attack, my escape artist dog saving my ass, returning home to find Matty gone. All of it.

When I was finished, I took a breath and glanced between the two men, who were both watching me like I was the most interesting bug they'd ever seen.

"Lily was the one who found the necklace, actually," I added with a flick of my hand, remembering the way she'd knocked the box of junk over and nudged that cursed necklace at me.

"Lily?" Leo asked, his eyes glittering with suspicious interest.

"My dog. Well, actually, I think she's at least part hellhound because she's been around forever."

They shared an indecipherable look before Hook turned to me. "How long is forever?"

Why the hell did it matter? I seriously considered pausing there and starting my own line of questioning, but since I was already in overshare mode, I just kept right on rolling.

"As long as I've been alive. I think she was around when my mom was a kid too, but I can't guarantee that. My mom loved to tell stories." My voice faded on the last sentence because she did love making up stories.

At least, I'd always thought they were made up. But so many of the stories her grandmother had written about were turning out to be true, at least to some extent.

What if my mom's stories were true too?

Sure, it struck me as odd that Lily had lived so long, but it wasn't any weirder than growing up fighting demons in city parks and back alleys. It was just life.

"Is that important?" I didn't see how it could be, but I felt like I was grasping at straws for anything that could help me get Matty home safe.

The two men shared another look, and I had to swallow down the sudden urge to kick them both in the shins. I hated being the odd one out around people who had known each other forever. It was like being a third wheel, all shiny and new, when the other two had worn and weathered together.

They were hiding something, though for the life of me, I couldn't see how Lily connected to any of it. Except maybe for the look in her eyes when the pendant first glowed to life. And the way she'd backed out of the room like she knew exactly what was happening.

Okay, yeah, that was strange and super suspicious, but it didn't mean it was connected to anything happening in that cramped room that seemed to be overflowing with rolled papers. They were propped against walls and stacked on top of cabinets.

"I can't say whether it's significant or not," Hook finally offered, pulling my focus with the way he ran his hand through his tousled hair.

For one fleeting moment, I saw the man I'd shared my body with not more than a few hours earlier. The longing in his eyes made my breath catch, but it was gone in a flash, replaced by a stone wall and an unreadable expression.

"Are you going to give me the necklace or not?" I asked, feeling more exposed than when I was sprawled on his bed, naked and at his mercy.

I also wanted an explanation as to why *he* was pissed at *me* for having it. And it would be nice to know what the magical, glowy rock actually was. Better yet, how it worked. If he wanted it so badly, he had to know those things, right?

Instead of answering, he ignored me completely, turning his attention to Leo. "I assume the demon is planning on coming here, rather than trying to lure us to the island?"

"Yes," Leo said, falling back into his leather chair with a manly harumph. "And you can count on her showing up with an army of her lost boys."

Hook's lips quirked up in the first hint of a smile. "That's fine by me. My men haven't seen a proper battle in ages and they're itching for a little action."

"Will she bring Matty with her?" I asked. It was the only thing I cared about. I'd steal the fucking pendant back if I had to, but I still needed to get my hands on my brother so we could get the hell out of dodge.

"I'll see what I can do on that front," Leo said. "But this will only work if she thinks she can use you against your brother. So, you're going to have to—"

I cut him off with a wave of my hand. "I'm his big sister. He's young and immature, and kind of a little prick sometimes, but he wouldn't let anyone hurt me if he had a way to stop it." And I would take his place if it came to that. A soul was a soul.

Hook stood and moved around the desk, keeping his eyes on Leo. "We'll work out a plan to separate her brother from the others and get them clear of the fight. It's probably better if you don't know the details."

Leo nodded his agreement but said nothing. When he turned to look at me, tilting his head, I could see the question forming in his mind. "How's your ankle?"

Oh, right. That. The memory of my ankle led my mind directly back to Hook's hands on my skin and his breath in my ear. The hard slide of his cock plundering my pussy.

"Better." My voice cracked on the word. The heat that was just starting to stretch across my cheeks bloomed into a scorching blush, but I refused to break eye contact. I had nothing to be ashamed of. "Won't stop me from getting a few shots in if it comes to a fight."

He eyed Hook knowingly, then stood and moved past me to the door. Over his shoulder he said, "She plans to make her move at sunset. Be ready." And with that, he disappeared into the darkness.

CHAPTER 40

"He's not going back to the island right now, is he?" I asked, turning to stare at the empty doorway.

"Why wouldn't he?"

"The sirens? You know, the creepy looking mermaid zombie things. Won't they eat him alive?"

His chuckle was soothing and vaguely condescending, which made it entirely frustrating. "He's killed enough of them that they know to steer clear. That might change if he ended up in the water, but as long as he stays in his skiff, he'll be fine." He moved back and sat on the edge of the desk, motioning to the chair Leo vacated.

I shook my head. "I'm not really in the mood to sit and chat with you."

"Still angry, I take it," he said, crossing his arms over his chest.

"You caught that, did you?" I shook my head again, gritting my teeth against the anger and frustration bubbling back to the surface now that it was just us.

The whole stupid situation had me feeling all sorts of vulnerable, and I didn't do vulnerable. People didn't hurt me because they couldn't, because I didn't let them in. But right then, everything I was feeling was coming from a place of hurt and I didn't like it one bit.

"Did you trick me into your bed so you could take it? Was it just a ruse to get a stupid magic rock? Because I'll find another way home." Those were some big words, considering I had no idea where to even start looking. Surely, since Petra was able to travel to my world, and I was able to travel to hers, there had to be other ways in and out of the realm.

Hook's features gave nothing away. Nothing about his posture or breathing indicated my question or my heightened emotions had any effect on him at all, until he reached in his pocket and pulled out the necklace. He let the pendant dangle from the chain in front of him, a look of longing following the gentle swing of the yellow-green stone.

I hesitated for a moment. Was it a trick? Was he taunting me?

"Give me your hand."

It took me a solid five seconds to convince myself to reach out. When I did, he cupped his outstretched hand around the backside of mine and set the pendant in my palm, folding my fingers gently over it and pinning me with a fiery gaze.

"If this is what you need to get home, then take it."

Why did I have the urge to thank him? He'd stolen the necklace from me. Took it from me while I was sleeping. I really wanted to ask what the hell was so special about the little glowy rock. Like why would he even bother with it, aside from its apparent powers of transportation? But for once, I knew enough to keep my mouth shut.

I also knew there was no way in hell I was letting him get his hands on it again. I pulled my hand free of his and clasped the chain around the back of my neck. The fire in his eyes flared when the pendant settled against my breastbone.

"What now?" I asked, my voice sounding more breathless to my own ears than I wanted.

"I owe you an apology." His eyes were still locked on the pendant, and I covered it with my hand to break the spell. When he finally looked up, there was confusion in his expression. Confusion mixed with something I couldn't quite identify. "Another apology. I shouldn't have taken it."

I took a step back. "No, you shouldn't have."

"It wasn't a ruse."

I chewed on my bottom lip. Some shameless, desperate part of me wanted to believe him, but once bitten and all that. "Are we going to work on that plan for freeing my brother or am I on my own? I'm good either way, but—"

He pushed away from the desk and looped his warm hand around the back of my neck, pulling me to him and capturing my lips with his before my brain had a chance to react properly. The kiss was deep and needy and deliciously hot.

My body started to melt in the space of a heartbeat, but he pulled back entirely too soon and pressed his forehead to mine, his breathing heavy. Why that reaction sent a shiver of excitement through me, I didn't know, but I wanted to chase that feeling.

"It wasn't a ruse, Never." He dipped his head and trailed his lips along my jaw. "No trick." His words tickled my neck as those lips worked their way lower, nipping along the sensitive flesh. "I want you more than I have ever wanted anything."

All too easily, I could see myself pressed face down, flat against his desk with my hands clawing for purchase while he drove that gorgeous cock of his into me. The image was as clear in my mind as if I were watching it on a screen. My anger, and hurt, and frustration all melted away with the heat of his breath on my collarbone and the flick of his tongue along my skin.

A gentle knock stole the moment away from me, and it was only then that I realized the door to that tiny little room had been standing wide open since Leo had left. Any of Hook's men could have seen what we were working up to.

Come on, girl. Get your fucking head on straight. The man might have some magical ability to make you wet and wanting on command, but that doesn't mean you have to give in to the lust.

I kept my eyes clenched shut and waited, hoping the intruder would see himself out.

"Sir?" William's voice was quiet and distant, and when I pried my eyes open, I saw why. He was in the doorway, but with his back to us. He really was the most gentlemanly sailor. "It's nearly sunrise. Should I have Cook prepare breakfast for you and the lady?"

If I could have stopped the wildly audible growl of my stomach in that moment, I would have. My cheeks caught fire at the sound, and Hook pressed his head to my shoulder, letting out a deep but distinctly disappointed chuckle.

"Yes, William. That would be perfect," he said, lifting his head. He pinned me with a delicious glare. "Any special requests?"

I couldn't seem to find my voice, or form words, so I gave my head a little shake and tried to will the flush from my cheeks. I was not usually the shy type, not quick to be embarrassed by anything, but even with both of us fully clothed, that moment with Hook was intensely intimate. Realizing anyone from his ship could have walked by and seen us, seen me on the brink of giving myself over to him, left me feeling exposed.

As if he could sense my discomfort, he pulled me around him so my body was partially hidden behind his. "Have Cook make it a large meal, would you? Afterward, we'll need to work out a new plan for getting Never's brother away from the demon."

William tensed visibly, but he nodded once. "Yes, sir. Should I have the food brought here or to your quarters?"

He took a few seconds before responding. "Here will be fine. Thank you, William."

I peered over Hook's shoulder as the other man disappeared from view. "What now?"

"Now we talk." He motioned to the chair.

My shoulders slumped. That wasn't exactly what my body had been gearing up for.

"I need to know what I can expect from your brother if and when the demon brings him here. And I need to know what I can expect from you."

I sank into the chair, reveling in the surprisingly soft leather and plush cushioning cocooning my tired body. "I'll tell you what I can." Within reason.

He didn't need to know that I was more than willing to sacrifice my own soul for Matty's. That was my personal Hail Mary. No one else needed to know I would make that trade before I let my brother condemn himself to an eternity at Petra's mercy.

The prospect of spending a soulless existence on that cursed island wasn't ideal, and lord only knew what weird, kinky shit the demon might come up with for me. But I wouldn't have a soul, right? Which meant all my worrying probably didn't matter. So what if she turned me into one of the lovesick puppies that followed her around and lapped at her skin like she was made of honey? It was better than leaving my brother to that fate.

He was still young, still had plenty of time to make a future for himself, and he could get by on his own. He might be a brat sometimes, but he was a smart kid. I'd socked away enough money to cover the rent until he graduated high school in a few months, if he was careful. And he would have Lily. She might not be able to get a job and help provide for him, but she would always stick by him, just like she'd always stuck by me.

So, that was plan B.

"Would your brother trade his life for yours?" Hook asked without an ounce of sheepishness.

"In a heartbeat."

His tongue darted out across his bottom lip, and he eyed me knowingly. "Would you let him?"

Oh good, he jumped right to calling my bluff. No cute little dance or hedging, just straight for the jugular.

"No."

His brow twitched up and his lips pursed, like he'd known exactly what I was thinking. "Are you planning on offering yourself in exchange for him, Never?"

Was I really so freaking transparent? Honestly, I thought I was better at keeping my shit to myself. "Would that work?"

His tongue traced the line of his teeth in a move that could almost be considered threatening, but the man had no reason to react that way to the prospect of me trading myself for my brother. Hell, it would mean we would be in the same realm for all eternity. If he really wanted me so badly, that should make him happy, right?

"Don't try it. I can see the gears working in that stubborn head of yours, but it won't work out the way you think it will."

"She wouldn't let him go?"

He shook his head and lowered to a crouch in front of me, bringing us to eye level. "You share the Darling bloodline. That's what the demon really wants, so it's possible, but I wouldn't hold your breath. She takes boys for a reason. They're easier to control, easier to manipulate. You can agree to give her your soul, but you have to be willing when the time comes." He reached out, gently grasping the pendant. "You have to open yourself up and allow yourself to be vulnerable for her to gain access to that part of you. Do you really think you could do that with her, knowing what you know?"

I stared at him, sinking into those light brown eyes. It felt like he could see better than I could see myself. "I would try."

He drew in a breath and let it out on a sigh. Letting the pendant fall against my chest, he stood and moved around the desk. "It doesn't matter what I say, does it?"

Hook dropped into his own chair and leaned back, crossing his arms over his chest. As if the distance and the desk between us weren't enough, he had to create that barrier with his arms.

"It does, if you help me find another option. All I have to do is get him away from the frat boys long enough to make this thing work." I tapped the pendant. "Then I can drag his butt back to our world, and all will be right in the universe again."

His eyes twitched at that, like he'd barely managed to hold back a flinch. "You make it sound simple, but you don't even know how it works, right?"

Asshole. Yeah, sure, call me out on the fact that I had no clue how the pendant created a portal and transported me or did whatever the hell it did to drop me in the sea in his world. That was super helpful.

"Do you know?"

He pressed his lips together. It wasn't a yes, but it also wasn't a no.

"What about Adon—"

That frustrated, pressed lip look turned feral at the mention of the other man, and I scrambled to correct myself. "Leo? He recognized it."

Hook shook his head again. "He knows what it is, but that's all."

That's more than I knew. "What is it then? Maybe that will shed some light on how to use it."

His gaze settled on the pendant, and he was silent for a long moment, long enough to make me want to squirm beneath that assessing stare. "Don't even think about taking it from me again," I said flatly.

Those whiskey eyes met mine and his jaw tensed, like he was offended by the thought. "Knowing *what* it is won't help you access the power of it, but figuring out how you made it work the first time might. Tell me again what happened, and this time tell me everything, every single detail."

HOOK

CHAPTER 41

Never walked me through the night of her arrival in my realm again, but nothing stood out.

No, that wasn't true. Lots of things stood out. Like what Petra was doing in her world in the first place. Someone would have had to summon the demon, that was the only way it could have made that trip, but Never was convinced it hadn't been her brother.

Who would dare meddle with that kind of magic? And why turn around and sic the demon on Never in the park? Petra and the Darling family had a history, yes, but what was the point in drawing them together again? What purpose would that serve?

Then there was her boyfriend. That stood out in a big, find-a-way-to-her-world-to-kick-the-shit-out-of-him-on-her-behalf kind of way. I considered it, briefly, but she didn't seem terribly upset by his betrayal. If she was, it was nothing close to the betrayal and rage pulsing from her when she'd stormed into my war room demanding I return her necklace.

Those things were all interesting to note, but they weren't helpful in terms of getting her and her brother home. We could separate the boy from the demon's minions, that I was sure of. We'd stolen plenty of the demon's captives in the past, but where I had always failed was finding a way to send them home. Every time.

Except for Wendy.

Now I understood it was the power she'd stolen from Anya that had helped her escape. The same power now dangling from Never's slender neck. My power.

"Knock, knock," William said, balancing a tray on each hand.

Scents of freshly fried bacon and lightly toasted sweet bread spread through the room, and Never's stomach rumbled loudly again. She turned the most enticing shade of pink at the sound, and I couldn't help but laugh. The woman was a world of contradictions. Bold and brash in all the best and worst ways, but her own hunger was somehow a source of embarrassment.

I stood and took a tray from William. When Never started to get to her feet, I motioned for her to stay put, set the tray in her lap, and lifted the lid. She leaned over the array of fresh food and inhaled deeply, her eyes fluttering closed as an inappropriate groan escaped her lips.

I glanced at William, feeling oddly protective of that sound. Not that I had any right. She wasn't mine to keep.

My first mate was already moving around the desk and setting up my breakfast, pretending like he hadn't heard that illicit sound. *Good man.* Always the professional, he was, but that only slightly tempered the ancient imperative rising within me that demanded I not only throw him out of the room, but that I cut off his ears for good measure.

No one but me should get to hear her make those sounds of pleasure. Except, as I had to keep reminding myself, she was not mine.

"Thank you, William." Despite my effort to sound civil, my voice carried a dangerous edge, and his eyes widened for a split second before his gaze dipped respectfully to the floor. When he lifted his chin, he kept his eyes on me, nodded once, and stepped out of the room without casting so much as a glance in Never's direction.

"You should really try to be nicer to him," she said, drawing my attention back to her. She dipped her fork into the fluffy scrambled eggs and bit them delicately off the tines. How she could give me such a judgmental look while she did that, I had no idea.

"I'm his captain, and I'm plenty nice to him when the situation calls for it."

She bobbed her head side to side and swallowed. "Then why did it sound like you were about to rip his head off? What, did he lay out your breakfast utensils in the wrong order?"

I narrowed my eyes at her, debating how to handle her when she was clearly goading me. She had an adorable smirk on her face that made my own lips curl up in the first hint of a smile. It was tempting to let me suck her into a little argument over nothing, but if we did that, she wouldn't eat, and we would either end up at each other's throats or tearing off each other's clothes. As much as my whole being longed for the latter, she needed food first.

"Eat, Never. We can discuss proper protocol for a first mate later."

She eyed me like she wanted to argue, but instead she lifted a slice of sweet bread to her lips and shoved it in her mouth like an animal. Her smile was triumphant until I gave her a little wink.

"Good girl."

She looked like she might choke on that giant mouthful of bread. Fortunately, instead of trying to talk, she just glared daggers at me from across the desk. That was fine. She could be mad or cranky or whatever suited her in that instant, so long as she finally settled down enough to eat. The woman had to be running on fumes, which wouldn't help her make smart decisions when the time came.

I was fully expecting her to launch into a tirade the moment she swallowed down the bread and chased it with a gulp of cool water, but she kept quiet, tucking herself into the meal with surprising enthusiasm. I ate slowly, keeping an eye on her tray as she devoured every morsel on it. When she'd finished the last bite and looked down, the disappointment on her face bordered on comical.

I slid my own barely touched meal across the desk and leaned back, patting my stomach. "I don't think I can eat another bite."

She finally looked up, spotted the pile of food still sitting there, and I was struck by the hunger lingering in those eyes. "Help yourself."

Again, she glanced longingly at her own empty tray. "No, I'm good."

"It'll just go to waste."

Never mumbled something under her breath but eyed my tray like a hawk zeroing in on its prey. I waited a solid thirty seconds before I lost my patience with her inner war and stood. I pulled the empty tray from her grasp and held the other out to her. "If you don't eat it, I will throw it overboard."

She glared up at me and yanked the tray from my hand. "Are you always so overbearing?"

"When I need to be, yes." And I wasn't about to apologize for it. There was no sense in her not eating when she was clearly still hungry, especially not after the hell she'd been through in the last couple days. I hadn't been much help on that front either, seeing as how I'd woken her up and taken advantage of her when she was tired and vulnerable.

I eyed the pendant resting against her creamy skin, just below the hollow of her throat. When I'd held it in my hands and it glowed to life, I'd told myself that moment was the first time I'd felt whole in a long time, but that wasn't true. Not really. Yes, it had been eons since I hadn't felt like a piece of me was missing, but that didn't go away when I picked up the pendant.

It was already gone.

That empty feeling had begun to fade when I'd first held Never in my arms on the beach. And the last of it had slipped away when I'd had her in my bed with my cock buried deep inside her. She'd had the pendant in the beginning, so I could chalk my initial interest in her up to the pull of the magic trapped in that innocuous piece of jewelry, but she wasn't wearing it when she was wounded and asleep in my bed. It was on the opposite side of the room then, hidden in a pile of damp clothing, and I was oblivious to its presence or proximity.

It was Never I was drawn to.

"What's on your mind, pirate?" She popped a piece of fruit in her mouth and tipped her head to one side, giving me an assessing look.

My mind must have wandered for a good long bit, because the tray in her lap was nearly empty again. "Just working out a plan."

She perked up at that, leaning forward with the tray and setting it on my desk next to the other. "For tonight? For my brother?"

Not exactly. I needed to find a way to keep her, but I couldn't just force her to stay. Holding a woman hostage was rarely the right choice, especially when she was counting on me to help save her brother.

She was only counting on me because she needed my help... because she wanted to go home.

"I'll need to coordinate with my men, make sure they're all in the right places when the time comes." I said it with an air of confidence I didn't feel. We could take on the demon on my ship, but a siege at sunset was a calculated complication, one that could prove particularly gruesome for Never and her brother if things went sideways.

"What about Matty?" She shifted in the chair, tucking her legs underneath her and leaning back. I could picture her like that on a lazy day with a book open on the arm of the chair, her hair tucked behind her ear as she scanned the pages with a contented little smile on her lips.

It was a pretty thought, but it was wishful thinking. I had no right to damn her to a life that wasn't really a life, in a world that barely existed, forever bound to a man who wasn't really a man at all.

I wrenched myself out of my spiral. "The demon plays dirty. She'll try to take you, and if that doesn't work, she'll try to trick you and your brother. She'll threaten your life and his, but I promise, Never, I won't let anything happen to either of you."

If I could help it. That was the key, wasn't it? If I failed in protecting her brother, she would hate me. If I failed to protect her? I didn't even want to entertain the thought. It wasn't an option.

She studied me for a moment like she had a question dancing on the tip of her tongue, then she covered her mouth with the back of her hand and let out a great, sighing yawn. "I need to get up and move around before breakfast puts me into a coma."

"Actually, why don't you stay here for a minute." I stood and stacked the trays on one hand, then headed for the door. "I'll take these back to the kitchen, have a quick word with my men, and then I'll come back in here and we can brainstorm a bit more."

Her eyelids were already drooping as she nodded. "Sure. I'll be right here." She stifled another yawn and settled deeper into the chair, resting her head on her arm.

The woman was tough, but she was in no shape to fight.

I stepped out of the room and pulled the door mostly shut behind me, leaving it open just a crack so the click of the latch wouldn't wake her when I returned. Then I dropped the trays off and called a meeting with my men, letting them know what has happening and what was expected of them when night arrived and the demon made its move.

Over time, the magic in the Nassa Realm infused a body with the ability to heal quickly. It prolonged life almost indefinitely. But it wasn't true immortality.

Petra could kill my men, just as I could kill the demon's soulless minions, but the demon and I were different. Cut from a different cloth, so to speak. A person could burn us to ash and scatter what remained across the universe, and it still wouldn't be enough to stop either one of us from coming back.

When I finally made my way back to the war room over an hour later, Never was still curled up where I'd left her, fast asleep. I lifted her as carefully as I could and carried her to my room, settling her on the bed and pulling the covers over her. She desperately needed rest, and this time I wasn't going to interrupt.

I watched her for a few minutes, making sure I didn't wake her, then I carried my chair over to the side of the bed, grabbed my book off the nightstand, and settled myself in for a long day. There was plenty I should be doing to prepare for the coming fight, but with William leading the charge, I had no doubt the ship and my crew would be as ready as they could ever hope to be come nightfall.

In the meantime, I wanted every second I could get with Never, even if those seconds were spent simply listening to her slow, steady breathing as she slept alone in my bed.

CHAPTER 42

I woke slowly, listening to the sounds of the room before daring to open my eyes. My right arm tingled maddeningly from laying on it wrong and a heavy weight was draped across my middle.

Where am I, and why the hell am I pinned down?

I opened my eyes a sliver but saw nothing. The room was pitch black. That realization did nothing to help the anxiety crawling through my insides. I tested the weight. It was soft to the touch but didn't seem to have much give, so I wrenched harder, trying to at least shift it even if I couldn't dislodge it entirely. Before I could try again, a masculine grumble stopped me in my tracks.

"Go back to sleep." Hook's voice was low and gravely, and entirely too delicious to ignore, even in my mildly anxious state. The weight anchoring me to the bed shifted, clamping tighter around my waist, turning, and pulling my back flush with his body. Flush with every solid inch of him.

I did a quick mental inventory. I was still fully clothed with my jeans twisted around my legs and my shirt rucked up just below my bra. I leaned back into him, taking some of the weight off my aggravated shoulder, and bit my tongue as the sharp tingles in my arm and hand intensified. Clenching and unclenching my hand in a fist helped encourage the flow of blood to something resembling normal, but it was slow going and I was left with an uneasy tickle along the length of my arm.

I desperately wanted to shake it out, to get up and walk around, or find some other activity that would get my blood moving. I could think of one or two that sounded appealing.

Hook buried his face in my neck with a groan, his breath hot against the sensitive skin. "Sleep, Never."

"My arm was going numb," I whispered back.

He mumbled something unintelligible and shifted so his hand was splayed across my stomach, but that was as far as he went. There was no slow slide up to cup my breast or teasing glide down to unbutton my jeans. I loved those jeans, but at that moment, I wanted nothing more than to peel them off and toss them on the floor so I could feel his skin against mine.

I reached back and let out a dissatisfied huff when I discovered I wasn't the only one fully clothed. That wouldn't do, not at all. I turned to see him, but with his face still pressed to my neck, I couldn't get a good angle. Not to mention the lack of light in the room.

A jolt of electricity shot up my spine and I tried to pull away. "What time is it?"

"Settle," he said, a soothing lilt to his voice like he was trying to calm a startled animal. "It's midday. You've only been asleep for a few hours."

"Really?" That didn't seem right. I felt surprisingly well rested for only a few hours of sleep.

"Mmhmm." He slid his hand up, tracing the lower edge of my bra with his fingertips. "Do you know you talk in your sleep?"

Not cool.

"I do no such thing." At least I hadn't, not since I was a kid.

His chuckle against my neck sent a shiver through me. "You do." The soft press of his lips pulled a moan from me. "Don't worry, you didn't say anything coherent. It was mostly just senseless babbling, though I'm sure I heard the word pirate more than once."

I was torn between urging him to continue with the kisses and smothering him with a pillow to get him to stop talking. It was embarrassing enough to know I talked in my sleep when I was little, but to find out I apparently still did it, and that he'd heard it?

A rush of heat filled my cheeks and spread down my neck, and it had nothing at all to do with arousal.

"I need to get up." I tried again to pull away from him, but he held me in place, propping himself up on his elbow to get a better look at me.

His lips were quirked up in a playful smile and I had to fight the urge to duck away from his gaze. "It was adorable."

Yeah, no. Of the many adjectives that could be used to describe me, adorable had fallen out of favor when I was about six years old.

I shoved half-heartedly at his chest. "Who are you? One minute you're a jerk, then you're ordering me around, then you seduce me with your whole—" I moved my hand in a circle in front of him "—pirate thing. Which shouldn't be hot in the first place because I've never been a fan of pirates."

"Because of the story with the flying boy and the wicked pirates?"

"Exactly. Then you stole my necklace."

Some of that delicious smile slipped away. "I gave it back."

"Which I appreciate. But I can't help wondering; What's your deal, Hook?" I slipped the name in secretly hoping he would pull away and give me an opening to escape his grip. Not because I desperately wanted to get away, but because the longer I laid there looking up in those eyes of his, the more I wanted to fall into them, to lose myself in them and him.

It was utterly irrational. Unreasonable. Not at all like me, even in the slightest.

He didn't flinch. Didn't bat a single enviable eyelash.

"What, the name doesn't bother you anymore?"

He gave me a little shake of his head. "Not so much, when you say it."

"Why did it ever bother you?"

"If I tell you, will you promise me you'll try to get at least a little more sleep?"

"Will you stay here with me if I do?"

Where the hell did that come from? I mean, yeah, some shamelessly sexual part of me wanted him to stay, but no part of me intended to actually say it out loud.

The fine lines around his eyes softened and he dipped his head, pressing a gentle kiss to my jaw as I tried not to sigh like a harlot. I failed, but his laugh was worth it.

"I'll stay for as long as you'll let me," he whispered.

There was no need for the whisper. We were the only two people in the room. The door was closed. And yet, those hushed words sent a thrill through me like nothing I'd ever felt. Hot and exciting, but also warm and comforting.

I didn't know how to take it or what to do with it, so I filed it away to deal with later, when I wasn't high on the man's scent and his voice and his heat. "Fine. Yes. If you tell me, I will attempt to sleep."

He watched me again, only this time it felt more like he was trying to decide how much he wanted to tell or gathering his courage. A little pang of guilt zinged through me.

"If you don't want to—"

He shook his head. "It's not a pleasant story, and I'm fairly certain you're not going to like what you hear." His voice faltered toward the end, but his gaze never left mine. "It stems from an incident that happened long ago."

I raised my eyebrows, and he nodded like he knew what I was asking.

"Before Wendy ever visited this place." He pulled his bottom lip between his teeth for a moment. "I was different back then, in many ways. I'd been stuck in this realm for what felt like an eternity, cursed with the responsibility of keeping the demon from escaping. It was— is—my punishment."

"For what?" There weren't many things I could think of that warranted a punishment that lasted an eternity.

"New rule: you're not allowed to ask any questions until I'm done. Got it?" His fingers had been tracing lazy lines across my stomach, but they stilled as he waited for my answer.

I managed a quick nod, because for some god forsaken reason, I couldn't seem to find my voice. Me. The girl whose mouth got her into trouble in every school and every job. It was infuriating. But the way he touched me sent tiny waves of tingles across my skin, a sensual tickle, if that was even a thing, and I absolutely did not want him to stop.

"Good girl." Those two little words did something unspeakable to me, and his fingertips resumed their slow, wandering drift across my skin. From the lazy smile on his lips, he knew exactly what he was doing. "When I was younger, I didn't like to play by the rules. I was always testing limits and doing my own thing. Eventually, I took my rebellion too far and I was sent here to keep an eye on the demon."

"Forced into playing jailer? I bet that went well."

His smile turned wry. "Indeed. The demon and I actually managed to get along for a while there, reaching something of an accord. I wouldn't say we ever became friends, but life around the island was mostly peaceful back then." He fell silent for a moment, his jaw so tense a muscle in it ticked in time with the damned clock. "Anya and I started spending a lot of time together."

Oh shit. I could already see where this was going, and I so didn't want the play by play of him bumping uglies with the glitter bitch.

"You two hooked up." There was no point in pussyfooting around it.

Even in the near darkness of his room, I could see the color drain from his face. He gave me a quick nod, then let out a heavy sigh. "Bear in mind, this was before I knew a lot of what I know now. There were no emotions involved, not for me, but we did learn to start trusting each other. Or so I thought. Until it became clear that Anya wanted more. She wanted me to claim her as mine, in a way that hasn't been done in eons. And I couldn't. Or maybe I wouldn't. I've asked myself that question a thousand times since that night, and I still don't know which it was."

"Maybe it was both."

"Maybe. Regardless, she didn't take the rejection well. She put on a good show, played it off like everything was fine. Then one night, when we were... having fun... she got the better of me." His hand drifted to his chest and the scar hidden beneath the smooth, silky fabric.

"She did that?" I knew I hated the wretched little bug, but that was the last nail in her coffin. I laid my hand over his and laced our fingers together.

He started at my touch and looked down, staring at our entwined fingers. "I still don't know how she did it. I was awake but couldn't move, couldn't fight back. She would have had to use some powerful magic to paralyze me like that, far more powerful than what she possesses naturally. She hooked me on a boat anchor and hoisted me up into her tree."

The mental image that spilled into my thoughts was horrifying. "But you were paralyzed, right? So, you didn't feel anything?"

He closed his eyes. "Oh, I felt it all, I just couldn't do anything to stop her. My mind was alert, but my limbs, my body, they were useless."

I wanted to be sick. What kind of monster would do such a thing? "How did you survive that? I get that you're not exactly human and all, but how does that even work?"

"I can't die," he said in a matter-of-fact tone.

"Because you're here, in this realm?" If the stories were even kind of true, that would make sense. This realm was supposedly like the fountain of youth.

He shook his head. "It's complicated, but no, my ability to heal has nothing to do with this place. I can still be injured, but before her, I healed quickly." He squeezed my fingers gently then pulled his hand away so he could show me the scar on his chest. "Anya couldn't force me to want her the way she wanted me to, so she carved out a piece of my power and kept it as a trophy. Then she left me up in that tree. Three days passed before my men finally found me and cut me down."

I winced, trying to imagine what came next in his story but seeing it play out in my mind before he said the words.

"It was enough time for my body to heal around the anchor. The only way to get it out was to pull it out the way it had gone in." I shivered at the confession, and he pulled me closer. "Hey, it's okay. It was unpleasant, but as you can see, I'm still here."

"But the scars. If you heal so quickly…"

"Because of the power she stole. Healing takes a good bit longer these days."

"So, when the sirens attacked?" I asked, flinching at the memory of the tears in his flesh and blood pouring from the wounds.

"That actually wasn't so bad in the grand scheme of things," he said quietly, stroking his fingers through my hair. "I've often wondered if the injuries from the anchor scarred because some part of me secretly wanted them to, so I would always have a tangible reminder not to make the same mistake again."

That was bleak, but I couldn't blame him. If someone I trusted betrayed me like that, I couldn't imagine ever letting anyone in again. Hell, I had a hard enough time of it as it was, and my issues came from my mom ditching me, not some psycho ex-lover hooking me like a fish with sailing hardware and literally hanging me out to dry.

Then something clicked.

"The name. Hook. That was her, wasn't it?" I'd never felt so sheepish in my life. There was no way I could have known just how much pain was tied to that name for him, but that didn't excuse it. I knew it was a point of irritation and I'd kept poking at it. "I'm sorry."

"Don't be." He pressed a firm kiss to my temple. "I actually kind of like it when you say it."

I couldn't help the smile that snuck up on me. "Better than Atlas?"

He stilled, the gentle brush of his fingers through my hair pausing as a deep hum rumbled through his chest. "Not quite."

I pulled back far enough to see his face. "You like it when I say your name." It wasn't a question because I could see the truth of it in his eyes. "Want me to say it again?"

He licked his lips. "I'd rather hear you scream it."

That one quiet statement sent a torrent of lust ripping through me, pebbling my nipples and making my core pulse. I tipped my head up, pressing my lips to his as I hooked my leg over his hips. "Is that a challenge?"

CHAPTER 43

The groan that echoed through the room gave me hope that we could forget the foolish agreement to focus on sleep and move on to more interesting things, like me stripping every bit of clothing off that delicious body of his.

I couldn't keep thinking about what was coming, or of the many, many ways everything could go wrong. It would drive me crazy. What I needed was a good, old-fashioned distraction.

I pulled myself up so I was straddling him and slipped my hands beneath his shirt. Sliding my palms up to his pecs, I lightly trailed my nails back down over those delicious planes of muscle. His gaze burned into me, and I didn't know whether to melt or rejoice.

Strong hands gripped my hips, and he moved me effortlessly, grinding his need up into my throbbing heat.

He felt so good, even when we were both covered in clothing. The next second he snaked his arm around, then lifted and turned, dropping me on my feet and holding me steady until I found my balance.

I was suddenly breathless. Electricity raised the hair on my arm and the back of my neck. Energy that seemed to originate from him, from his lips and his fingertips, soaked into my skin through his touch. His hands roamed over me, tracing dual lines of fire up my abdomen as he slowly, gently worked the fabric up my body.

I lifted my arms and the deep sound of approval he made shot straight to my core. Why was his approval such a turn on for me? I didn't think I had a praise kink, but I craved those sounds from him.

He dropped the shirt to the floor and leaned back, gripping my waist in his large hands. The man made me feel downright dainty. His thumb traced a line of ink up the plane of my stomach, and I sucked in a breath.

"I want to know about these," he said, loosening his grip with his other hand and letting the tips of his fingers trail lightly up, over my bra to the gnarled tree tattoo peeking over my shoulder.

His voice and his touch were undeniably sexy, but I didn't want to talk about the meaning of my ink. Some of it was teenage angst. Some of it was meant to bolster me up when I was feeling weak. Some of it, honestly, just felt right at the time. But I wasn't in the mood to explain it all.

I wanted to feel, not think, so I shook my head. "Not now."

His eyes flashed darkly, as though he thought he could make me spill my secrets with the dangerous look. Not going to lie, part of me wanted to, but the liquid heat pooling inside me overpowered his silent command. I leaned back in his grip, giving him some of my weight as I twisted my arm behind me and popped the clasp on my bra. His gaze immediately dropped to my chest.

"You're not fighting fair."

"Why would I want to? In a fair fight, you would easily get your way," I teased.

"You would enjoy my way." The confidence in that statement should have come off as cocky, and it did, but the pull of it was undeniable.

The man had already proven he knew far more about a woman's body than any of my previous lovers. I wavered for a moment, caught between wanting to take control and the foreign desire to hand it over. His natural authority called to me, urging me to give into him in every way. It was a terrifying feeling.

He must have sensed that jolt of fear, because he pulled me gently into his chest and pressed his lips to my ear. "Easy, Never. I won't hurt you."

A chill shot through me, an erotic slice of ice through the heat. "That's not what you said last night." My mind raced even as my lips could barely form the words.

"I'm pretty sure last night I did hurt you." His hot whisper fanned the fire in my veins. "And you loved every second of it."

Asshole. He didn't have to call me out like that. But he wasn't wrong. Every hard thrust had been excruciating ecstasy.

"Do you have any idea how enticing you are?" He pressed his face into my hair and inhaled deeply. "Say you'll give yourself to me, right now, and I promise I'll make you feel that way again."

I melted with the request. Melted and bristled, because I was still a fully functional, independent woman. The thought of just giving myself to a man, any man, grated against my entire being. But a warring part of me wanted exactly that.

He pulled back, the fire in his eyes dangerously compelling. "I'll give you a minute to think about it." A mischievous smile quirked his lips. "In the meantime, don't move."

His hands slid down my waist, and his rough knuckles grazed along the skin just above the top of my jeans. He flicked the button and it slipped free of its little hole with ease. The zipper followed, unbearably loud in the silence of the room. His palm was a delicious heat as he slid his hand between the fabric and my sensitive skin.

I was frozen in that place, caught in limbo between two things I desperately wanted: control and release. Hook moved around behind me, keeping one hand anchored less than an inch above my slick heat. All he would have to do was slide his hand down the tiniest bit. Just a little farther.

The moment I felt the heavy warmth of his chest against my back, my resolve faltered. His other hand snaked around my front and my bra was tugged free, the straps sliding down my arms bringing a whole new set of nerve endings into play. In half a heartbeat, his hand was back, tracing a line up my side to cup my breast.

He slipped his other hand lower, finding my swollen clit with ease as he pinched my nipple. The dual stimulation set my whole body alight. My head fell back against his shoulder, and I sucked in a sharp breath.

Had I been breathing at all before that? It sure as hell didn't feel like it.

Pleasure spiked through me again from those two lush points of stimulation, and when he pinched my nipple harder, bringing me right to the edge of pain, my knees nearly gave out.

"Fuck," I whispered harshly.

He pressed his palms flat, one against my pussy and one to my rib cage, as he pulled me tight against him. The length of him pressed into me, a wicked reminder of what I had to look forward to if I played this right.

His voice was nothing but pure heat and desire against the shell of my ear. "Your minute is up. Yes or no?"

For the love of Pete. It wasn't that simple. Was it? Could I just give in for an afternoon and let him do as he pleased? I'd done it once and it was glorious. It was also reckless and dangerous and another night like that might just ruin me for all future men. Not that I planned to have a throng of men chasing after me. But still.

"You're overthinking it," he said, kissing my neck as his hands got back to work.

Pleasure built on itself with each pinch and each stroke of his fingers, and an orgasm unfurled inside me. Not violent, not explosive, but so intense I gripped his wrists to keep myself upright. If it wasn't for the way I was leaning back into him, I would have collapsed into a puddle at his feet.

Panting and boneless, I reached back and threaded my fingers through his hair. "What are you?" Because he wasn't just a man. No man had ever given me that kind of easy, fluid orgasm. Hell, I'd never given myself one, and I was pretty familiar with my own body.

He stilled. All I could hear was the thunder of my blood coursing through me and the endless ticking of that invisible clock. Tick. Tick.

"Yes or no?" he growled.

Fuckity fuck. "Can we just—"

"Never." My name was a warning. He wasn't playing. If I didn't give in, he would put an end to things. I could feel the truth of that in his touch.

"Yes." The word was out of my mouth before I could think to stop it, and he didn't waste a second.

His strong hands anchored me to him as he walked us slowly backward, his tongue tracing the shell of my ear and sending a wave of shivers through me. When we stopped moving, he slid his hand up and pulled mine away from his head.

"Keep your hands at your side."

Every rebellious instinct in me told me not to follow that order and I had to ball my hands into fists to comply. "I don't want to play this game if I don't get to touch you."

"It's too late to negotiate terms," he said darkly.

Somewhere in my post-orgasm haze, I managed to find my bossy voice. "No, it isn't."

His heat disappeared from my back for what felt like an eternity before his lips were there, kissing a line down my rigid spine. It felt hot and cold at the same time, and I wavered on my feet.

"You like that." It wasn't a question, and I wasn't about to answer.

I meant what I'd said. If he didn't let me touch him, I would end this. His fingers hooked the waist of my jeans and tugged them down, dragging my undoubtedly damp panties with them. His lips continued their slow, southerly exploration down one thigh as he wrapped his strong fingers around my ankle and gently lifted, sliding my jeans clear. He repeated the move on the other side, and I was officially butt naked in front of him, wearing only my pendant as he sprinkled hot kisses up the back of my thigh.

I yelped when his teeth sank into my right ass cheek and I instinctively batted at him. "Not cool." The effort and the words were weak, but it was the protest that mattered.

He laughed but didn't chastise me for the movement. Instead, he licked the spot he'd bitten and kissed it softly. "And here I thought you enjoyed the biting."

"Not on the ass," I shot back, twisting to look at him. "Who does that?" And when did he have time to lose his clothes? Fuck me, he was gorgeous.

Of course, he took my question as a challenge. His eyes narrowed and he grabbed my wrist, pinning it behind my back so I had a clear view of what he was doing back there. He let me watch as he bit me again. It wasn't hard and it didn't hurt as much this time, but then, it hadn't actually hurt the first time either. He'd startled me more than anything.

He licked and kissed the spot again. "See, not so bad."

My breath was coming in short pants as he stood slowly, keeping my wrist pinned in place. When I tried to turn, he grabbed my other wrist, adjusting his grip so he held them both in one strong hand.

"I wasn't joking about the touching," I said breathlessly. It was exhilarating and frightening being at his mercy like this, a love-hate moment if ever there was one, but not being able to touch him was frustrating me beyond measure.

"I know," he said, threading the fingers of his free hand into my hair and tugging my head back. He rained hot kisses down my neck and shoulder, lightly grazing his teeth over my skin. It was an exquisite kind of torture, and my insides quivered in anticipation.

The next moment, his grip was gone from my wrists, and he spun me to face him. In a fluid movement, he hoisted me up like I weighed nothing. I greedily wrapped my legs around him, grabbing his hair with both hands and holding him there as our lips crashed together. Heat bloomed in my chest.

No, that wasn't quite right. Not in but *on*.

I pulled back and looked down to see the pendant glowing brightly. Brighter than I'd ever seen it, even when the damned thing had brought me here.

"What the fuck?"

CHAPTER 44

Hook saw it too and when I met his heated gaze, his pupils exploded into that deep black well of want. The darkness pulled me in. Bright orange light pulsed around the edge, but I wanted the darkness.

I shifted my hips and the head of his cock nestled against my opening. I wanted to impale myself on him, to take him to the hilt in one smooth move, but he wouldn't let me. His grip on my hips was solid, those strong fingers digging into my flesh in a way that would absolutely leave bruises.

He lowered me just a little, then lifted me, setting a slow pulsing rhythm as my slick arousal spread over his cock. With every pump, I sank lower, until it felt like I might explode from the pressure of him stretching my inner walls.

I pressed back, digging my short nails into his shoulders and adjusting my angle, giving my body that extra little space to take him deeper. He bottomed out and ground roughly into me, sending a flutter of chills through me, racing out from my core to the tips of every finger, every toe. My orgasm crashed over me, bringing my nipples to hard, almost painful nubs as every inch of my flesh caught fire.

I writhed against his hold, riding the wave for everything I was worth, and just when I felt him thicken inside me, right on the edge, he pulled me up and off him, setting me on my feet.

"Whoa." My knees, my ankles, pretty much everything from the waist down wobbled, but he didn't let me fall. "Why did you stop?" I could hardly find my breath, let alone a coherent thought, but I managed to bite that one out clearly enough.

Hook ran his tongue over the edge of his teeth and smiled wickedly. "Because I'm not finished with you yet."

He guided me to the settee and I sat, my shaky legs giving out so I fell the last few inches. "We're going to ruin your fine upholstery," I said, running my hand over the rich fabric.

"Fine by me." He settled his hands on my knees, gently prying them apart. Then he hooked his hands under my hips and pulled me right to the end of the seat. He didn't say another word before he turned that fiery gaze on my pussy and dove in.

He was merciless with his tongue and lips and teeth, driving me to the edge of orgasm before backing off with soft kisses and gentle touches. The third time he did it, I raked my nails down his forearms hard enough to leave a mark.

"Are you trying to torture me?" I asked between pants.

My body was a million sharp points of sensation, and the pleasure coiling inside me threatened to shatter into the worst pain I'd ever experienced.

"Yes." His voice was a low, pussy clenching rumble.

I moaned. "Why?"

His tongue flicked my sensitive clit and I jerked, digging my nails into his arms again. "Because when you get what you want and leave this realm tonight, I want you to remember this. I want this moment between us to be branded in your memory for the rest of your existence."

Not fair. Saying things like that was not fair at all.

I closed my eyes and shifted my hips, trying to find the friction I needed, but he pulled back, robbing me of his talented mouth. "For fuck's sake. You're killing me, pirate."

He pressed a kiss to my inner thigh, then nipped at it playfully. "So dramatic."

"Not being dramatic." The tension inside me pulled tighter and I groaned. "Atlas, please."

Everything went perfectly still. His breath, my heart, even the air in the room. Before I could react, he had me off the couch and sprawled on the floor, the plush fibers of his fluffy rug creating the perfect softness against my back.

He settled his big body between my legs, grabbing his cock by the base and sliding the head through my arousal. Up and down, up and down, each stroke over my sensitive clit making that hot coil inside curl just a little bit tighter.

I let my head fall against the floor with a thump. He really was killing me.

"Never." Again, he used my name as a warning and my body reacted instantly, tensing up even as my arousal inched higher.

"Please," I whispered. I'd always thought I was the kind of woman who would never beg. He was proving me wrong. When I looked up to see his nostrils flared and his gaze wild, I realized it wasn't the 'please' he was responding to.

A new kind of heat snaked through me, and my mind blared a warning. He was slipping, barely holding onto his control, all because I'd said his name. What would happen if I said it again? Gods only knew, but damned if I didn't want to find out.

I mean, how bad could it be if he lost control?

If it was anything like the night before, I would enjoy every brutal minute of it.

I bit my bottom lip, reveling in the feeling of him between my legs and that feral look in his eyes. "Please, Atlas."

His growl rumbled through the room, seeming to vibrate the air itself. The pendant flared back to life the moment he sank into me, burying his thick length all the way to the hilt. I cried out, the pleasure and pain too much to bear silently, and he did it again. And again.

"Atlas," I called his name, and with each iteration he drove me higher, reckless, relentless, until I was sure I would break in two. And something did break. Or crack. Something new and raw bloomed to life in my chest and my back arched with the sensation. It wasn't pain, exactly, but my lust-drunk brain couldn't think of a word to describe it.

He sank down over me, tangling his hand in my hair. He whispered evocative words in my ear in a language I'd never heard before. It sounded meaningful. Important. Then his grip tightened to the point of discomfort, little jolts of sensual agony tugging at my roots as he drove his cock home once, twice. Another inhuman growl shook the room and a shock of pure power slammed into me.

I shattered.

My world went completely black for a beat before exploding in an ocean of light and color and sensation. I stared up at him, barely able to process thought as his gaze locked to mine. The orange rings around his pupils were gone. All that was left was the darkness.

HOOK

CHAPTER 45

With Never wrapped in my arms and the day slipping through my fingers, I could almost justify what I'd done. Almost. I knew the moment it happened, the moment she gave herself over to me completely, and the joy that filled me was a revelation.

No wonder Anya was desperate to have a piece of me. But where she'd taken a piece of my magic, I'd taken something far more valuable.

Of course, in the aftermath of that wholly selfish moment, I couldn't help feeling like a monster. There was one little detail from my story about Anya and the anchor that I hadn't shared with Never, because if she knew, she might not leave.

Knowing what I did about her, she would give me back the pendant and try to find another way to get her brother home.

But she needed to leave. This wasn't her world, and I wasn't the kind of person a woman like her should ever end up with, especially after what I'd just done to her.

It would keep her safe. It would prevent the demon from taking her in exchange for her brother. But I was pretty sure she would never forgive me.

When Anya had stolen a part of me, when she'd carved a piece of my magical heart from my bleeding chest and held it up like a trophy, I understood what was happening. There was no gray area, no question. I couldn't do anything to change the outcome, but at least I understood what I was losing.

With Never, I could have stopped her.

I *should* have.

Instead, I was reckless and utterly selfish. Taking her the way I did was likely the most selfish I'd ever been in my long life, and I should have felt absolutely miserable about it.

I certainly wasn't proud of myself. There was still a tiny sliver of decency buried way down deep that was rattling its chains at what I'd done. Laying a godly claim to her soul was unforgivable. But even if I could turn back the incessant tick of that old clock and undo it, I wouldn't.

She'd offered me that piece of herself, and even if she didn't know that was what she was doing, I'd taken it, greedily. My one consolation was that when she went home—when she left this place forever and returned to her world—she would be taking a small piece of me back with her.

Quid pro quo.

I didn't want to wake her. The moment she'd been working toward since she first stepped foot in my realm was on the horizon, but that selfish part of me wanted to keep her in bed, curled up with her warm skin pressed against mine.

She'd slept for a few more hours. It was fitful, filled with dreams that had her mumbling and jerking every now and then, but it was still probably the most sleep she'd managed since her brother had gone missing. Maybe that was why I was having a hard time convincing myself to rouse her.

A loud knock at the door did the job for me.

"Sir, it's time." William's voice was muffled through the thick wood, but the urgency was clear.

Never didn't stir with a sleepy grumble or come slowly awake with a long stretch. Not my girl. She shot up, wide awake in the space of a second.

"Just a minute," she yelled toward the door.

She looked down at me with a mix of emotions flickering across her features and I waited, hanging on the edge. Did she realize what had happened between us? If she did, wouldn't she be angry?

The look in her eyes spoke of sadness and longing. There was a little confusion in there too, but then she leaned in and pressed a soft, chaste kiss to my numb lips.

"I need my clothes." She slipped out of my grip and off the bed and started throwing on clothes like she was in a race against time.

I stayed where I was, blinking like an idiot for a moment. She'd said nothing. Not a word about what had passed between us only a few hours earlier, and I wasn't sure whether to be relieved or insulted.

"How are you feeling?" I asked, sitting up and tossing the covers aside.

She hopped on one foot trying to get the other in the leg of her pants and nearly crashed onto the loveseat when she glanced over at me. After she finally got her foot stuffed in the hole and started hitching the pants up her thighs, she shot me a glare.

"Clothes, pirate, put some on." She motioned toward me, encompassing my naked frame with a flick of her wrist. "All of that is entirely too distracting."

Her reaction to my nakedness smoothed some of my ruffled feathers. She wouldn't have reacted like that if she was angry with me, right?

"My apologies," I said, careful not to let a drop of remorse leak into the statement. I wanted to make my way over to her and pull her into my arms, to steal every second I could, but she was working herself up for a fight.

The meeting with Petra would be tricky. The demon's hands were tied in one way; it couldn't take the brother's shadow without permission. Well, it could, but his soul would be next to worthless by the time the demon ripped it free. Which meant it would use every trick up its evil sleeve to get the kid to hand it over of his own free will.

Never pulled her shirt over her head and tugged it down. "Can I let him in?"

I gave her a quick nod, pulling on my own clothes and fighting to maintain an air of calm around me. She was whipping herself up into a frenzy and pulling me along with her. "Yes, please."

She stalked over to the door with her boots in her hand and yanked it open. "Are they here?"

William tipped his head toward the deck. "On the beach. It looks like at least half of Petra's army is out there."

"Did you see my brother?"

"Petra hasn't been spotted yet, nor has your brother."

"Can I see?" she asked, dropping onto the loveseat and yanking on her boots. "Do you have a scope or something I need to look through?" She was on her feet and facing off with William in the next instant, pelting him with questions he clearly didn't have answers to.

I edged up behind her and laid what I hoped was a reassuring hand on her shoulder. "I'll be out in just a minute, William."

Never tried to shrug away from my grip to follow him, but I tightened my hold enough to stop her.

"What? I'm good." She motioned to her fully clothed body. "Good to go."

She was antsy. I understood that, but I couldn't have her running off half-cocked and mucking everything up. The woman seemed to run almost purely on instinct, and if I knew anything about her, it was that her instinct would be to protect her brother at all costs. "Remember what we talked about. The demon likes to play games."

"I got it." She tapped her temple. "I'm ready. I know what I need to do."

"So, you know you're not going out there yet."

She shot me a glare so vicious it was hard not to take personally. "Never, this is the plan we discussed, remember?"

"I can't just sit here." This time when she pulled away, I let her go. She paced a small line back and forth between the bed and the table. "How will I get to Matty if I'm hiding in here? What's to stop Anya from dropping those lost boys right in here with me. I can take one or two on my own, but I don't like feeling trapped. It doesn't usually end well."

From the state of my room during her first night here, I hardly needed a reminder. "The pendant, you're sure you can make it work for you again?"

She offered me a curt nod, but I could see the hesitation in her gaze. "I'll figure it out. It worked once, right?"

I pulled her into a tight hug. "It'll be better if she doesn't see us together like this."

That was part of the reason I wanted her locked in my room. The other part had to do with what the lost boys could do to her if they got their hands on her. Anya couldn't step foot on my ship. In fact, she couldn't hover within several yards of it, but if one of the boys managed to grab Never and pull her overboard, there was nothing I could do to stop Anya from getting at her in the water.

She wrapped her arms around me and squeezed, burying her face in my chest. "This is it then?"

I pressed my lips to the top of her head. "This is it."

She pulled back and looked up at me. "Then kiss me like it's your last chance, pirate."

I didn't need any more of an invitation than that. I took her lips in a kiss that vaulted down to my toes and back, soft and sensual, and desperate in a way I'd never felt before. She met me stroke for stroke, taking as much as she was giving as the hole in my heart bled with longing.

When I finally broke away, her eyes stayed closed, and she dropped her forehead against my chest. "That was *some* goodbye, pirate."

"Yeah," I said on a sigh. If I could have stayed like that for an eternity, I would have, but with every passing second, the tick of the clock grew louder.

CHAPTER 46

Lost boys appeared on the deck of Hook's ship one by one, materializing into existence like something out of a science fiction movie before spreading out in a defensive semi-circle. At least, it looked like a semi-circle from my limited point of view. Hook wanted me to stay in the room with the door locked, but a girl could only take so much.

I needed to know what was happening.

Which was why I was standing at the door with it barely cracked open, just enough to get the lay of the land. How else was I going to know when to jump in and save his ass if it looked like his side was losing? And if Petra did have the proverbial cojones to show up with my brother, I didn't want to miss my shot at getting him the hell out of this cursed realm.

Sure, I still didn't know how the stupid necklace worked or even if it would take us both back. My hope was that if I could hold on to Matty and make the thing work, it would just, poof us back, kind of like the way Anya tossed people to different places.

Which brought me back around to the question: Was the necklace really hers?

Follow up question: Was I the bad guy for holding onto it?

That would have made for an interesting twist, and given Leo's reaction to it on the island, it was a possibility. What if the rock was the thing the pixie needed to escape this realm? What if she was one of those souls like the lost boys, trapped by Petra and forever doomed to flit about in service to the demon?

She could only zap people to a couple different places. The fact that one of those places was Hook's ship was all fucking kinds of special, but that little detail didn't matter, not to me. What mattered was the pendant and what I could do with it.

Was the magic in it more powerful than what the glitter bitch wielded?

I could dream.

I pressed my hand to my hip, checking again, for the umpteenth time, that the pendant was still tucked safely in my pocket.

This would work out. It had to work.

On the deck, a dozen of Petra's frat boys stood their ground with the largest one demanding the pirates release me. For as big as the guy was, Leo would have towered over him, except Leo was nowhere in sight.

Even if I'd been an unwilling guest on the ship, the lost boys all appeared to understand that the other men would never freely give them what they wanted. The two factions seemed to hate each other on principle. Then again, they had been at odds for a few years, give or take a lifetime or two.

I couldn't make out everything that was being said, but the words ceased to matter when the fighting started. My view of the action was woefully limited and every time I started to inch the crack in the door wider, I heard Hook's voice in my head telling me to stay put and stay safe. I tried to listen to that hot, gruff warning, feeling the heat of his breath on my ear as he whispered it to me before slipping outside.

I tried.

Between the clanging swords and the taunting shouts, there was a constant struggle, with the lost boys pushing Hook's men toward the railing and the pirates drawing Petra's guys closer to the center of the deck. It didn't take long to figure out the lost boys' goal was to pitch the pirates overboard. With the sun on its way down, the sirens would be out in force and those carnivorous sea monsters would be all too happy to tear any of them to shreds.

Not exactly a genius plan, and Hook's men had clearly been down this road a time or two, but the thought still made my skin crawl. Fortunately, I didn't have long to dwell on it before William stumbled into my field of view with a sword skewering his stomach and blood pouring down his front.

Fuckity fuck fuck.

I yanked the door open, grabbed him by the collar and hauled him into the room with me.

"Miss, no! I must stay and fight."

"With a sword sticking out of your gut? I don't think so." I examined the position of the sword. It was entirely possible the blade had sliced through several important organs, but maybe that didn't mean anything in this realm. "Can you die or are you like Ho—the captain?"

William blinked at me a few times as though he was having trouble processing the question. "It's complicated. I'm not like the captain, not by any means, but it would take quite a bit more than a sword through my middle to kill me. The same goes for most of us on the ship."

Interesting. "Most? If I were to be wounded like that, would I die?"

He nodded once. "It takes time for the realm to work its magic. Years."

There went that idea, and now I had so many more questions that I would probably never get an answer to. "If I pull the sword out, will you still be able to fight?"

He nodded again in that curt, yet respectful way he had. "Yes, I'll be fine."

"Is the captain immortal?" I wrapped my fingers around the hilt of the sword as I spoke, trying to keep William's attention on the conversation.

For all I knew, he might have suffered this very injury a hundred times before. A sword to the midsection might be nothing more than an irritating flesh wound to a man like him, but damn, it looked like it hurt. Sweat beaded his wide forehead, and his brow was pinched, though he was clearly trying to hide his pain.

"Yes." His voice hitched on the last word. He knew exactly what I was doing.

"How long have you two—" I gripped the handle and pulled back as smoothly as I could "—known each other?"

William let out a breathy groan and doubled over, pressing his hands over the wound now pouring blood from his abdomen.

"Never mind. New question. How long will it take to heal?" I looped my arm around his waist and tried to guide him to the loveseat, but he resisted.

"Not long now that the blade is out." He pulled up the hem of his shirt and showed me the wound. While it looked gory as hell, the flow of blood was slowing, and the flesh was already starting to knit itself back together. As an added bonus, the man was surprisingly ripped under his stuffy first mate clothes. We're talking at least a six-pack with a hint of a happy trail peeking over his linen pants.

"Holy shit. Is it always that fast?" I caught myself reaching out to touch his stomach but pulled back when he stiffened. "Sorry."

The wound was almost completely healed. There was still blood staining his clothes, but the part of his skin where he'd been stabbed was sporting an angry pink scar that was fading by the second.

Hook's injuries two nights earlier had been worse than William's, I would grant him that, but there still seemed to be a pretty big difference in the rate of healing.

William sniffed and turned his attention to tucking his shirt back into his pants before setting his belt right.

"Tell me the truth. If Hook gets hurt badly enough, can he actually die?"

"I don't believe so. It is possible *something* can kill him, but he hasn't found anything yet that will get the job done."

I'd asked for the truth, but if William realized what he'd just confessed to me, he didn't show it. Maybe I misunderstood. To me, it sounded like Hook had been trying to find a way to die. As in actively seeking out his own demise.

I wanted to ask about that, but was it really any of my business? I couldn't imagine being immortal. There was a cycle to life, a give and take. Dying was part of it. I was cool with that.

Hell, back in high school, I was pretty sure I wouldn't live to see twenty. When that landmark came and went with me still breathing, I swore I'd never be afraid of death. Obviously, there was some fear involved, what with the potential for pain and all. I didn't want to be burned alive or gut shot and left for dead, but that didn't mean I had any reason to fear the inevitable.

But to have that taken away? To know I would never be able to end my own suffering even if I wanted to? That was a deeply depressing thought.

"I have to go, miss. Stay in here, no matter what happens." He turned his back to me without another word, flipping his cutlass in his hand as he headed for the door. The man might have been a first mate in title, but he sure moved like a warrior.

"What if she doesn't show? How can you all be so sure of what she'll do?"

He looked back over his shoulder. "Not to worry, we will get your brother back to you, one way or another." With that, he slipped out the door and pulled it shut behind him.

CHAPTER 47

Roars of anger and hair-raising battle cries swelled in the room for the half-second the door was open, but no one tried to shove through. The battle was raging and as far as the lost boys knew, there was no risk of me charging out to lend a hand.

I was supposed to be a captive. I had to stop forgetting that. It didn't matter that my skin was crawling just sitting in there. And it definitely didn't matter that there was a deep, growing need trying to pull me from the room, a tug in my chest that demanded I grab my dagger and defend... what? The ship?

I crept forward and pulled the door open a crack in time to see two of Hook's men wrestle one of the frat boys over the railing. His scream as he plummeted to the sea made my stomach roil, but I stayed where I was, like a good little captive. From the look of things, the pirates were holding their own just fine without my help.

Goody for them.

Of course, that was before the entire deck shook violently and Petra appeared in the middle of the fight with Leo by her side. He was holding my lanky, six-foot-tall brother in his arms like a fainting damsel. Matty was either dead or out cold, because he didn't move a muscle.

"Stop!" Petra's voice was commanding, and every head on the deck swiveled her direction, including Hook's. "I'm here for the girl. Hand her over and we'll be on our way."

Hook stayed as he was, mid-strike but with his gaze on the demon who looked like a diva. "No. She's my prisoner to deal with as I see fit."

She raised a hand, and Leo stepped forward. One long, very sharp claw extended out from her index finger, and she threaded her other hand through Matty's hair lovingly, then yanked his head back, pressing that deadly talon to his throat.

Hook lowered his sword a touch and stepped away from the man he'd been battling. "It makes no difference to me what you do with the boy. If he was foolish enough to summon you, then he is responsible for his own fate. But the girl is mine and she stays on the ship."

The claim sent a strange shiver through me, a mixture of anticipation and something more primitive. Petra plumped her lips like she was about to blow him a kiss, then she smiled.

"In that case." She drew her talon a short way down his throat and blood welled around the fresh wound.

It was a test. Everyone on the ship knew it. My skin was on fire with the need to intervene, to shove her away from my brother and gut her where she stood, but I didn't. Miracle of miracles, I held. Barely.

No one else on the deck moved. Even Hook, whose expression was as bland as I'd ever seen it. Either he was very good at masking his emotions, or he really didn't care what happened to my brother. And why should he? It wasn't like he'd met Matty or got to know him. My brother was just a kid to him, another damned Darling who was crazy enough, or foolish enough, to summon a demon like Petra.

I still struggled with that. Matty wasn't the type to go digging through old books looking for spells, and I couldn't recall a single time he'd shown more than a passing interest in our lineage.

The demon studied Hook for a long moment. Whatever she saw in his orange eyes made her nostrils flare. She reached for my brother's shirt and tore it down the center, revealing his chest. All five fingers on her right hand extended out into those shiny black claws and in the space of a blink, she sank them all at least an inch into my brother's chest, sending rivulets of blood rolling down his pasty skin.

I slapped my hand over my mouth to muffle my scream before the anger took over. It was like a switch flipped and logic left the building. Big sister bitch mode, activated. I shoved through the door and marched straight toward her, ignoring Hook's angry hiss.

"Give him to me," I demanded, putting as much calm authority in my voice as I could manage. It didn't sound too bad, given the way my hands were shaking at my side.

"Ah. There you are." She scanned me up and down, then let her gaze drift around the deck, pursing her lips ever so slightly when it landed on Hook. Then she turned back to me. "I was led to believe you were here against your will, but that does not appear to be the case." Her honeyed voice was dripping with venom.

"I wouldn't read too much into what you're seeing at the moment," I said, forcing myself to maintain a calm posture despite the adrenaline coursing through me, ratcheting up my heart rate and making my palms itch. "I was kidnapped and hauled on this ship. I'm pretty sure they've let me wander around because they don't see me as much of a threat." I waved a hand toward the men without taking my eyes off her. "I mean, look at them. There's not much a girl like me can do against all that muscle, right?"

Petra's smile curled up on one side like a villain from an old cartoon. "Oh, I doubt that's why you're not chained, but by all means, keep talking. I do enjoy the sound of your voice."

Okay, what the hell was she up to?

"Give me my brother." There was no trace of politeness in that demand. I was done playing, and I wanted to make that abundantly clear.

Petra tipped her head to one side, letting her claws retract and cupping his slack cheek in her hand. "I'm afraid I can't do that. He has something I need."

"That he has already refused to give you, right?"

She narrowed her eyes. "How would you know that?"

"I'm clever like that. Or maybe I'm psychic." I took a step forward, putting myself between her and Hook. He growled something from behind me, but I blocked him out and focused my fury squarely on the demon. "My brother shot you down." I glanced around the deck with a shrug. "I can't say I blame him. I mean, come on, who really wants to spend an eternity shackled to a slut of a demon and trapped in this tropical hellhole?"

I gave her two full seconds to respond, but she only continued to stare at me with those big, emerald green eyes, so obviously a glamour now that I'd seen the demon hidden behind the mask. I shook my head in disgust. "That's what I thought. You're only here because you think you can use me to get to him. Bad news, sister, ain't gonna happen. He's a sweet kid, but he won't pick me over him." I tapped my chest. "I know this because it's how I raised him. Survival comes first."

I felt, more than saw, the pirates and lost boys edging in closer around me, pressing into my personal space with their big sweaty bodies, bleeding testosterone and vibrating with tension. Every soul on that deck was on edge, waiting for a signal. Waiting for what would happen next.

"But don't you worry, demon chick, I'm going to make you an offer you can't refuse. Let my brother go, free and clear. Agree to never even set your beady black eyes on him again, and you can have me instead."

"Never." Hook's voice was thick with warning.

I cut him off with a swipe of my hand through the air. "This is a limited time offer, hot stuff. Take it or leave it."

CHAPTER 48

Petra's lips quirked up in a wicked smirk and she motioned me forward with the crook of her finger. My legs were wooden as I took those last few steps to close the gap between us, and the sound of every footfall echoed across the deck. If I looked, I wouldn't have been surprised to see every single man behind me holding his breath.

Leo must have sensed something because he backed away slowly with my brother in his arms. I didn't trust the man, not in the least, but if Hook was working with him, he had to have some value as a decent person, right?

Sure, why not? It wasn't like I'd only known the apparently immortal pirate for a grand total of three days. It was perfectly sane to jump to conclusions about not just him, but also the kind of people he chose to align himself with. Totally reasonable.

Petra's eyes on me felt like an unwanted caress. It was all I could do not to reel back and slap the bitch. Or cut her. If a guy at a club had looked at me like that, I probably would have thrown my drink in his face. In her case, it made me want to slice her open and watch her innards spill out all over that lovely wooden deck.

She looked me up and down like she'd done a few times since our first meeting, like she was taking my measure. Was that the way butchers looked at cattle during an auction?

I dared a glance to my left and was met with Hook's fierce glare. That's when a whole new fear sank in. Could I really spend the rest of my life a stone's throw from the man and never see him again?

It wasn't like he'd really tried to stop me. Sure, he'd said my name in that dangerously sexy tone of his, but that was it. Just my name. He hadn't intervened, hadn't contested my offer.

And why would he?

We were nothing more than a fling, a distraction from the reality of his eternal duties. Thanks for the sexual romp, Never. Good times. Enjoy being the demon's lap dog for the rest of your existence.

"You have a very interesting energy around you, girl." Petra's voice dripped with sensuality as she edged closer.

In her current form, with the glamour, she smelled of coconut oil and something floral. I wrinkled my nose. She'd gotten close with the smell, but something about it was off, like the glamour wasn't quite strong enough to completely cover the rank demon stench. It reminded me of those ladies who spent too much time in tanning salons. The way they smelled always had a manufactured edge to it.

I had the presence of mind not to comment on it, but only because I was holding my breath. Things got especially challenging when she leaned in close and sniffed along the too sensitive skin of my neck. When Hook had done that, it had sent a thrill through me. With her, I was torn between shrinking away and turning to rip her throat out.

Then I thought of her teeth. Not the island beauty's teeth, but the demon behind the mask. A shudder rippled through me.

This was not a moment for weakness. I mentally clamped down on my body, doing my best to trap everything inside, refusing to let another tremor surface and become a fear the demon could latch onto.

"Familiar." Her breath against my skin was an assault, and affront to my senses.

Suddenly, my choice to offer myself in place of my brother felt entirely justified and incredibly, epically, stupid.

"I haven't had a shower in a day or so," I managed to say, though I didn't quite get the snarky edge I was going for. "Are you into BO?"

Petra sniffed again and pulled back, looking a touch confused. "I smell power. Far more than the boy could ever dream of possessing. I don't know how I missed this at our first meeting." She cast a glance over my shoulder, nodding at someone behind me.

With my skin crawling painfully and every instinct inside me demanding I either tear the monster's head off or grab my brother and run for our lives, I could barely manage a civil response. "Then we have a deal?"

Hope, and fear, and a horrifyingly selfish sadness filled the space between us as I waited for the demon to seal my fate.

And still, Hook didn't argue. He didn't intervene. Not a single word slipped past his lips.

I had no right to be surprised. Our connection, that tenuous link, was a purely physical thing. That's all it could be after just three days, and it was ridiculous for even a small part of me to wish I was wrong about that.

Petra grabbed me by the jaw and narrowed her eyes. "I require a taste first. Then I'll make my decision."

Shit. Ew. Fuck. I'd really been hoping the slutty demon didn't go for chicks. *So much for that idea.* She leaned in and pressed a surprisingly gentle kiss to my lips, teasing with her tongue along the rigid seam of my mouth.

It was nauseating.

A familiar growl startled a gasp out of me, and Petra didn't waste the opportunity. Her tongue slid inside as her long fingers looped around the back of my neck in a lover's hold, a surprisingly strong hold.

It wasn't like I hadn't kissed my fair share of women. Humans had the potential to be beautiful creatures, regardless of sex, and I'd been curious in my late teens and early twenties. The difference then was it was always consensual.

This was not.

If I'd had any inner doubts about that, the tug I felt deep inside me was all the reminder I needed. It felt like a string was tangled around my insides and Petra was pulling on the end of it, testing the strength of the line.

The strange sensation made me wobble on my feet and Petra yanked her head back, staring at me with daggers in her eyes. Those fake, glacial irises morphed to black and back again so fast I barely caught it.

"What?" I asked, trying to hide the nausea coursing through me. "Am I not doing it for you?"

"Nice try, girl." She shoved me off and I reeled backward, absolutely certain I was about to land on my ass on the deck. Instead, I hit a muscled wall. Strong hands wrapped around my upper arms holding me steady until I found my footing. Warm leather and sunshine filled the air around me and I inhaled greedily, letting it wash away the demon's stench.

Petra's gaze locked on the man behind me. "You think you're awfully clever, don't you, Captain?"

I was missing something. I twisted to try to get a look at him, but his grip on my arms tightened. "What is happening?" I demanded.

Silence crept across the deck, with only the sounds of the night breeze knocking the ropes and pulleys for the sails against the mast giving me any indication that I hadn't suddenly gone deaf.

Petra's expression shifted from angry to viciously amused, and her gaze darted between me and the big man behind me. "She doesn't know."

If he hadn't been holding me so carefully, I wouldn't have felt the way he flinched at the observation. Or was it an accusation?

"What don't I know?" I tried to pull free of his grip, and this time he let me. Neither demon nor man made a move toward me as I equalized the distance between the three of us.

"Oh, she truly has no idea." Petra's voice dripped with condescension.

"Would anyone care to explain what the fuck is happening here?" I asked, trying desperately to stem the flow of adrenaline that had me feeling like I was vibrating in my skin. When no one ventured an answer, I pinned my gaze on Hook. "What is she talking about?"

He tore his eyes off the other woman long enough to give me a look so weighed down with guilt that I had to fight the urge to go to him and soothe whatever the hell was wrong. His lips pressed into a thin line, and he gave his head a little shake. That was it. That was all the answer he offered me before turning his attention back to Petra.

"Oh, this is just too precious," Petra cooed. "And after all these years." She opened her arms wide, encompassing everything around us. "After millennia. I didn't think you had it in you."

Her laugh grated against my nerves in the worst way, and I reached behind me, pulling my knife from the waistband of my jeans. I was inclined to stab her in the throat just to stop the sound.

"You truly are embracing your pirate lifestyle these days. I have to say, I'm oddly proud." This time Petra's smile bordered on admiration. "There may be hope for you yet."

For fuck's sake. I drew in a deep breath and stepped up to Petra. "Do we have a deal or not?"

She licked her plump lips. "Not. You have nothing to offer me."

"I offered you my soul. You *just* said I'm powerful. How is that nothing?" I asked, swallowing back the panic rising in my throat. That was my bargaining chip. My only one.

She paused, drawing out the moment and playing on the drama of it like a pro. "You can't give me something that doesn't belong to you anymore." She cast a knowing glance at Hook.

Dread coiled in my stomach as a chill raced down my body from head to toe. "What is she talking about?" I asked, directing my question at him. The way he refused to acknowledge me only fueled my growing agitation. "I will cut you, pirate."

Petra's laugh echoed across the deck and the rest of the situation came back to me. We were a spectacle every person on the ship was watching. "You tricked her. How wonderful," she teased.

"It wasn't a trick," he finally said, his voice low with warning.

Her expression shifted again, taking on a menacing scowl. "Whether it was or not, she's no good to me as a trade. But she may still be useful as a bargaining chip." She flicked her hand in a circle, setting the frat boys in motion.

I flipped my blade in my hand and lunged forward, slicing a deep gash across Petra's neck, fighting a gag when her black blood erupted from the wound. It splattered my face and spilled in sheets down her body. Her shriek was so loud it felt like my ears were bleeding, and I stumbled backward.

CHAPTER 49

I backed up another step, not looking behind me as I moved. Leo was nearby, murmuring something low and foreign, but violence erupted around me, drowning out his words.

Then I heard it. Matty's voice.

I glanced over my shoulder and spotted him. Leo was setting my now conscious brother on his feet, and my heart leapt right before it launched into a frenzied gallop.

He looked dazed, but the moment he spotted me his eyes cleared and he straightened up. A smile bloomed across his face, and he started to say something before Leo grabbed him and shoved him behind his big frame.

I had to get to him.

I couldn't tell if he was shielding my brother from me or the other frat boys, at least not until Matty's gaze landed on Petra. She was positively fuming. If this were a cartoon, little tendrils of smoke would have been curling up from around her head. Her carefully constructed glamour flickered, letting her true appearance bleed through the island beauty facade.

I didn't think, I just ran, shoving past men locked in battle with zero regard to who I was pushing out of my way.

A hand wrapped around my wrist, and I spun, dagger in hand ready to strike. It was through sheer force of will that I didn't plunge the blade into Hook's neck before my brain registered who he was. Will and luck. I managed to stop my swing just a few inches short, but he didn't flinch. His eyes were pinned to mine, pleading.

"It wasn't a trick, Never." His voice was little more than a whisper over the din of the fight, running beneath the sharp clang of battling swords, but I understood the words perfectly.

Understood and didn't care.

In that moment, all I cared about was my brother. I yanked free of Hook's grasp and shoved the nearest body out of my way. I scanned the deck. When I couldn't spot Matty immediately, my stomach did a panicked little shudder.

A few excruciating seconds later, I saw his shock of curly brown hair hiding in a corner. Leo was still in front of him, and when he spotted me, he tipped his head back, motioning me forward.

Maybe the giant Adonis was on my side.

A beady-eyed frat boy shoved me aside, but hard enough to knock me off balance. His sneer was almost comical, until I righted myself and kneed him in the groin. He bent in half, gasping for air, and I shoved the blade down, burying it to the hilt in the soft spot at the base of his skull. His body crumpled like a deflating balloon, and I moved around him.

Matty stared at me wide-eyed from where he was crouched. Even Leo gave me an approving little nod as I eased past him warily, still uneasy about where his alliances truly fell. As long as he didn't get in my way, it didn't matter.

I knelt next to my cowering brother, turning my back to the wall beside him and looking out at the melee. "Are you okay?"

"You just killed that guy," he said, his voice wobbling.

"I stabbed him, yes, but he's not dead." I said, scanning the action, watching for an opening. Petra and Hook were locked in a battle of their own, but the demon refused to let go of the glamour, morphing between beauty and monster every few seconds.

"He looks dead," Matty said. He glanced down at the small streaks of red racing down his chest. "Am I bleeding?" He reached up to touch a spot but didn't quite have the nerve to make contact. As if the pain had only just registered at the sight of his blood, he curled forward. "Ow."

I shifted my hips and pulled the pendant from my pocket, willing the damned thing to glow to life. When nothing happened, I had to fight the urge to chuck it against the wall.

"Follow me," I said, grabbing Matty by the wrist.

"What? Where?" he squeaked.

Did he actually think he was safer curled in a ball in a corner while a legendary pirates-versus-lost-boys battle raged across the deck of Hook's ship? Probably, since he didn't know the plan.

I leaned in close and pointed, keeping my hand low so it wasn't glaringly obvious to everyone around us. "Do you see that door? We need to get in there."

"And then what? Where the hell are we anyway?"

I shook my head. "Later, Matty." I laced my fingers through his, the way we'd done when we were both much younger. It didn't feel the least bit strange. "Come on."

The fighting men seemed to move away from us on instinct as we ran, and maybe they were. Maybe the instinct to keep a buffer around them was so ingrained that they didn't even realize what or who they were shifting away from. Either way, I was grateful. Well, I would be grateful later. There was still entirely too much adrenaline pumping through my body for me to be anything other than on alert and on edge.

I only had to stab two more frat boys before we reached the door, and both of those were basically warning slices. For every pirate there was a lost boy, and the men were falling and getting back up like toddlers on a playground, minus the high-pitched screaming.

No, wait, that wasn't entirely true.

A piercing cry filled the air, a woman's cry of pain. It sounded like she was being tortured in the most horrible way, but I knew better. It was a trap. The demon was trying to use her fake feminine softness to draw Matty back to her, and it was working.

"God, what are they doing to her? Never, we need to help."

"No, we don't." The door was right there, just a few short steps away, and I yanked his arm hard, knocking him off balance as he reeled after me. I swung the door open and shoved him inside before his misplaced chivalry got us both killed.

Life really was an unfair little bitch sometimes. Every single soul on that cursed ship couldn't die, save for me and my little brother.

Not cool, universe.

I kicked the door shut behind us and shoved him back when he tried to move past me to get back out. "She's not human, Matty. Did you not see that?"

His resistance faded slowly as recognition dawned on his young features. He was a big kid, big enough to be mistaken for someone old enough to buy beer every now and then, so it was easy to forget sometimes that he was, still, just a kid.

"She's a demon parading around in a woman's body," I said.

He backed away from me and I flipped the latch, locking us inside.

"I saw that." He shook his head like he was shaking off a nightmare. "I did. Why did I want to…" His voice faded.

"Help her? Because that's what demons do. They'll use any trick in the book to lure their victims, even the dirty ones." I moved back toward the bed and pulled the pendant out again, glaring at it.

"What is that?" Matty edged closer, dipping his head to examine the small, dull stone.

"It's like Dorothy's ruby slippers, sort of."

I think.

I didn't add that we didn't have some amazing witch dressed in pink tulle giving us step by step instructions on how to make the damned thing work.

Of course not. That would have been way too easy.

He reached out and touched it with just the tip of his finger, pulling back like the thing might bite him. "It doesn't look like much."

He was right. It was as dead as a little rock could be without crumbling to dust. I needed to remember how I made the stupid thing work the first time. I'd had it in my hand, and I was thinking about Matty and it just… came to life.

"Give me your hand," I said, wiping the blood off my dagger and tucking it in the waistband of my jeans. Something heavy slammed against the locked door, rattling the thick wood barrier on its hinges, and I nearly stabbed myself in the ass when I jumped.

Alarm shined in Matty's light brown eyes, and he slapped his hand over mine. "What do I do?"

"Think about home." I shook my head. "No, more specific. I don't want to end up in the middle of the pond in the park. Think of our apartment, the living room, us sitting on the couch watching TV. Got it?" I squeezed his hand.

"The couch? Sure," he said, sounding more unsure than I was comfortable with.

"This is important. I don't know what will happen if we think of different places, but I doubt it'll be good. Think of the couch in the living room." I glared down at the little stone and focused all my energy on it and that ratty old couch.

The air around us shuddered, but nothing else happened. The pendant emitted the faintest glow, so we were doing something right, but it wasn't enough.

"Think, Never," I mumbled to myself. "What was different?"

Matty watched me warily. When another weight crashed into the door, we both flinched, and I nearly dropped the pendant.

"Fuck!"

Matty unlaced his fingers from mine and reached for it. Instinctively, I pulled back. His face flickered with some emotion, maybe disappointment, but he must have read my unwillingness to part with the thing because he backed off. "You're sure that's the thing that will send us home. It couldn't be anything else?"

I shook my head and closed my eyes, trying to remember the night I arrived. "It was definitely this," I said.

"What did it do when it worked the first time?" Matty asked.

"It glowed, super bright. The air got all watery. I was startled when that happened, and I dropped it. When I picked it back up, it was smeared with blood. Of course!" My eyes flew open. "I was bleeding and it got on the pendant." I pulled the dagger back out and opened a small cut in my palm before eyeing him. "Your turn."

He hesitated a moment before trying to reach for the knife, but I pulled it away with a shake of my head. "You're already bleeding."

He looked down at the gouges in his chest. There was a moment when I thought he might actually faint. His face was quickly turning a questionable shade of green, but then another body hit the door hard enough that something cracked, loud.

He wiped his hand across his chest with a hiss. "This is crazy. You know that, right?"

"You have no idea, little brother. No idea." I held out my hand for his, laced our fingers together, and squeezed. "There's no place like home."

His laugh was terrified and weak, but at least he wasn't petrified. "When we get back, you're so buying me red shoes."

"Whatever you want, just focus," I said, turning all my attention to thinking about home. Of course, it wasn't all about that beat up old couch or our shitty little apartment, because that's just not how the human brain works. Thoughts of Hook snuck in as the air around us thickened and shimmered. I caught the familiar scent of our apartment, faint at first until it spread and overtook Hook's alluring scent.

The outline of our television and the second-hand entertainment stand it sat on started to form in front of us, and Matty stared at that shimmery image like a kid seeing Santa for the first time.

"It's working!" I couldn't hide my excitement, but I felt a deep sense of regret too. Sadness.

I shoved it away. My goal had always been to get Matty home, to keep him safe. That would always be my priority.

Another hard blow smashed the door to pieces and Leo, bloody from the battle, rushed forward, yelling something I couldn't hear over the drone of the magic encasing us. Two steps behind him was the man of my dreams, Hook, reaching for me.

Then it was all gone.

CHAPTER 50

I landed on our couch with a thud, kicking up a puff of dust and dog hair. My vision was still a little fuzzy, so I squeezed my hand hard to make sure Matty was with me. His responding wince sent a wave of relief through me.

I blinked about a thousand times before the TV and the rest of the room finally came into focus. Then I let my head fall back, and sucked in a few deep, calming breaths.

"How are you feeling?" I finally asked, rolling my head to look at my little brother. His eyes were closed, and he honest to god looked like he was sleeping.

A groan slipped out. "Like I just woke up from the weirdest dream."

I laughed, ignoring the small ache in my chest at knowing I'd never see Hook again. That was probably for the best, wasn't it? He could go on doing his thing in his world, and Matty and I could pick up where we left off in ours.

Speaking of... I needed to find Lily. Goddess only knew how long we'd been gone. Was time in Hook's realm the same as time in ours? Was it just three days?

Lily was a tough pup. Clever enough to let herself out of the apartment. And she had an automatic feeder in the kitchen that was still at least half-full when I'd left.

"Lily?" I called, letting go of Matty's hand and trying to get up.

It didn't go so well. The moment I leaned forward, a wave of dizziness knocked me back, but that only lasted as long as the silence did. Only until a low, hair-raising growl bled through the room.

"Lily, honey, it's just us." I gave my head a hard shake and forced myself to my feet.

It was sketchy for a second. I had to hold out my arms like a kid on a balance beam to keep myself steady, but once I was up, my senses sharpened rapidly.

Another low growl had me turning slowly toward the sound.

Had we been gone so long that she'd forgotten who we were?

No, that didn't make sense. Dogs remembered their people for years after they'd last seen them. Every heartwarming video on the internet of a soldier coming home from war proved that.

Lily was in the hallway with her head low, her hackles up, and her teeth bared in an unmistakable warning. She was big for a dog, and a terrifying sight for anyone on the receiving end of those sharp fangs. If even an ounce of her attention had been focused on me, I might have cowered, but her attention was locked squarely on Matty.

"Lilybug?"

I wheeled around at the deep voice to find a large, golden skinned god standing in my living room, directly behind where my brother was sitting.

Oh shit. I'd somehow managed to drag Leo along for the ride, and now my dog was preparing to rip his gorgeous head off. *Crap, crap.*

Before I could make it around the couch, Leo was dropping to his knees, holding his arms out toward her. "Lilybug, is it really you?" His voice was unsteady, like he was unsure of what he was seeing.

Her furry ears twitched, and a little of her snarl faded. Then my normally dangerous and viciously loyal companion whimpered like a puppy and shuffled forward just like one of the dogs in those reunion videos. All giddy with the wildly wagging tail that had her hind end swinging. When she reached Leo, she popped up on her back legs and plopped one paw on each shoulder.

"I thought I'd lost you forever," he whispered, burying his face in the fur of her neck.

So, yeah. I was a little confused.

I glanced over at Matty, and he had about the same look on his face. Then shit got really weird.

While Leo was hugging her, the fur on Lily's body seemed to pull back even as the fur on her head lengthened. Her paws elongated and her limbs stretched. Every joint in her body shifted position in a way that should have been impossible.

In a few confusing and alarming seconds, my beloved dog, my constant furry companion for my entire life, morphed into a tall, curvy, entirely naked woman.

What in the actual fuck?

Note from the author: I totally get it if you hate me right now. Honestly, I hate *myself* a little bit for that cliffhanger, but I promise it'll be worth it.

Why?

Because things are just heating up for Never and Hook...

ANOTHER DAMNED SERIES: BOOK 2
ANOTHER DAMNED PIRATE
MYKA BOUND

Torn between two worlds,
haunted by the pirate I left behind,
and the real battle has just begun...

One click to snag your copy of
ANOTHER DAMNED PIRATE

ACKNOWLEDGMENTS

First, I owe a big thank you to *you*, yeah you, the person reading this sentence right now: Thank you for spending your valuable time with my stories!

To my editors and beta readers, you all are the best.

And to my fellow authors, you lot are my inspiration. I will always be grateful that you've chosen to share your stories with the world.

myka BOUND

ABOUT THE AUTHOR

In case you couldn't tell from the story you just read, I love writing gritty romantic fantasy filled with magic, monsters, found family, and damaged characters who are willing to sacrifice everything for the people love.

I'm also awkward as hell, love quoting the 80s and 90s movies I grew up with, and I'm not afraid to get my hands dirty.

I live in the Rocky Mountains with my lumberjack-looking husband and our pack of rowdy rescue dogs. And yeah, I'm a *total sucker* for the rough-around-the-edges type.

Website: www.mykabound.com

- facebook.com/mykabound
- instagram.com/mykabound
- bookbub.com/authors/myka-bound